South of Market

A Novel

Jeffrey Peel

Copyright © Jeffrey Peel 2025

All rights reserved. No part of this publication may be reproduced, stored in a retrieval system, or transmitted, in any form or by any means, electronic, mechanical, photocopying, recording or otherwise, without the prior permission of the publishers.

To my wife, Liz, and my two big children – Jessica and James. They all make me hugely proud and helped me immensely to get this thing finished.

South of Market

Chapter 1: Rahul Vaidya

Let me tell you about the life I left before coming here to Silicon Valley. I'm telling you this story in English. It's my mother tongue. My Dad always preferred to speak English, certainly when out and about in Tellicherry. Even at home when I was a kid our day-to-day chatter was Englishayam - a mishmash of silliness and puns based on both English and Malayalam. My Dad always liked to use little-heard American words like 'faucet' and 'diaper'. It was showing off, of course. My Dad worked for an import-export business, so he'd deal with Americans on the telephone and even started to use email to communicate with Americans and British before he retired. So, he'd use silly American words, and we'd laugh and hijack them and use them too.

So, what was my life like? Frankly, it was good. Kerala is the best of India. There really are few places in the world more blessed than Tellicherry. And my childhood was one of bliss most of the time. My Mum and Dad, both, were fanatical about cricket. Still are. And, of course, you've probably heard about the famous Thalassery biryani, which has Kaima and Jeerakasala rice instead of the usual Basmati. Thalassery, by the way, is another name for Tellicherry, my hometown in Kerala, India.

Anyway, yes, the Thalassery biryani. My goodness, it's the very best of biryanis. And it's the thing I miss so much about home. Especially my Mum's weird version of it. She'd only make it every so often - for special times. Like the time she made it for my sister when she came back from San Francisco with her baby girl - two years before I, too, left for Silicon Valley.

My sister in America, you see, is four years older than me. Like me she studied at the College of Engineering at Thalassery. She's a system engineer. I'm more of a classic coder guy. My sister was the first of the brood to leave the nest. My other siblings - 4 of them - all still live and work and thrive in various parts of India.

So, as I was saying, I had a great childhood. I had the classic, caring parents. I was encouraged to get an education, and my parents encouraged me to seek out the lights of America once I graduated from college. And while at college I still got to swim in the four rivers that flow through the area or take my Dad's car (when he'd let me) to Muzhappilangad beach. I had a nice girlfriend for a while I was at college. But we agreed it would be better to go our separate ways and lead our own lives once I decided to leave for America.

But I still haven't really told you much about my life in Tellicherry. Maybe it's because of what is happening here in America and how my life has changed. Maybe I'm beginning to forget what my life was like in Tellicherry. Because the thing about the internet is that it blurs everything out. It blurs out the local. It blurs our memories. Of course, it's not really the internet, as such. I shouldn't blame technology. It's not the technology's fault. We created it, after all. But like all technologies we tend to make them work against us, strangely. I wonder why we do that?

But technology is, clearly, why I came to America. I'm a technology guy, I suppose. But I'm also an Indian. And, as an Indian living in America I'm not so much a technology guy as a 'Dev'. It's all because of the H1-B visa.

Let me tell you about the H1-B. These are a special type of visa (and I say, 'these', because an awful lot of them are given to Indians). My boss used to say that America needs them because America just doesn't produce enough good quality people and that its education system fails most who go through it. H1-Bs are supposed to be given primarily to people who have skills or qualifications that aren't readily available in the United States. But, these days, instead of hiring in creative talent, or Nobel prize-winners, it's mostly about Python developers, or blockchain bros, or just about any Indian who can make the grades. Like me, I suppose. And that's why I came to America, out of Kerala, 14 years ago, in 2014.

And I joined a start-up. Nothing like this was or is happening in India - startups hiring people on the strength of funding from VCs. Don't get me wrong. India is doing very, very well now. But the startup I joined in Palo Alto had just closed a B-round of $100m. And, honestly, I can tell you, when I did my first Skype call with the Head of Developer Talent, I wasn't even sure that she knew what the firm did. It was all, "We don't want you talking to anyone else, now". And then I had a couple more calls and I was on my first ever long-haul flight out of India to Doha and on to San Francisco.

It was fortunate, as it turned out, that I chose to work where I did. The CEO of the firm I work in now was often in our offices. He was, at the time, CEO of one of our 'technology partners'. He was also on our advisory board. That's the way Silicon Valley works. It's like the CEO knows someone who knows someone and can get an introduction to the VCs like Kleiner or Mayfield. And, yet this all happens in one of the most economically divided states in America. We're lucky in Kerala - it's one of the wealthier parts of India. But we have poverty, and crappy towns and villages with dirt-poor people. But so it is here in the Bay Area too.

After Covid San Francisco went down the shitter big-time. The vagrants, the Fentanyl-deranged and the crackheads moved in while the retailers and commuters moved out. It was pretty shit in 2014 with the homeless lying in doorways and around Union Square. But it's a fucking shithole now. Elon Musk closed his Twitter offices in 2024 - they were down in SOMA - and moved to Texas, just like Joe Rogan.

There's a lot of graffiti here - but fewer and fewer people to over-paint it - they're too spaced-out. But, when Twitter moved out of the city, it was like the writing was on the wall for San Francisco. There's hardly any tech downtown now. Most of the best-known firms still huddle around the main Bay Area highways.

South of Market

Drive up Route 1 and you'll see the names of towns that used to be sleepy Spanish-named suburbs of the City but now are home to some of the Tech giants that everybody has heard of. Towns like Palo Alto, or San Mateo, or Santa Clara.

But the price of real estate - even when I arrived - was well beyond a boy from Tellicherry. I rented, initially, in Oakland. But astonishingly, I was able to buy a small place in Santa Clara County on the strength of the stock options I was given by my first employer - that little startup that was acquired by Oracle for $2billion three years after I joined. Frankly, I could barely believe my luck. My stock allowed me to acquire a little 'Cape Cod' two-bedroom house for around $350,000 - in cash. It was just seven hundred square feet, but I was home and dry. I also got my Green Card shortly after that. My real estate agent recommended a good visa lawyer and, again, I got lucky.

But those lucky events were just links in a chain of events that have, mostly, worked in my favour. When I bought my little Cape Cod house in Santa Clara County I was still living alone. But it didn't feel that way shortly after I moved in.

The house I bought was one of a strip of little Cape Cod dwellings that were essentially starter homes for young professionals living alone (like me) or young couples. And one of those couples moved into the house next door just a matter of days after I got my keys. In fact, I clearly remember the day they moved in. It was a

Rahul Vaidya

Sunday, and it was late Summer. The Sun was well-up and was streaming into my bedroom. I was willing myself to get up for a morning run. But I heard some commotion outside and peeked through the window. Outside was a U-Haul truck. And jumping out of the passenger side was a young woman wearing white shorts - very short white shorts - super-white sneakers and a little vest-top. She had a very dark tan and bleached-white-blonde hair. In a few moments she was joined outside the front door of her new home by the truck driver and her partner, I presumed. He was something of a Tommy Lee lookalike with lots of tattoos. And to all intents and purposes they looked like they were going to shoot a porn video rather than take possession of their new home.

I'll admit that, with the arrival of Tommy and his Pamela Anderson lookalike girlfriend, or wife, I knew not which, I had to make myself known as soon as possible. So, I threw on a t-shirt and a pair of beach shorts and thundered bare-footed downstairs.

Luckily, they were having problems with the keys and were standing looking somewhat irritated with each other as they took turns trying the keys.

"Hey there neighbours," I said, and Pamela looked at me with a beaming smile and loads of wonderfully perfect teeth, California-style.

South of Market

"Hey, Hello!" she said as she fumbled, dropping the keys in Tommy's big, tattooed hands. "I'm Anna, lovely to meet you."

The teeth were not those of a Californian girl, in fact. Yes, they were perfect, but her accent was very definitely English - a people not noted for their perfect teeth - something I'd noted in the office where we had quite a few English ex-pats.

"Oh, my goodness," I said, "you're British."

"Yea, and you're Indian I presume. This is Alex."

Alex smiled and made a kind of saluting sign with his hand. But we had made contact, and I helped them find the right key and Anna and Alex became my best buddies, as well as my neighbours.

Anna was from Swindon in Wiltshire and had worked for Aether Semiconductor's UK operation before coming out to work in marketing for the company in Santa Clara. Alex was, it turned-out, not in Tech but had ambitions to get in. He was more of a day trader and also played in a rock band and dabbled in coding. He had, in common with most of the most super-successful Bay Area entrepreneurs, he claimed, dropped out of college. He'd done a few semesters at Stanford and had met a few cool people but dropped out and joined a 'founders' program'. He was still searching for an idea. He'd met Anna only recently, he said.

There seemed to be an oddness to their relationship, I'll be honest. Tommy Lee and Pamela Anderson, fair enough. But these two? A hot girl and a tattooed college drop-out day-trader? But the thing is, the Bay Area's 'diversity' has an oddness about it. All sorts get together. And I pretty much figured that this was just another odd coupling among a sea of odd couples. The good thing for me was that they were cool. And they seemed to be happy with me hanging about. And they seemed to think of me as a Tech Bro. 'Result,' as Anna was fond of saying with a big, perfect orthodontic smile.

And it was a good year, 2018. It was August, I think, when I first saw Anna's beautiful legs emerge from the U-Haul. It was a great Summer - warmer than average. Anna and Alex were fond of inviting friends around. Mostly I was invited over. We drank lots of wine. Although Alex was quite a stoner. Weed, and drugs generally, are not my thing. My family never really drank alcohol that much. We had the odd beer to wash down my Mum's biryani - but my booze consumption went up quite a bit when I landed in California.

There was, and is, a huge amount of wine snobbery in the Bay Area. There are lots of professionals with lots of money and a need for the trappings of wine brand identity. When I was interviewing for a job with Twitter the interview took place over lunch. The HR guy who interviewed me ordered a bottle of Screaming Eagle Sauvignon. It was very pleasant, but it must have been $1,000. And he didn't even offer me the job. In fact, I didn't even hear anything after the interview. Those guys, as Anna would put it, were and are wankers.

But I digress, I still haven't told you anything about what I do in this crazy place. Let me tell you. I don't do very much. You see, it's really not that hard to code these days. We give the impression that we're all super-high-IQ people - the type of people that Donald Trump used to talk about. In fact, that's why, we all presumed, that he buddied with Elon Musk in the early days, when he was elected in 2024. Elon, he used to say, was one of those super-intelligent people. Although I did read a Reddit thread where most thought that guy couldn't code for shit and didn't even know what GitHub was when he bought Twitter.

But that is why being seen to be a super-high-IQ person is such a big deal in Silicon Valley. Just think about it, every tech dude you know wants to be seen to be a super-high-IQ person. But, let me let you into a secret. They're not.

Well, I am. I came through the Indian system. The College of Engineering at Thalassery is not the most top-notch college in India, by far. But, still, getting into any pretty highly rated tech college in India is not easy. Getting into IIT in Madras is near impossible. In fact, I've met some of the alumni from there. And they're very, very smart. But here's the thing, it's really not that hard to shine in coding. Because, in fact, now more than ever, we don't even code. We sort-of need to know what we need to do. But, these days, we don't really need to edit code. We can just talk to large language model AIs, and they'll generate the code. We can say, hey dude, I'm getting some strange artifacts when I ask yada to draw a helicopter and the AI will be like, "Here you go dude, this'll fix it. I can see what the problem is."

It's all about energy, you see. With AI all of the best Tech dudes haven't been working on products as such. They've been working on AIs that essentially take all the collective intelligence of the best of the Indian technology colleges and consolidate it into a collection of AIs that do all the work - but only we, really, can instruct them. If we can't we'll ask an AI how we can. It's super cool. But this is only possible with energy. It takes huge amounts of energy to run the server farms, which serve up the AIs. That's why energy is all there is really. It's also why California is such a shithole. It can't produce enough energy, you see. The AIs are the new gods. But like all gods they need sacrifice, fire and power.

So that's where I am now. I'm working for an energy company. Who would have thought it? I'm not even really coding anymore. When I started, yes, I was all over the tech side of things. But it's more about the fact that I come from Tech that they wanted me to focus more on business development – even running the whole company depending on the circumstances. Just 14 years ago I was in Kerala, now I'm helping to lead a company building so-called small nuclear reactors. And, based on the last funding round, that means I am, on paper at least, or in pixels, worth quite a lot of money. Although other things have made my life rather more important than my stock.

Now we're selling the small nuclear vision to Tech firms running big data centres. Larry Ellison was talking about small nuclear power plants for his data centres years ago. But it took the second Trump administration to really give the technology the green light. Now our turbines are under construction - in London and in Washington State. But who knows what the future holds. Constant war in the Middle East makes our selling job easier. But not in a good way.

But back in 2018, when I joined the business, things were very different. It was just two years before the Covid Psyop that almost crippled the fiat monetary system. We were lucky that we'd raised our second round at the tail-end of 2019 - bringing our total investment to $200m. We also got quite a few bitcoin investors. By 2025 our bitcoin investment - which we held in cold storage - was worth almost as much again as bitcoin reached well over $100,000.

Part of the reason for bitcoiners being interested was because they wanted to piggy-back bitcoin miners on the back of our customers' capacity. And that's quite a bit of capacity. Our earliest turbine designs that we pitched were supposed to produce around 300 Megawatts of electricity - that's about seven or so million kilowatt hours per day. But while that's enough to power hundreds of homes it's only enough to power around two or three massive data centres. So, we're getting interest from multiple operators who want to use spare capacity. Bitcoin is essentially crystallised energy - or so they used to say. But that was useful for me. I got to know lots of bitcoin billionaires.

Anna took a keen interest in what I was doing, needless to say. She told me that her job was seriously fucking frustrating since Nvidia cornered the AI market - so she was changing direction, career-wise.

"Seriously, Rahul," she told me at one of her parties just a few weeks after we'd met outside the Cape Cods for the first time, "I need to know more about what you do. My career is changing direction. I need to keep on top of what's the new, new thing."

She had a very tactile way with her. She touched me on the arm as she quizzed me on who she needed to speak to in the Bay Area. "Why do you need to speak to them?" I asked. Then she squeezed-up her face a little and her freckles danced over her perfect little nose.

Chapter 2: Anna Sussex

Why California? Well, my Dad visited a lot - on business - and I suppose I just knew that it had to be part of my life too when I was of an age to get a job or book a flight. He would sometimes fly all of us out: my Mum, me, and my two brothers. I'm told that my first visit to California was when I was just 5 years old. I obviously can't remember it. But there were many other visits after that. Sometimes we'd fly to LA and make our way up the coast. Sometimes we'd make our way further South to San Diego. But invariably, we'd end-up in San Francisco - or, more particularly, Sausalito.

I asked my Dad a few times why he loved it so much. And it was always about the landscape, the ocean and also the vibe. Those trips were during the days that California was where everyone wanted to be. That's not so much the case now, of course. And we know the reasons now. But those reasons are all about the cities and the downfall of the cities. But the ocean is still there and Route One is still there.

Those childhood visits for me meant staying in little clapperboard B&Bs in places like Carmel or Monterey. Even when I was at the LSE in my late teens my Dad would call me just before the end of the last academic term of the year and ask if I wanted him to send me a ticket to San Fran so I could join them in California for the Summer. I always accepted. And it was usually just the three of us: me, my Mum and Dad. By that time my older brothers had long since moved on with various girlfriends and wives and were probably holidaying in Tuscany or playing golf on the Algarve. But, for me, California was what the Summer was. And it was idyllic.

And, honestly, I'm not even sure why. But I was hooked. And I knew that it was pretty inevitable that I'd live there one day.

My Dad worked in data communications pretty much all of his career and ended up being Global CTO of a Sequoia funded startup based out of Santa Clara. He used to stay in the Marriott Hotel in Santa Clara, and we'd end-up spending a few nights there on our various visits. This would give my Dad a chance to get a few days of business in - to justify his expensing of at least his own airfare. Although I suspect there was quite a lot of creative expense claiming relating to our family visits. Perks of the job, I suppose.

The Marriott in Santa Clara was far from being a resort hotel. It, and several other big-brand hotels in the area, served the needs of most of the tech companies that were packed into the various business parks on Tasman Drive, Hacker Way, Great America Parkway. Facebook was there, Cisco Systems, 3Com, Aether Semiconductor, Hewlett Packard. And the Marriott Hotel accommodated the great and the good that came and went constantly.

It wasn't a particularly salubrious hotel. The Westin on Great America was more impressive and had much more light. But the Marriott had a very Spanish feel and had, I seem to remember, a very good TexMex restaurant within strolling distance with amazing pico de gallo and chips.

My Dad, being an engineer, wanted me to follow him into tech. Tech left both my brothers cold. One became an accountant and the other studied law and was working in corporate finance. And when I announced that I was going to study PPE at the - according to my Dad - very 'lefty' LSE he just assumed that I was a lost cause. But I wasn't, as it happened. California and Tech were incredibly alluring. The allure was something to do, of course, with the phenomenal wealth that could be made. But it was more than that. It was a world where I knew I could do very well if only I could find my niche. The key question was how a girl with a BSc in PPE from the London School of Economics could get into Tech. Thankfully, my Dad provided the answer. The problem was that the answer was in Swindon. Fuck.

As you'll understand, chips are everywhere - and I'm not referring to the ones served with salsa. Aether Semiconductor - as the world's most important semiconductor firm - knew that it was becoming geopolitically very important. The UK was, and still is, the centre of gravity for information technology in Europe and across the Commonwealth states. In fact, given the richness of its engineering talent there are many who think that while Silicon Valley provides the capital, the UK provides the technical brilliance, along with the Indians. Well, this was my Dad's view anyway. And this is how he articulated it to me.

Anyway, and I'm not sure how it came about, but my Dad emailed me a job description of a role at Aether Semiconductor which very much looked like government relations. Since graduating I have been working for Burson Marsteller in London on a number of relatively small accounts, and mostly B2B. So, a government relations role at Aether Semiconductor's European HQ seemed quite a step-up for me. But I'll admit that a move to Aether seemed very attractive.

The interview didn't add much meat to the bones of the job description. I didn't really have much idea what I was expected to do even after they offered me the job - after three interview rounds, the last with a panel of interviewers involving people from across the company. But there was lots of reference to Brexit.

I joined Aether Semiconductor in June 2015 - almost exactly a year prior to the Brexit vote. And, as it turned out, I joined a team that was assembled for the very purpose of ensuring a Remain victory when the referendum was held. I'll be honest, I hadn't really taken a particular position on the subject. But I was left in no doubt about the position I should adopt.

The company had actively scaled up its public affairs team. And, as an alumnus from The LSE, with experience from Burson and a 1st Class Honours Degree in PPE from the LSE under my belt I was considered the perfect candidate to help give voice to the Tech community: that the United Kingdom has to remain a member of the European Union.

"So, what's your view about this Brexit thing, Dad," I asked him when I visited my parents for Sunday Lunch a few weeks after landing my new job at Aether Semiconductor.

"I think it's probably best not to rock the boat, Anna. I think the UK has long lost its importance in the global pecking order."

"You think?" I asked. "But why do you think that the Tech industry needs to make its view so forcefully on the matter? Do you not think that coming across like we know what's best for the little people of Britain that we might annoy them so much that they'll vote the 'wrong way'?"

"You could be right. But your role is to do your best. You're the new kid. You'll learn a lot from this experience."

He wasn't wrong. But what I learned from the experience wasn't quite what he had expected.

On the Monday morning after the conversation with my Dad over Sunday lunch I had to attend a meeting with a group called London Friends of Tech. It was a group led by a former Microsoft Executive who had apparently done pretty well in Tech circles and wanted to "give back" to the industry. He had assembled many members - mostly by word of mouth and the "network effect". LiFT, as the group referred to itself, had managed to convince several of the leading UK based Technology companies to sponsor it. It had arranged many events - involving politicians and opinion-formers - and the numbers attending had been increasing markedly. It had also taken an aggressively pro-Remain position - claiming that over 90% of its member "friends" were diametrically opposed to Brexit.

LiFT's self-appointed Chair, Cliff, was a slim, tanned and slightly effete man, probably in his early sixties. He attended the meeting with two adoring women - one from LiFT's PR agency and another from a sponsor and London based software startup that had received investment from a "Sand Hill Road VC".

Cliff was very animated during the meeting and used profanities quite a bit - especially when referring to Nigel Farage, Leader of the Brexit Party. Various Conservative Party "Vote Leave" advocates were treated with disdain. Cliff even called one a "Cunt" - his PR blushed at that point and smiled meekly into the distance.

But we were left in no doubt that we were to consider LiFT as being dependable advocates and to be called-upon should we need industry expertise. Similarly, they would call upon us should they organise any 'Tech for Remain' conferences.

The next year of my career involved lots of this type of thing. Meeting after meeting felt like we, as a Comms team, were being programmed and reprogrammed, as to the lines that were to push. But eventually I found myself zoning out, mentally chanting, "LA, LA, LA" to myself rather than succumb to the MK Ultra type conditioning.

It wasn't as though I became an active campaigner for Leave as such. I never really felt that strongly about either side of the argument. But I did find myself naturally gravitating towards the opposite viewpoint. I had to keep convincing myself that this job was eventually going to be a route to California and to some form of Tech or entrepreneurial stardom.

You see what I have on my side is this. Yes, there's the degree from the LSE and the big tech brand on my CV. But, and I'm not ashamed to say it, I'm hot. Look, there's no point pretending that my parents didn't give me certain advantages in life. Both my parents were definitely at the upper end of the attractiveness quartile. So, it was inevitable that I'd luck-out in the looks stakes.

So, I know that I kept my head down, didn't challenge too much, that ultimately, I'd get my ticket to ride. I had two further years after the Brexit vote stuck in bloody Swindon. But then, thank God, my manager summoned me to his office and told me that there was a role available in Santa Clara if I'd be interested. And there was no visa issue. And that was it, I was off to Santa Clara, and they even offered to put me up in the

Anna Sussex

Marriott Santa Clara for the first month until I could find myself somewhere to live.

I was just a week into the new job in Santa Clara and was having a glorious long sleep into my first lazy Sunday morning when my work cell phone rang. This was to be my first conversation with Sebastian Cox.

"Hello, is that Anna?"

"Yes, who's this?"

"Hi Anna, this is Sebastian Cox. We haven't spoken before. And I'm very sorry for disturbing you on a Sunday. But I thought this might be a good time to catch you. Do you have a moment or two for a quick chat? I got your number from your email autoresponder."

"Er, yes, but can you tell me what's the nature of the call?"

"Yes, of course, Anna. I'll be brief. Let me explain. I'm in the talent search space and am working with a client who might need your skills. I was wondering if you might be able to have a coffee with me so that I might explain more."

I was a bit flustered by the call. And I wasn't sure how to react. Sebastian had a strange mid-Atlantic accent and was very smooth.

"Perhaps I should explain, Sebastian, that I've only just relocated to California from the UK. I'm starting a brand-new role here so I'm not sure that I'd want to discuss another role when I haven't really done anything much here as yet."

"No, I fully understand Anna. But I have to say, that you come highly recommended. What I would say is that I really would recommend having a chat. I can guarantee that you will find the conversation very valuable."

"My goodness," I answered, slightly disarmed by this degree of charm so early on a Sunday morning. "Can you tell me who you're working for…I mean, who is your client?"

"Yes of course you can, Anna, but I'd probably want to keep the answer until we meet. Where are you staying in the Bay Area?"

"I'm at the Marriott in Santa Clara. Just for a few days until I get somewhere more permanent."

"That's ideal Anna. Could I buy you breakfast in the morning? I can highly recommend the Huevos Rancheros there. They're my favourite. Shall we say 7am?"

And that was it. We agreed to meet, and he gave me his cell phone number and email address. And a website address.

The website didn't tell me very much. He appeared to run his own headhunting firm but there were no published vacancies or client details. The only photograph was one of Sebastian. He looked quite suave and was wearing a dark suit and skinny tie in the pic. Very corporate America.

When I checked-in for breakfast the following morning Sebastian had already arrived and was at the table. He had already ordered orange juice for us and a large pot of coffee.

"Anna, it's an absolute delight to meet you," he said as he stood up, quite formally and shook hands with me across the table." I noticed him looking me up and down. I had no idea what was appropriate to wear and had opted for a skirt suit, not too short, and heels, not too high.

"So, have you decided to go for the Huevos Rancheros?" I asked him.

"Absolutely," he said, "and will you be joining me?"

"I'm not really an eggs in the morning person. I think I'll go for Oatmeal. And, anyway, you have me intrigued so I need something easy and quiet to eat."

After more small talk around eggs, beans and oatmeal Sebastian finally got to the detail of why we were having breakfast.

"You'll be aware, Anna, from your recent experience in the UK that the Brexit vote didn't exactly go the way that the great and the good wanted. The experience you gained there will have told you that the public, across most of the Western democracies, are losing faith in what is increasingly referred-to as the mainstream media."

"Yes, I'm very aware of that. But surely you must know that I was part of the losing team. I didn't even manage to convince the voting public in Wiltshire that they should vote to remain in the EU - never mind the voting public across the UK."

"Yes, we appreciate that. But that had nothing to do with your skills. We're definitely of the view that it was only because of the skills of people like you that the vote didn't go even further in the Leave direction."

"And who are 'we'?"

"Ah that's a good question, Anna. I represent a media group that is funded by a variety of people - including a major New York based Hedge Fund that's very keen to grow its presence in alternative media. One of the things we noticed was that lots of people who we didn't expect to come out in favour of Leave had a lot of visibility by building their own social media and even podcast profiles. My clients think that in order to win more eyeballs they can't rely on traditional media to the extent that they used to."

"But surely the BBC, the news agencies, and American networks, very firmly pinned their colours to the establishment position? They blocked out any dissenting voices to the best of their ability. But, sorry to change direction, why is your client so fixated on Brexit?"

"Ah, that's an even better question. My clients like control, Anna. And the Brexit vote marked the point when the media organisations didn't deliver. Remember that commercial media jumps to the tune of the big advertisers - and they're mostly big corporations that like control. The Brexit vote was a big surprise for everyone - and showed that the networks weren't delivering."

"But I don't work in alternative media. I just peddle the line and hope for the best."

"But that's the point. You don't just hope for the best. I sense you invest a lot of yourself into what you do. Can I ask, how did you vote in the referendum?"

"Goodness, that's a cheeky question Sebastion. What happens at the ballot-box stays at the ballot-box."

"Well perhaps. But I suspect you may well have been arguing against yourself to a degree during the campaign. I've spoken to some of your colleagues who tell me that by the end of the campaign you felt that you were losing but you stuck with it and with the lines to the bitter end."

"I did. That's true. But I was paid to do what I did. I booked interviews with Tech Execs and the media. Frankly, many were badly prepared and arrogant. Most refused to have anything to do with those 'alternative' commentators. So, the material I was given wasn't exactly great."

"Look, we get that. But the reason I'm speaking to you Anna is that we need to create a new media that's prepared to protect various interests. We can no longer rely on traditional channels. So, my clients want to create their own alternative media. That's why we need you. You have all the attributes. You're beautiful. You have dual British and American citizenship. You're highly intelligent and have stunning academics. We're prepared to give you a new toolkit so that you're always on the winning side. Oh, and if you can give me a quick decision, we think we'll be able to sort out your accommodation needs here in Santa Clara."

I was genuinely astonished at this turn of events. The guy, as far as I knew, didn't even have a copy of my CV. This wasn't a chat as such, it was more of a pitch, and this guy was doing the pitching. "But what's the agenda? What do you want me to do exactly?"

"We need to redress the balance. There's a culture war going on, for example. The woke agenda is gaining ground."

"What's that?" I asked? It was genuinely the first time I'd heard the term. Remember, this was 2016.

"I'm sorry. Woke means, I suppose, 'politically correct' but in a very lefty liberal way. I suppose the best way to think of it is the liberal media's obsession with identity politics. But a lot on the right are concerned about a lurch to the politics defined by an emerging liberal elite. You experienced this to an extent during the Brexit referendum debate. The media seemed reluctant even to allow the argument for Brexit to be made. Trump has characterised this as 'fake news'. It means that alternative views are systematically stifled. Discussions can't be had about draining the swamp."

"So, what would you want me to do? I must admit, I'm a little bit at a loss as to why you've approached me. There are others who would probably be much better qualified. For goodness sake, I studied at the LSE. It's probably the biggest hotbed of lefty, politically correct posturing - or woke as you call it - in the UK."

"I understand that. But we watched the debate you chaired in London - hosted by Bloomberg I think it was - and were very impressed by how you gave balance to both sides of the argument. There were some pretty big names in that debate, on both sides - but you were very effective in calling out the absurdity of the Remain position. I don't know your politics. But you were, quite frankly, head and shoulders above any of the mainstream media in being fair and non-patronising. We have been doing our due diligence."

"My God, you have. I'm very flattered, obviously. But can I ask, what would you want me to do exactly?"

"Well, Anna, we would want you to create, from scratch, one of the highest traffic political broadcasts outside of mainstream media. The technology is evolving, obviously. At the minute people consider podcasts to be a bit niche, audio only. But we reckon that more and more people will start watching alternative media content on YouTube, for example. And we want to make up lost ground by giving them long-form content. That means long, incisive interviews."

"With whom?"

Sebastian's answer to that question was absolutely the clincher. I was, at the time, in my mid-20s with just a few years of experience. I didn't even regard myself as a journalist - I was a PR hack with an interest in politics and economics and tech. But I was still at that stage in my life where I was more interested in drinking cocktails and striking a pose at the Redwood Room Bar in the Clift Hotel in San Francisco than doing anything particularly serious. But Sebastian was offering me a life-changing opportunity. There was no possibility that I could refuse this.

I now know, of course, that unlike Sebastian, I didn't do my own due diligence. In fact, as soon as I finished breakfast, parted company with Sebastian, and called my Dad, I knew that I should have asked more questions.

My Dad's first comment was, "Who is this guy, Sebastian?"

But even he admitted that a $100,000 signing bonus, and a $150,000 salary, and a share of YouTube revenue and the provision of free accommodation in Santa Clara, were reasons to defer the due diligence questions for some time in the future.

I signed my contract a week or so after my first meeting with Sebastian. And a month or so after that I was moving to my new home with an in-house studio. And a Producer called Alex. Our Head of Content, Xavier, suggested that I be vague about our relationship.

"We want to keep things as anonymous as possible. You'll be able to roll out of bed into your studio. Alex will be coming and going so we don't want to raise any suspicions with the neighbours. So perhaps give the impression that you're a couple. Alex is more interested in weed and boys, by the way. So, he won't be getting frisky with you."

"That's good to know," I answered, slightly disappointed that my hopes of a fit and horny sidekick was not part of the package.

The company had already ID'ed a cute little Cape Cod house that was much bigger inside than it looked from outside. A large extension had been built on the rear of the property and was now kitted out with a fully soundproofed sound studio and slightly edgy interview set with green-screen and lighting rig. Alex had his own little mixing desk and there was a little green room with a fridge stocked with some lovely California Chardonnays and lots of Coke Zero.

The first day we arrived at the house I met our neighbour, Rahul, who had just moved into the house next door. It was such a relief to know that I had such a sweet, non-American, neighbour. I'd always had a thing about Indian men - and had gorged a lot on Bollywood films when I was at the LSE - which had many Indian students very fond of holding curry and beer parties or Bollywood cinema evenings. I even attended some Bollywood dance classes.

But my problem was that I wasn't quite sure how to tell Rahul what exactly I was up to in the world of new media - all based out of my own studio, in the house. I wasn't sure what I was up to either.

Chapter 3: Rahul Vaidya

So, I'm a Developer. And I come from India. I'll be honest, I never really paid much attention to current affairs when I first came to America. But America is an odd place and most people in California have an unhealthy interest in politics. Even back in 2016. And then there was Trump being elected. California was essentially a blue state although Tech always had more of a whiff of self-styled Libertarian about it. Tech was the last remnant of the Wild West, after all.

Remember that 2016 - and Trump's first election - was just 8 years after the Great Crash. Trump's second inauguration in 2015 came just days after the wildfires in LA destroyed Tinseltown and its power over American culture - along with Governor Gavin Newsom's career. But, in an odd way, the demise of LA also marked the end of Silicon Valley calling the shots. But even in 2016 the centre of gravity was shifting. Tech seemed incapable of producing anything particularly wonderful.

Ironically the Brits had already identified the new, new thing even back then. I met my CEO for the first time at a drinks party organised by the British Consulate in San Francisco in January 2017 - shortly after Trump's first inauguration. A bunch of British entrepreneurs were in town to meet and greet the locals. But I was there because I needed a new job. Then I met Mark Carlisle.

Mark was a working-class boy made good. He always seems just slightly drunk - regardless of whether he has drunk any alcohol. He's default tipsy - which gives him licence to be cheeky, provocative, and disarming. Coupled with his impeccable dress sense and quaint English manners he was the ultimate Englishman abroad.

"Do you know who owns this house?" he asked me. I didn't, but he did. "Do you want me to tell you?"

"Yes, that'd be good," I answered.

"It's actually owned by a chap I used to know, slightly. He started a social media site for kids primarily and then sold it to one of the big media groups for a stonkingly large amount of dosh. Are you British?"

"No, I'm Indian."

"Well, I kinda gathered that but I was just wondering if you hailed from Birmingham or Leicester or somewhere."

"Yes, understood. But no, I come from a place called Tellicherry in Kerala. But I've been here for a few years. I think I'm representing America here this evening. There are a lot of us, feeding the beast, as they say. Indian devs I mean. What line of business are you in?"

"I'm in the energy industry. My company is hoping to sell lots of small nuclear reactors to your colleagues here in the Bay Area and across America that want to mine bitcoin or run AI data centres. It's a very lucrative sector, we think. Except for the bloody regulators and eco-warriors and carbon fanatics."

"Indeed," I replied. "When I first came to America, I was a bit naive. But the more I know it the more it feels like it's a stage-play. I drive a car that runs on gasoline. Or petrol as you'd say. But now that's regarded as a political statement. Some people, I know, think I should be driving a Tesla or at least a Prius. It's bizarre."

Mark Carlisle looked at me, raising one side of his mouth into a wry little smile. He then took a gulp of the Irish whiskey from the tinkling cut-glass lowball that he'd been nursing for some time as we spoke. "Hmm. I think you and I should talk. I might have a job for you. Something tells me we might be kindred spirits."

Mark and I swapped emails over the next few months, finally meeting again properly in the Summer of 2017. He suggested The Clift. He was staying there. This time he wasn't part of a delegation or anything. He was there with some of his senior team. The intention, for this trip, was to establish the US HQ and team. And that's why he was meeting me. But he wanted to tell me his back-story and better understand mine.

"Rahul, I wanted to meet you because I need really good people. But I need to explain something to you about our business. In fact, it's not a business as yet. It's more a concept. Possibly a philosophy. But it's certainly not a cult. In fact, the reason this company came into existence is because I'm a bit concerned about things.

And I'm not suggesting here that my concerns are magnanimous concerns about the state of the world. No. I have concerns that things are moving away from us in ways that might, ultimately, undermine our existence as free individuals. Let me explain."

I was genuinely captivated. This was far from the opening gambit of an US corporate HR-driven interview. This guy had passion. I loved it. And something told me that I was about to start a new stage in my life with this odd Brit. And so, Mark outlined his life and his philosophy.

"My view of the world, Rahul, is based on one simple premise. We must never be slaves. We must always be masters of our own destinies. If we're in debt, we're controlled. If we're controlled, we have no agency. Loss of agency is the greatest loss. The fact is that in the UK - and I use the UK as an example of a relatively affluent democratic Western nation - most people have hardly any money. Average savings, even among people who have worked most of their lives and are aged over, say, 50 are just a few thousand pounds. Many people retire but still have mortgages or rent to pay. About a third of the UK adult population have savings of around a hundred pounds or less. But they typically have huge debts. And so they become dependent. Millions of people in the UK are working poor, billions across the world. Millions receive benefits because they can't afford anything and have to work as well as receive handouts. But the consequence of this is that they are being constantly stressed, constantly concerned, constantly unable to escape the trap of relative poverty. They become slaves because they can't challenge their masters: their employers or their governments.

"Now, I graduated from university in the late 90s. I got myself a decent enough job, working for an electricity generator. It was far from inspiring. But it gave me time to read. I've learned more after leaving formal education than I learned when in it. When the crash happened in 2008, I wasn't entirely surprised. I'd read enough to know that we had built huge fragility into the economic system. The sub-prime mortgage collapse, and the collapse of the derivatives market - itself created to cover-up the sub-prime mess - was a bellwether that indicated that something was terribly wrong with the system. I call it Phase 1 of my own journey towards discovery. I know that money had become debased, the financial sector was being manipulated for the benefit of the few, and that the ordinary Joe paid for the bank bailouts. So, I took an interest in the cypher-punk movement. I started a bitcoin node. I bought bitcoin. I knew I needed a hedge. And, working in the energy sector, I accepted the argument, without question, that Bitcoin was the crystallisation of energy. Proof of work. So I bought bitcoin. Lots of it. And I waited. I waited years. I'm still waiting."

At this point he stopped talking and asked me if I wanted another drink. He had already downed two large glasses of Jamesons. But he decided to move onto Bushmills. He took a few sips of Bushmills single malt. Looked me up and down and complimented me on my shirt. It was from Banana Republic. I gulped a large mouthful of Bombay Sapphire and Tonic and prepared myself for the next instalment. He continued...

"I appreciate, Rahul, that you're probably wondering why I'm telling you all this. I appreciate that I've been rambling. But there is a point. And the most important point is that what I'm doing is all about money. It's not about me making money. I've made a lot of that. It's really about making a bigger point. And the point is this. I know that the system always works to the advantage of the few. And I don't like the few. This doesn't make me an anti-Capitalist or a Socialist. Quite the opposite. It makes me a champion of the individual. But I'm not an altruist. I'm just annoyed. I'm making an intellectual case. If there's centralised control of anything - money, business, culture, or society - it creeps me out. And there's something in me that has to say something and do something. Being part of the matrix simply doesn't suit me anymore. I've been quietly red-pilled. And the only means by which I can do anything about the matrix - pulling people out of their stupor - is to challenge a system that I find offensive. And the only way I can do that, I've concluded, is with energy."

At this point I had to seek some clarification. "So, are you saying that you're not in this for money?"

"I am. Well, I mean, it's not the main objective. Let me ask you to accept that *I've* accepted all the arguments for bitcoin - well with a pinch of salt. Bitcoin takes a lot of energy to mine and the rewards for that mining decline over time. Energy is expensive and getting more expensive - because it's controlled by supply cartels. And bitcoin is delimited in terms of supply. You know all this stuff. Now, I accepted all that. Because, if you think about it, this is a libertarian wet dream. If you hold coins, the value of those coins can only get greater over time if there's a demand for the coins - especially if the coins can be converted into fiat at any time and the dollar is getting more and more inflationary. So, bitcoin becomes the ultimate store of value. But then I started to notice something else. The argument for store of value started to drown out the libertarian argument - that this was a democratising currency. Instead, bitcoin started to be positioned as a hedge against the dollar's demise. Certain venture capitalists have been actively pushing bitcoin. I sense that, soon, Wall Street will be all over this. And now the eco-warriors are saying that we need to use 'green energy' to produce bitcoin to avoid massive hikes in fossil fuel prices in an uncertain world etc. - and that fossil fuels are bad.

"So that was my cue, Rahul, to start exiting some of my bitcoin positions to create a startup that's not in the business of mining bitcoin - but is in the business of creating energy outside the grip of the cartels and Wall Street. We have received some angel investment. We're well funded. But our objective is to help businesses create value from cheap, readily available energy, outside the clutches of the mob. We're not pursuing a low carbon agenda. We're pursuing a cheap energy agenda - the same agenda that was pursued by those who built Britain as the economic powerhouse of the world."

"I'll be honest. Our focus will, ultimately, be on India, Africa and Asia - individual national economies whose resources have been pillaged and have never had any type of industrial or post-Industrial revolution. We want to create an off-grid mind-set - a decentralised, energy-driven future. But we know that we're going to challenge so many entrenched positions - and, indeed, the entire, America-dominated geopolitical world order. In effect, we're declaring war on the establishment. So, the key question I have for you is, why would you want to join us?"

Then Mark paused, looked at me expectantly, and waited.

I had no idea that things would go in this direction. I'd had a few Skype calls with him prior to this meeting. He was well aware of my experience and, I suppose, I must have confirmed that I was the 'good fit' that he expected for Carlisle Energy. But this pitch was designed to leave me in no doubt that this was a man on a mission. I'd decided, already, that this was also a man I wanted to work with. But I wanted to know more about his motivation. Why was he doing this? And why was I so important?

He leaned back against the glass topped bar and looked round the room. "Isn't this a beautiful room, Rahul? There's something wonderful about this bar. The redwood panels are beautiful. The drinks, while expensive, are perfectly poured. The staff are impeccable. But this is a uniquely characterful hotel. It's probably owned by some group or other, but it has its own *savoir faire*. It knows what it stands for. Yes, ultimately, it wants people to come here and talk and drink and sleep in the rooms - none of which is cheap. But it's not like any other hotel. It didn't just happen. It ended up being what it is because of the people who come here, each one getting something slightly different from the experience. And over time, very subtly, it finds its groove and the synergy emerges. In order for any organisation to gain the respect of its patrons it needs to please them. It's all about mutual respect.

"I was born into abject poverty. The reason I escaped was because my parents wanted me to succeed. I did well at school. They encouraged me to do even better. I was really lucky that I was able to get into a very good high school, and I was hot housed by some really exceptional teachers. I was the first person in my family to get a university degree. I was exceptionally lucky. Nearly all of my peers at university were from upper middle-class families. Meanwhile, I left behind just about everyone who was important to me when I was growing up, including my parents, both of whom died well before I had the financial wherewithal to give them any luxury in their final years. I wasn't able to properly say thanks to the people who made me. But don't get me wrong. I'm not a Socialist. I believe in capitalism. But we live in a world that operates an elitist closed shop. Banks fail but are bailed out. Nations fail but can print money that hard-working strivers pay for through inflation or chronic disease. Governments now define our culture, our loyalties and our freedoms. And politicians have become B-list actors, telling us what's good for us as they go to war using our children as human shields.

"Governments now, routinely, take wealth by force and keep the producers of it - as Ayn Rand once wrote - bound, demeaned, defamed, and deprived of honour.

I'm incredibly lucky. I was lucky enough to have the parents I had. I was lucky enough to make lots of money very easily. And now I want to make a company that removes the power - literally - from the organisations that want to centralise it and control it. I want to give it back to the people. I may not succeed, but I want you to help me to. Does that make any sense?"

Chapter 4: Anna Sussex

I'll be honest, I wasn't entirely comfortable with the process of being turned into a minor celebrity. It turned out that I wasn't the only one being given the star treatment - although my 'new media' colleagues weren't exactly generous giving me tips about how to get off the ground. My job, it appeared, was to compete with the 'traditional' media for A-list guests - especially MAGA fanboys and girls. By the end of 2018 my personal reputation was growing, according to Alex, but I wasn't convinced that my viewing audiences justified my enormous salary and the growing support team at 'HQ' in New York. When I asked Alex to tell me how my traffic compared to 'the others' - meaning my fellow podcasters - he was vague. "To be honest Anna, they don't really give me their numbers, I just get a rough pecking order in terms of earballs."

"Earballs?"

"Yes, that's what they call combined audio listens and video views. You're well up there in terms of video views. But you're not doing so well on Spotify and Apple - particularly in terms of long-form."

We both knew that video views were low - right across the board. Who would want to watch two people having a chat on YouTube? My numbers were higher, according to Alex, because I had a growing fan-club of male MAGA types who wanted to fuck me. He didn't say this. He was too politically correct to state it as it was. But he certainly encouraged me to wear tight sleeveless tops and sent me a link to Kim Kardashian's nipple-bra advert. He said he was joking when I replied on WhatsApp with "WTF Alex?!"

But, aside from podcasting, and terrible viewing numbers, 2018 was a good year. Rahul and I were able to swap notes about our relatively new jobs and the strangeness of our respective employers. While both of us had been anointed as 'high flyers' it didn't exactly feel like that. Both of us were struggling to understand what was expected of us. Both of us were essentially outsiders and our positions felt precarious even though neither of our employers were expressing any dissatisfaction.

It didn't take me long to tell Rahul about my odd 'working at home' arrangement - and about my professional relationship with Alex. He was relieved, he admitted. Although I was slightly taken aback when he told me he thought Alex and I looked like Pamela and Tommy. "I don't have huge silicon tits though," I pointed-out. He blushed and tried not to look at them.

Rahul and I became 'a thing' very quickly. It was almost impossible for us not to be 'a thing'. We were neighbours. We had two houses beside each other and six bedrooms between us. He was a dreamily attractive Indian man with an incredible six-pack, long black hair and was a heterosexual in California - quite a rarity. And he told me constantly how hot I was and how astonishingly beautiful he found my accent and my body. There was only one way this relationship was going, and it involved just about every one of the bedrooms in both our Cape Cods.

The first time we made love was on the beach at Half Moon Bay. It was uncharacteristically warm. I think it was in late September 2018. We had been sunbathing and swimming at Gray Whale Cove. I knew, of course, that I was driving him wild. We'd brought a picnic. We'd found a spot where there was no-one nearby. And after nibbling on a few sandwiches and drinking a glass or two of Chardonnay we rolled out our beach towels and I told him that I needed to tell him something.

"You know I'm European, right?"

"Well, you're English. And you helped secure the British exit from the EU."

"Yes, yes, I know that. But you know how I come from Europe where we're much more laissez faire about sunbathing and stuff. St Tropez etc. Brigitte Bardot."

"Hmm. Yes. I'll go along with you. But you're English. Not French."

"Point taken. But I'm referring more to the laissez faire sunbathing aspects of European culture." By this point I was undoing my bikini top.

"So, you're saying that you want to go topless." His mouth fell open slightly.

"Oh no," I said, as I stood and removed my bikini G-string, "I'm not saying that at all."

And that was the start of it. We had sex everywhere and every which way. Rahul was highly creative in terms of suggesting some of the oddest sexual positions - but claimed he had never read the Kama Sutra. And after a literally exhausting two-hour stint of multi-orgasmic, weird positioned and hunger inducing sex we lay wrapped up in each other's bodies and I suddenly announced one thing that I wanted him to do with me that didn't involve sex. I wanted him to help me buy a car.

"What type of car do you want?"

"I don't know. But this is California. There's the ocean. We're both young and hot. I want to show off. I want us to be able to cruise into Carmel and have a lazy lunch at the Hog's Breath Inn. What's the best car to do that in?"

"Oh, I know exactly what's the best car for that, my beautiful, blonde girlfriend. Now, come with me." He stood up. He was still stark naked and sweaty but stretched out his arm and offered me his hand. "We're off to buy you a Miata."

And that's exactly what we did. I was now, officially, living the American dream. Not only was I an English girl in California with a beautiful Indian boyfriend, capable of getting into some weird sexual positions, I also now had a little Japanese sports car, in red. Life was good. Even if my podcasts and vodcasts were shit.

Although that was about to change. And it was all because of Rahul.

The problem I was having was that I was perhaps trying too much to please my bosses - even though I didn't quite know who they were. All my interactions were through Alex or the HQ team - including my 'bookers'. My assumption was that in trying to do what was expected of me I was defaulting to guests who were die-stamped neo-Nationalist Trumpian idiots - or dead-behind-the-eyes people from free market "think-tanks".

"You need to be yourself, Anna," Rahul advised me when we were heading out for dinner one evening - in the Miata, roof down, along route 101 to Palo Alto. It was difficult to hear him, so I asked him to shout. "You need to be yourself more," he yelled. I asked him to explain. "It needs to be about you and not your guests. You need to start telling stories, from your perspective. Your guests are just bit-part players. You're the star. You're the intellect and the talent. Get somebody on the show that you can have a conversation with. You ask the questions - you can drive the narrative and the engagement. Flirt. You're great at it."

He was right, of course. So, I contacted a friend of mine from back in the UK who was CEO of a tech firm - one of the few who had gone out on a limb and stated publicly that he'd be voting for the UK to leave the EU. Trump and Nigel Farage had already made public their bromance following the Brexit vote. So, I figured that I could do a show that would focus on why Americans should give a fuck about Brexit.

I bounced this off Rahul. He liked it. But then he came up with another idea. "That sounds like a plan. But try this. Before you introduce your guest, set the scene. Do a monologue to the camera. Give your viewers the background. Communicate your passion. Give them the context."

I bounced the revised format idea to the New York team, and they loved it. They advised me to pre-record the monologue so that they could tee-up teasers across social media. And, astonishingly, when the teasers went out, I was contacted, via Twitter, by a Producer from Fox News. I was asked if I might be a panellist on Fox & Friends - to discuss Trump's interest in Farage and Brexit.

And after the Fox package went out my Twitter following grew like crazy. The 'bromance' show was also the first to get over 100,000 views on YouTube within a week. By early 2019 I had close to 1m subscribers on YouTube and was regarded as one of the 'Top "new Right" commentators according to Tucker Carlson on Fox.

Anna Sussex

Meanwhile my little car inspired me to write a monologue about 'freedom' - that I intended to set the scene for an upcoming episode. This is what I wrote:

I'm British and a relatively recent arrival so I may well be newly fangled about living in America - especially in this part of America. For many, California - and especially coastal California - represents the American dream. Recently a good friend of mine suggested that I get myself a little Japanese car with a soft top so that I could properly experience the Pacific Coast road here in the Bay Area, San Francisco. And, I must admit, the feeling one gets zipping down Route 1 and watching the waves crash along the shore is one of the best.

But liberty is delimited here. California is no longer a place for beatniks and refuseniks. More and more, it has succumbed to compliance and collegiate thinking. There's a creeping political correctness even in the type of car we choose. Mine is a tiny little thing with just 2 seats and weighs just a few hundred pounds. It explains why it's so nimble around those coastal roads. But it's powered by gasoline. Increasingly it seems to be a requirement - instructed by the 'powers that be' - that we should drive electric cars. Or, as I prefer to call them, battery cars.

Battery cars aren't proper cars - they're toys. They need to be plugged-in and recharged for hours so that they can carry around their passengers and enormous batteries. There's no freedom or liberty in that. But the gas-powered and tank-filled car has, within it, the potential of hundreds of miles of open road - with only an occasional need to stop to refuel. And the refuelling, of course, is easy - given the compact power that lives within gasoline - or petroleum as we prefer to call it in Europe. Gasoline is supplied to us via a very well refined - pun intended - decentralised network. The smallest town has a gas station. It's unlikely to have a battery charger for a Tesla.

But we need to think hard about how else our freedoms - and our liberty - may be under attack from the politically correct powers that be. We need to be ever watchful. My protest against the nonsense that is global warming driven by man-made carbon dioxide is to drive a gasoline-powered car. But what other evidence is there that our freedoms are under attack?

A few days ago, I read an article in a British newspaper written by a fine investigative journalist. This journalist had been moved to read a report published by a United Nations organisation called the OPCW - the Organisation for the Prevention of Chemical Weapons - which had investigated the purported use of chemical weapons in the city of Douma by Syrian government forces against its own people. Various senior politicians had concluded that Syria had, indeed, based on the report, gassed its own citizens with Chlorine gas dropped from an aircraft. But the politicians hadn't done what this fine journalist had done - namely read the whole report. Had they done so, they would have discovered that some scientists had produced a dissenting assessment - that the Chlorine gas canisters had been placed where they were discovered in the City of Douma.

Of course, this was not the first instance of journalists and scientists uncovering difficult dissenting evidence - that didn't fit a narrative used to justify Western strikes on nations where the regime was deemed to be in need of forced change. Here in America do we know, definitively, based on the 9/11 Commission Report, who caused the twin towers to topple in Manhattan on September 11, 2001 - justifying the so-called War on Terror called by George W Bush? Or, in my home nation, do we know, definitively, what justification Tony Blair had to go to war with Iraq - other than the dossier compiled by his Head of Communications, Alastair Campbell?

Because if it's the case that these reports are used to justify war and huge loss of life - of our own soldiers and the citizens of foreign lands - where is the evidence that we're being presented by the truth and the whole truth?

I sent the draft to Alex the night before we were due to record an episode. I think it was Episode 48 or so. Our recording sessions were pretty turnkey by that stage. Alex typically had my monologue loaded up on autocue ready for me to record and have it in the can prior to my live stream and guests. But this particular morning when I entered the little studio ready to record Alex looked odd. He was sitting at the mixing desk when I entered the room. I popped my headphones on and chirped, "Hey Alex, how are ya?"

"Anna, we have a problem. There's a problem with your monologue. HQ doesn't like it."

"WTF Alex? Since when did you start submitting my content to New York?"

"Erm, since forever, Anna. Listen, I'm as amazed as you. They've never blinked so far about any of your stuff. They've expressed some views in the past about your British English, but that's about it. But, today, they went fucking nuts. Said that this can't go out like this - in its current form. They want a call. They said not to be worried though. They think you should be able to adjust it and be well ready for the stream. Xavier says he can do a call whenever."

Alex set up the call and put Xavier on speaker.

"Hey Xavier," I said, trying to sound chirpy, "what's goin' on?"

"Hey Anna. Listen I'm sorry about this but we have a bit of an issue with your introductory piece for the show today. It's nice but it makes certain people here very uncomfortable."

"It makes them uncomfortable? Who does it make uncomfortable?"

Anna Sussex

"Well, some of our sponsors, Anna. This isn't a criticism of you. It's more about the messaging. We don't want this to go out like this. Listen, the line I'm getting is that they want you to stick to the initial brief when you joined us - to give voice to Libertarians and to make the Libtards uncomfortable. But we don't want kinda excessively opinionated pieces that are too critical of certain people. Especially the governing establishment."

"Sponsors? I didn't think we had any sponsors."

"Come on Anna, there are always sponsors. We're all paid to do this. Our sponsors want us to stay on the rails. Listen, I've taken the liberty of editing your script a bit and adding some notes suggesting other directions you could take. You're really good at what you do. You should be able to amend it easily and record in good time prior to the stream. Best of luck - I'll trust you to make the changes."

Looking back on this event is difficult for me. I gave them what they wanted. Or rather didn't give them what they didn't want. This was, clearly, not an act of journalistic integrity. But, then, I wasn't a journalist. I was a young PR executive who didn't really have anywhere to turn. I had no money - apart from my salary - and had a company-provided house and place of work.

Creatively, of course, it hurt.

When the live stream went out, and the programme was in the can, I headed into Alex in his little studio. "Hey babe, he said."

"What am I going to do, Alex? Should I look for another job?"

"You could, absolutely. But why? Listen, we're just the hired help. It's no different here to working on Fox or for the Wall Street Journal. The media stinks like the worst shitters."

"But why have they hired us, Alex? I thought we were the alternative media…all about toppling empires."

"You gotta be jokin' Anna. We're here to give the idea that there are people stickin' it into the big boys. But there are only the big boys. And people understand that the mainstream media is owned and operated by the corporations that fund it. Just look at the junk adverts for crap food, drugs and mobile phones. Every celebrity interview has an agenda - like pushing a book, or movie or app. So, the establishment knows that there has to be a counterculture to provide alternative views - because they are losing audience to new media. But they have to watch these alternative views on video streaming platforms funded by the same adverts. Have you heard of the Overton window?"

"Yea. My Dad used to bang on about this. It's the acceptable discourse, the parameters within which everything has to be discussed."

"Your Dad was right. But the parameters aren't set by the viewing public. They're set by those on high - the corporations and their masters. The establishment. The view I take is that I'll take the money for doing what they want of me. Outside of work I do everything I can to switch off. I smoke a bit of weed. I'll get a new tattoo. I'll get a massage. I'll play some music. They can go fuck themselves if they want to get inside my head. But you're a total babe Anna. You're hot. You're fuckin' bright as hell. But you have to realise that you're here to play a part. The part you play is the one they pay you for."

I knew, of course, that Alex was right. I hadn't built a reputation as an investigative journalist. I had no particular integrity to uphold. I couldn't believe my own stupidity that I'd been hired for something other than the fact that I was easy on the eye, had a funny British accent and could hold my own in an interview. I wanted to be more than this, but I knew that for the time-being at least, I'd need to be compliant.

Thankfully, Rahul made the situation even easier for me. He suggested that I meet with his boss, Mark Carlisle. He suggested that Mark might even be a guest on my show. And so it was, that just a week or so after I had my mini-crisis, I met the infamous Mark.

Chapter 5: Mark Carlisle

When Rahul called me and asked if I'd meet with his girlfriend, Anna Sussex, I was particularly delighted. He'd mentioned her name to me a few times and I found it very amusing to hear that she was a podcaster living right next door to him. I made a point, of course, of listening to some of her shows. Or, rather, watching them. She was a very attractive woman - but most definitely not in the mould of the usual plastic 'anchors' on mainstream media. I am biased, of course. She was clearly extremely well educated and extraordinarily articulate. And British. But the thing that struck me when watching her interviews was her inability to 'shine'. Her guests often sounded like they had a number of stock, boilerplate type 'messages' that they had to get out. Don't get me wrong, they sounded good. They were 'on point' in terms of making the case for Austrian economics or sounding off about Murray Rothbard and what a genius he was. But there was no passion, no interest in debate beyond bashing Socialists. And this left Anna simply muttering, "absolutely" or "you're right about that". She had nowhere to go.

When I chatted to Rahul, he made the point that Anna could be a great asset - he suggested I might be a guest on her show. But he also outlined the dilemma she faced.

"She feels trapped, Mark," he said when I routinely asked how she was doing. We had just finished a business planning meeting in our boardroom. We jokingly called it our boardroom, but it was the one and only meeting room we had at that point in our new offices walking distance to Union Square in San Francisco. I asked him to clarify as we made our way out of the building to get a coffee at a place on Geary Street.

"Well, she was firmly put in her place. You know how she starts her shows now with a monologue? It's been part of the reason why she's become so popular. People now share these, routinely, on Instagram and Twitter. She's got a great way of coming up with a pithy phrase and the Libertarians and MAGA lot - increasingly - just love them. People are now making memes featuring her one-liners. But when she wanted to question the mainstream narrative about Syria, she was told to get back in her box. Don't get me wrong. She's no great authority on Syria. Her point was more about our need to question the narrative. That was all. So, since then, she's had to tread carefully."

I didn't find this particularly surprising. But I was keen to find out more. "I'd love to meet her, Rahul. Can you set it up."

"Sure," he said. "Although please go light on the charm, Mark. She's mine."

I could, of course, understand Rahul's concerns. When I finally met Anna a week or two after that meeting, I was even more impressed with her in person than her on-screen persona. We met in Palo Alto in Il Fornaio. I had arrived first and spotted her stepping out of her Miata. She was wearing a black shift mini-dress and very white tennis shoes - and had an incredible tan. When she entered the restaurant, I think that every single diner - of both sexes - strained to check her out. I waved at her, she waved back at me, sunglasses in her hand.

"Anna, I am very honoured to meet you. What can I get you to drink?"

"Oh, a glass of Honig Sauv Blanc, please," she whispered to the waiter who had accompanied her to the table.

"You clearly know the wine list."

"I do indeed. Well, I don't really. But Rahul and I recently visited the Honig vineyard, and I tasted their Sauvignon Blanc. I liked it and I know they have it here. But that's the world for you these days. Sales promotion tactics work. They gave me a mouthful of their Sauv and they have me for life. Or until I visit another vineyard."

"Indeed. But just before we get into that, my surname is Carlisle - a town in England that I've yet to visit. Your surname is Sussex. I presume you've been there."

"I have. In fact, I've many friends who live in Sussex and I've spent a bit of time in the County, on and off. When Rahul mentions you, he always calls you Mark Carlisle in full. It has a nice ring to it."

"Yes, I like my name. The Americans don't pick up the fact that my surname is also the name of an English city. You know Americans…they know nothing really about anything. Unless it's on CNN or Fox."

"Yes, I like mine too. In fact, they even grow wine in Sussex now. Global warming for you, I suppose." She raised one side of her mouth slightly into a slightly cheeky smile before sipping her glass of wine.

"You mentioned 'sales promotion' tactics earlier. I gather from Rahul that you may have been sucked into something of a sales promotion trap by your employer."

"Yes, and I'm so grateful to you for meeting me. I'm not sure if you can help at all. But it does feel as though I've been sold a pup as we say at home. This was a marvellous opportunity they gave me. To be honest, I feel like something of an imposter. I'm not really a time-served journalist. When they offered me the role, I suppose I should have asked more questions. I know that you'll have a perspective on things. I'm really keen to hear it."

Anna spent about the next hour getting me up to speed on her predicament. At a certain point I realised that the situation she was describing was not a personal one. It was much more fundamental than that. Anna had talent, beauty and intelligence. Therefore, she was effectively purchased - to do the bidding of her masters. And this required her to suppress her own abilities and intellect if it didn't serve their needs.

But her more fundamental realisation was that she was not alone.

"Here's my problem, Mark. It seems that anyone who is deemed to be successful - not just in the media - is controlled. They can buy just about anyone. I don't mean "buy" as in corrupt activities. In my case they simply had to give me a very large sum of money as a salary and bonus and housing. But, I know, in the scheme of things, this is nothing for them. But I'm kinda on their side. So, I can't understand why they won't allow me to have any personality, any freedom. We're supposed to be alternative media. Isn't that why they wanted me?"

At this point, I laughed out loud. But I could see that Anna was very embarrassed. Her cheeks flushed and she swigged her wine.

"Oh, Anna, I'm so sorry. Believe me, I'm not laughing at you. It's more because you *are* me - it's uncanny. I have the advantage of age. But, believe me, I had been asking myself these questions for decades. I found my answer back in 2008. Do you want me to tell you about it? It may help."

I ordered us two more glasses of wine.

"Prior to the financial crash in 2008 I found myself questioning the logic of what was going on in the financial markets. House prices in certain cities here in the States were going crazy. People were trading these weird and wonderful financial products that no-one understood - such as mortgage-backed securities. Traders were getting seriously rich on the back of a huge property bubble. When all of this was happening the little, tiny townhouse I had in England was probably valued at several £millions. It's not worth that even now. You've probably heard your parents and other people my age talk about this. But the thing that got me at the time was not that something very strange was going on in the markets. No, it was the fact that I came to the conclusion that we were being given terrible information. No-one was challenging why these things were going on. For most people with any common sense, it was clear that we were being played. There was clear collusion between the banks, the trading houses, the government and the media to obfuscate. No-one - apart from the most obviously fraudulent - really took the rap for what went on. A few banks collapsed. But they were scapegoats. The banks were bailed-out - at huge cost - but no-one really took the blame on either side of the Atlantic. But it was clear that there was a group behind the scenes that was pulling the strings. It was clear that the banking system was just a front. It looked to me that the entire financial services industry wasn't just rotten, it was an organised crime syndicate."

Anna looked at me with her head slightly cocked to one side. "But who, are you suggesting, was in the syndicate?"

I looked around Il Fornaio, noting the slight whiff of Basil and parmesan wafting around the place. "At first, I thought it was the bankers and central bankers, primarily. But then it became increasingly obvious to me that if you stripped away all the most visible players there had to be another power at play to co-ordinate all of these people so quickly. Government leaders, bankers, financial journalists were all in unison very quickly. The toxicity at the heart of the system had to be cut out very quickly - and stability restored. But remember, as far as I could see, the Western financial system had been on the verge of collapse. And then it wasn't. And, for me, this was the first time I had realised just how important some people had become and the extent to which they could manipulate for their own gain. It also showed me that, effectively, there was no such thing as government anymore. There only was 'the system'."

Anna looked at me with a confused look. "Yes, I know all this stuff. I watched the *Big Short*. But I'm not quite with you as to why this is relevant."

For a second I thought we were out of sync a bit. It was perhaps a generational thing. But I looked at her - and her youth and beauty - and realised that perhaps I was coming across as just a bit patronising. For Anna, the system had, so far, only given her some pretty significant breaks. So, I decided to change direction slightly.

"Do you know much about the people you're working for?"

"Not much," she replied. "It's funny, but when I discussed the job with my Dad - before I'd accepted it -

he asked me something similar. But we concluded that they were giving me a hell of a break. I didn't want to look a gift-horse in the mouth."

"Yes, I fully understand that. In fact, had I been you at your age, I would have done the same thing. But now that you've had this, erm, editorial set-back, it might be time to take stock a little bit. But I appreciate, we all have to play the system a little bit, to find our feet. It's the only system we've got. But I want to return to what I was going to say earlier. But before I do, can I ask, where did you study? I think Rahul said you studied at the LSE?"

She nodded and turned her lip up a little. So, I continued.

"Yes, then you won't find it offensive if I say that the London School of Economics has a very particular macro-economic perspective. It's a university that was essentially born out of the Fabian Society. One of the founders was George Bernard Shaw. But you'll know that, so I'm not going to labour it. Sorry, that was an unintended pun. But my point is this. You'll know that one of the LSE's original roles was to create a business and political elite that adhered to Fabian Society values. So, it stands to reason that the institution doesn't exactly focus on monetary economics on its syllabus."

"You're right about that," Anna interjected, "although, again, I chose the LSE because it has an incredible reputation, and I knew it would look good on my CV if I could manage to get a first. I played the game and regurgitated the syllabus. But I took much of the lefty stuff with a pinch of salt. And I had a great time - even if I do have a massive student load to return to if I return to the UK."

"I'm sure you did. But even your student loan is a neat example of what happened after Black Monday in 1987, and then the dot com crash and then the great crash of 2008. My coming of age happened slowly over those years. For me it was the witnessing of a slow car-crash. The financialization of everything, the sequestration of assets, the bank bailouts, the printing of money, the massive increase in money supply. I concluded - probably in 2009 - that the system was being rigged in favour of the people that they probably wanted you to become a member of - the global elite. In short, if you play the game, if you ignore the signs, if you don't ask too many questions about who's pulling your strings, you'll undoubtedly do very well inside the system. But the question to ask yourself is, can you stay sane in the process?"

"So, what did you do, Mark?"

I found her question very disarming. I was half expecting to tell her at some point. But the way she asked me, and the result of a few glasses of wine, was that I found the question made me instantly very sad. Because at the back of my mind I wasn't sure that I should be offering the red pill to this beautiful, intelligent young woman. But both of us knew that there was no going back.

"I decided to keep one foot inside the system and one foot out, I suppose. The thing I'd noticed, Anna, was that I couldn't trust the media anymore. Even when I was growing up it was a truism that we shouldn't believe everything we read in the newspapers. Some were supposedly lefty - or liberal as the Americans would say - and some were right. But after all the obfuscation and cover-ups and arse-covering it appeared that everyone was lying - and the media had become a propaganda machine. No-one was willing to say that ordinary people were being raped, and their property rights were being trampled over by a cabal of thoroughly evil people. It seemed to me that nothing was done - really - after the crash in 2008 to correct the system. The financial system was on the verge of a global meltdown, but it was patched-up with sticky-tape like a shopping mall after a massive bomb had exploded in the middle of it. Everyone could see that the mall was totally fucked but the traders just swept up as best they could and carried-on. But inevitably, the mall would collapse."

"But surely, there are people who can see that the whole thing is teetering, though? There must have been more people than you, asking pertinent questions?"

"There were, of course, Anna. But remember, there only is one game in town that pays the bills. There are too many vested interests at play to challenge the system. No-one wants to bite the hand etcetera. And the other thing that happened was that the propaganda campaign started in earnest when the bank bailouts started. Some of this was just about making the media a stenographer for the preferred lines. But they needed to pretend that there existed a counterculture that wanted to create a new system. And so, we saw the emergence of bitcoin. This was the ultimate limited hangout."

"Now, you've definitely piqued my interest, Mark. But what's a limited hangout?"

I proceeded to explain the idea of a limited hangout - the controlled release of part of the truth while hiding the actual truth. I also explained, as best I could, the Watergate scandal from whence it originated - the role of the CIA in creating the term. "And as for bitcoin, well, it was a classic, superlative, brilliant example. Do you want me to tell you why?"

"Yes please. I'm loving this."

"Well, it really is the stuff of crazy. We don't know if the protocol, published by this mysterious character, Satoshi Nakamoto, was created by the CIA or whether they effectively outsourced it. There are various conspiracies floating around. But frankly, I don't care. In my view, the people most likely to cause the most problems after the 2008 crash needed something to keep them amused. Bitcoin was, in that respect, absolutely brilliant. Conceptually, it was difficult for the average Joe to get their heads around it. But for very smart, troublesome, libertarians, it was utterly brilliant. It allowed a new band of brothers (they're nearly always men) to talk endlessly about a new anti-establishment counterculture. And it was decentralised. Everything bad about the old financial system was centralised. But, just think of it, as if by magic a new currency just emerged because of the genius of this enigmatic man, Satoshi. He had created a digital currency, and its members could use it to buy stuff - even weed and guns - and set up trading exchanges using this new, undiscoverable and private money. And, it was totally digital, and it was a deflationary currency because its supply was limited. Whoa...Nirvana for cypher-punks."

"And, so, what's the problem? Why was it a limited hangout? Oh, and wait a minute, I thought you'd told Rahul that Bitcoin was the salvation. I take it that you've done something of a U-turn on this, Were you not one of those that thought that this was a new nirvana?"

"You're totally right. Also, I need to be more careful what I say to Rahul, obviously everything I tell him gets back to you."

"You can bet on it," Anna quipped back with a glorious big smile - more for Rahul than me.

"Hmm, you're right. But after the Silk Road was shut down it was clear that bitcoin's destiny was to be a store of value. You'll remember from even your LSE syllabus that money that's not transactional is not really money. A store of value applies to gold, sure. But even it is, potentially, transactable if made into little coins. But that move to a store of value alone made me rethink. There was an agency about it. Someone was pulling strings. There was an obvious organisational purpose behind it. It felt very like the moves to dematerialisation that also happened in asset management markets in London and New York after the big bang."

Anna looked at me blankly. "I can explain. I'm sorry, I know what I mean, but sometimes I need to explain a bit more what I mean. This stuff isn't easy. Few people know how the markets work - they're highly complex but there has been a land-grab going on since the creation of the Fed and the Bank of England. But, in a weird way, bitcoin shows just how unexceptional it is. Because it is being given the same treatment that was applied to other assets."

"What do you mean? Surely assets are owned by the people that own them."

"Well, you'd think so. But that's not the case. In fact, the land-grab started back in the 1930s when Federal Reserve banks became the mandated banks - others operating outside the cartel were forcibly closed. And then, of course, in April 1933, Roosevelt issued an Executive Order insisting that hoarding of gold would become illegal - and that all gold should be handed over to the Federal Reserve banks. That process has been going on ever since. But it's been much more subtle. But it means that there's been a consolidation in the holding of assets. Few people who invest in stocks and shares now hold paper. They hold some vague rights to the assets that are held by centralised custodians. In effect, asset holders are issued with tokens. Just like money."

"Yes, Anna replied, "you're talking about fiat money."

"Exactly. Fiat money is simply a token that can be used to pay off a debt. The government prints the tokens. Money is made out of thin air - hence the term 'inflation'. But, as with all tokens that used to have a physical form, those tokens are being held in digital databases. If you own a home, you used to be provided with the deeds to the property - a kind of paper-based ledger showing the passage of the property from one owner to another. Now, in most Western countries, the system of ownership based on paper trails has been replaced - dematerialised - by land registration entries on centralised computer systems run by the government mob. Big, illiquid, assets are now being tokenised making it possible for the assets to be bought and sold. And, with the emergence of derivatives markets, pretty much any asset concept, no matter how bizarre, can be traded using digital tokens of quasi-ownership."

"My God, Mark, you're going deep down the rabbit hole," Anna said, with a slight look of exasperation on her face. "I was hoping for something a little more light-hearted in this conversation. But, anyway, if I can drag you away from your libertarian economics 101 session, can you tell me why bitcoin is being given the same treatment? Surely, it's still the closest thing you have to a parallel system."

"I used to think that. But there are two things that keep niggling me. One is this: why do we know about it? Why do we know about bitcoin? Just think about it, it's the only digital currency that most people have ever heard of. Why is that? It's because it's a limited hangout. The establishment has made it what it is. This doesn't happen by magic. As you know, people and ideas only become famous when the media machine makes them such. Celebrities can be made - or broken - with surgical precision given the nature of the media machine. Do you think you'd have over a million YouTube followers had you not been given the star treatment? Well, the same thing applies to bitcoin. It was made. It was provided with a counterculture. And it can be torn down in an instant.

"Also, Anna, and I hope you'll award me with some type of gold star for leaps of logic here, there's that store of value thing. If bitcoin is a store of value - that is, in a long enough time period, it only gains in value, how is its value defined?"

Anna looked at me, slightly perplexed at first, and looked at the ceiling of Il Fornaio, thinking. Then, after a moment or two, her eyes locked onto mine and she said, "Okay, I get you. Dollars. Bitcoin only has value because of fiat."

"That's my girl, Anna. That's why you and I are going to make some trouble. The thing is that the Federal Reserve controlled establishment could bust it whenever it wanted. The Silk Road trading exchange was busted and all the bitcoin on that network was sequestered by the Feds. It turned out that it was pretty easy on a public network, to figure out who was trading what. But the thing you have to remember is that the Fed and the central banks were and are buying time. Bitcoin was a diversionary gap-filler allowing the 'powers that be' time to get their various schemes together to start thieving even more. But as soon as I heard about Bitcoin - and it was probably around 2010, a couple of years after the Satoshi paper was published -I started buying it. Because I knew that this was going to be one hell of a bubble. I have a lot of bitcoins. And they're now trading at $10,000 a coin. But I know, fundamentally, that they're worthless. But, Anna, here's my idea. You're working for a bunch of libertarians. They want you to stay on message. I'd suggest that it's time that you started having some fun with them.

"But to make sure you have some skin in the game, I'm going to give you something. I have a gift for you." I handed Anna a little gift bag that I'd hidden carefully under the table behind my feet.

Anna lifted the little gift-wrapped parcel out of the bag and carefully unwrapped it. Inside was a little electronic device, little bigger than a smart phone. "What is this she asked?"

"Well, Anna, that's called a cold storage device. It's a secure method of storing bitcoin. On that device is 10 bitcoins. And they're now yours. I'll send you the various access codes you'll need when you choose to sell them. But you are now the proud owner of $100,000 of bitcoin. You can keep that device - and the coins - as long as you want. But what I'm proposing is a strategy whereby we keep your employers sweet, as long as possible, have some fun and possibly make some money in the process. Because, Anna, I think you might, inadvertently, be working for the CIA. So, what do you think? Do you want to start playing with the big boys?"

Anna smiled and sipped some wine. "I like your style, Mark Carlisle. I thought you were going to tell me why I'd offended them by mentioning Syria. But now it turns out I'm a double agent using bitcoin as my trojan horse. I like it. I like it a lot. But when are we going to talk about the Middle East."

"Ah, Anna. That will require much more alcohol, and much deeper rabbit holes. We may also need a little more time. But I sense it's time to end this lunch. Can I walk you out to your Miata?"

Chapter 6: Rahul Vaidya

Anna was a bit all over the place after her meeting with Mark. "He does that, I said. "Sometimes he's a bit obscure. Sometimes I don't know if I'm on my ass or my elbow with him."

"I think I agree with him," she said while toying with a bowl of yogurt, "but I'm not sure what I agree with."

"Are you going to eat the yogurt?"

"I don't know. I just don't know."

"About the yogurt, or about Mark?"

"Both. American yogurt is terrible. God, we need to start making our own. We could strain it like the Greeks do. Apparently, you can use coffee filters."

"Yes, okay. And Mark? What do you not know?"

"Well, for one thing, I almost feel like I'm working for him now. Like what's with the bitcoin thing?"

"He loves that kinda thing. Sometimes I get the feeling he's like making up a play as he goes through life - and he has the lead part. He really likes to do really crazy shit like that that just stops people in their tracks."

"Yes, but I don't like the idea that I'm suddenly required to be his understudy."

"I really don't think you are, Anna. In fact, you know you aren't. You're flattered. I was flattered. He's very good at making people feel really important - like they're important actors in a very important play. Like a play by Chekov or somebody like that from India. Like Cho Ramaswamy."

"Well, I was never one for Chekov. And I've never heard of, er, Cho. But you're right. It was flattering. But I suspect he thinks I'm hot and likes the idea of being my mentor or something. Isn't that a bit sick?"

"Look, you could be right. But what's the harm of taking the direction he suggests? All he's suggesting is that you start making stars of the bitcoin community. But you'll have your work cut out. Finding any who can string more than a few sentences together and aren't addicted to porn will be difficult."

"Fuck me, Rahul! That sounds just lovely."

But I'm happy to say, Anna pitched the idea to her editorial guy, and he liked it. In fact, she did her research and even widened the net a bit and started interviewing a wide array of Tech Bros - even a few women. By the end of 2019 she was building quite a reputation for herself as the bitcoin queen. She was chairing panels at bitcoin conferences, discussing how bitcoin might just be the basis of an entirely new, parallel, economy. Her YouTube channel was given a new audience of crypto-Libertarians, amateur economists and Wall Street analysts - all bedazzled by my girlfriend's beauty and her access to this new, weird world. But then a bunch of videos started appearing on Twitter of Chinese people pretending to fall down dead in the streets.

Now, if things were going well for Anna in late 2019, things were going even better for me. Mark and I were on a massive expedition to convince everyone who was anyone in tech that we were approaching a cliff edge. It was - what is called, in the business - FUD. Fear, Uncertainty and Doubt. That's what we were doing. Sowing fear.

Let me explain. The way systems were developing required what is called real time computing. This was all being driven by the fact that more and more devices were being hooked to the internet. Internet traffic was increasing steadily - supported by ever increasing data capacity on the networks. And with every tech wave there was a growing need for real-time service. Social media allowed millions - billions - of people to create their own content. Video streaming on demand required ever larger servers to stream the movies or cat videos. Artificial intelligence required grids of super-fast computers to serve content, no matter how silly, as it was needed. Just think about it, millions of children across the world, all requesting an AI, at the same time, to generate their homework for them. That requires a vast amount of computing capacity. And energy.

Meanwhile, in London, New York and San Francisco, a new breed of hedge fund was emerging that needed to be able to trade really, really quickly - dipping in and out of currency or equity or cryptocurrency markets - taking positions and changing positions - creaming off little bits of 'alpha' as they went. Oh, and they needed to build machine learning models to be better at doing this, in real time.

Meanwhile, everything and everyone became internet enabled. Cars, boats, fridges, washing machines, tablets, doorbell cameras were all becoming "smart". Data was, and is, flowing everywhere and control is required of everything and everyone. This real-time computing model is enormously expensive to run. Thankfully people were willing to pay. The problem was - and is - that the energy systems haven't kept pace. We offered a solution - and were willing to take very large amounts of consulting income from companies that wanted - needed - to know the full extent of the problem. We were selling a nuclear solution but first needed to terrify our customers.

This process of terrifying people required lots of presentations to concerned Boards. We were rapidly assembling a team of analysts and consultants - nearly all products of the finest business schools. Our typical fee income, per customer, ran into the £millions. By late 2019 we were working for dozens of paying clients employing consultants in London, San Francisco and New York - and a growing team in 3 support centres in India.

Rahul Vaidya

Mark and I were in New York in December 2019 when the news about a new falling-down disease was beginning to break. In fact, it was on most of the bulletins pretty much in unison. Mark had spoken at an Energy Futures Conference, and we'd organised our own briefing session at the Carlyle Hotel on Park Avenue for after the event. We'd both arrived early. The room was being made ready by the hotel staff, and we were semi-disinterestedly watching a CNN report from Beijing about an outbreak of a respiratory disease in Wuhan.

"My God, they keep doing this Rahul," he said as he screwed his face up at CNN's typically sensationalist reporting. "Remember when it was Ebola, or Bird Flu or Dengue Virus or whatever the hell…how long will it be until the WHO has declared some type of emergency?"

"You're right," I chipped-in. "In India people die all the time from total mystery shit but it's mostly because they're malnourished. Why do they have to do this scare story stuff all the time? Like, seriously, we get these health scare stories almost daily. What the hell's going on?" But that was about it. We exchanged a few passing remarks. We assumed this would be just another health scare story competing against all the other babble on the news networks. Then we focused on the reason we were at the Carlyle Hotel.

"On the subject of the media, Rahul, we have Eve Lassiter here this evening. She's a freelancer but covers energy markets for quite a few trade and business titles. Should you meet her at the drinks reception, could you send her my way? She's a carbon bullshit queen, and progressive politics darling. Literally loathes Trump but supposedly is close to certain GOP senators in more ways than one. In fact, don't worry. I should ask our new PR. Have you met her? In fact, here she is."

I turned to look at who had drawn Mark's attention away from me. Jenny McIvor had just walked in. It was my first meeting with her. Mark had appointed her as our US based government affairs person. She'd joined us from an agency based in DC. At the time, I had no knowledge of 'government affairs'. I had no idea that people could make a living doing this type of thing. I'll be honest, I was much more comfortable when Mark was dealing with these types. Even in 2019, I still considered myself an imposter. I was a Developer now doing business development. I preferred technical discussions to conversations over Krug about who was sleeping with whom on Capitol Hill.

Jenny was astonishingly impressive. She was as tall as Mark in her Louboutins. Her legs were sheathed in sheer black and her black suit was pin-sharp Chanel. Her hair was razor-cut and shiny. And this is how she pretty much always looked at this event and the many others she organised for us from then on.

But it was her ability to get together a room-full of people who, according to Mark, were seriously A-list that impressed him the most. Or so he claimed. But there was no doubting that she was very, very beautiful in an extremely scary way.

When Jenny approached, people responded. They had little choice. She had the darkest of brown eyes - almost black - that were made-up with absolute precision. She was fond of wearing an over-extended, Arab-style brow-line that made her slightly quizzical looking or confused, depending on her mood.

Mark introduced me. "Ah, yes, Rahul, I'm delighted to meet you. I've heard so much about your technical brilliance. I'll need to seriously pick your brains. We need to get a session in the diary so that I can get much more up to date on all the stuff I need to know." But at that point her attention was caught by Eve Lassiter. "Eve. Oh my God it's marvellous you could make it. Can I please introduce you to Mark and Rahul. These guys you must meet."

Eve refused to even pretend to be pleased to meet us. She didn't even offer a hand to be shaken. "I'm sorry I won't be able to stay long. Before too many people arrive, would it be possible for me to have a chat with you guys. Perhaps we could sit in that corner?" She pointed to the corner of the room with her head. She had a small rucksack with her and was rummaging in it - and pulled out a notebook and a recording device. Jenny made clear that she wanted to join us to listen-in. And so, the four of us gathered in the corner of the room. Eve grabbed a hotel chair and positioned herself in the corner and motioned that we should get ourselves chairs. We arranged ourselves in an arc and looked at her expectantly.

Jenny immediately tried to take ownership of the situation and was first to speak as Eve fiddled with her recorder. "Thanks, Eve, for popping in…" but was immediately ignored by Eve who looked straight at Mark and ignored Jenny's gratitude.

"Mark, I'd like to know what this is all about. I mean, what's your endgame?"

Mark looked at her, his arms folded and looked at the ceiling for a few moments. He then tilted his head down and fixed his eyes on Eve who was now staring at her notebook. "My endgame? I'm sorry, what do you mean?"

"I mean you must be in this for a reason. What's your reason? Is it all about making money or do you have a political agenda?"

"Well, I suppose all businesspeople have an agenda. Obviously, we have to make money, or the business would not sustain itself. We don't take money from governments. That's in our DNA. So, in that way I suppose it is something of a politically motivated business. We also don't sell what we have to offer to governments. They tend to get in the way of what we want to achieve."

"So, what is it that you want to achieve?" Eve persisted. "What is it that *you* want to achieve?"

Rahul Vaidya

The antagonism between the two of them was very obvious. Jenny glanced at me and winced. Mark shifted in his seat slightly and leaned forward in his chair.

"What I want to achieve, Eve, is very simple. I want to build a business. I'm funding that business mostly by myself. I'm employing people. Great, hardworking people like Rahul here, like my teams here in the USA, in the UK and in India. We're keen to provide a new way of providing energy to wealth creators so that they're not dependent on government monopolies or politically appointed oligarchs."

"Ah, so you do have a political agenda."

"As I said, Eve, all businesspeople have a political agenda. I just happen to believe that mine is all about reducing dependence on corrupt governments in thrall to corporate interests. I would have thought that you and I would be at one in that ambition, given your interest in progressive politics and all. Haven't you been involved in progressive politics yourself?"

"This isn't about me, Mark."

"Isn't it? Journalists always use the defence that their involvement in politics is never a subject that should be on the table. Would you not say that most of your colleagues would pretty much despise everything I stand for because it doesn't fit with your collective narrative? You write for just about every establishment paper. You have to ensure that your content is fit for purpose. But do you ever question why the narrative you and your colleagues push always suits my competitors - governments and corporate interests? Why do you never challenge the orthodoxy about the climate emergency or the strangulation of business by tax and regulation, or the establishment's stitching up of the financial markets or the fact that workers - strivers - never seem to get their heads above water? Surely someone so wedded to the left would want to see the ordinary guy, or gal, doing just a little bit better? Isn't that a way for the left and the right to unite?"

"So, you see yourself as a champion for the little guy now? Mark, from where I'm sitting, I see a guy who has made a fortune. The system has been very kind to him. You're a rich white British guy who has benefitted from being born into a democracy, with free speech. But now you're biting the hand that fed you."

Having delivered what she, no doubt, thought was a killer blow question, Eve sat back in her chair, folded her arms and smiled. Her little voice recorder sat in her lap and her rucksack was propped against her chair. She was wearing a pair of quite baggy jeans and a mohair jumper. Her hair, well sprinkled with grey, was slightly tousled and her face was slightly flushed. She wasn't exactly an unattractive woman, but her focus was clearly on her work, which was, in itself, something of a statement. We were all sitting in a function room in a five-star hotel on Park Avenue. The room had been hired by Mark. The four of us were all sitting in the corner because of Mark. Our collective attention was focused on Mark.

"You're right, Eve, I'm enormously privileged. I was dealt a very good hand. I was born into a stable family, and I did quite well academically. But, regardless, I *was* educated. So many children here in America are denied the opportunity to get a decent education - and the establishment wants to keep it that way. Ivy League colleges - like the one you attended - are beyond the reach of even the most talented kids in this society, because money matters more than talent.

"Honestly, I don't know why I'm motivated to do what I do. Is it because I believe, fundamentally, in the benefits of nuclear power over fossil fuels? No. I'll only ever drive a fossil-fuel powered car, I'd imagine. Do I believe that I'll succeed against the establishment where others have foundered? No, probably not. I'll probably end up as another frozen corpse not that far from basecamp on my own, personal, Mount Everest. All I can say is that I don't want to spend the money I've made on me. I want to give *it* a try - and I'm not even sure what *it* is. I may have chosen the wrong face to climb. Who am I to say?

"But something tells me that if I can break the stranglehold that the establishment has over choosing who is to be successful and what constitutes a good social order then I'll have done something useful. The problem that I have though, Eve, is that it may just be the case that no-one will get to find out what my perspective is on things. You represent the establishment and all the corporate vested interests. All you have to do is to walk away from here, delete that little sound file on your recorder and tear up your notes. That's the way it works. Choosing to ignore the disrupters is always the path you choose. It may be that you know, deep down, that there's no way your editor will run this story. You're probably wondering right now why you made the trip. Perhaps you were keen to impress Jenny, here, because she might end up working for someone much more important. Or perhaps you'll pitch the story and it'll be accepted. The story may run but I suspect I won't come out of it well. What's it to be?"

"My God, Mark, you're adopting a very defeatist attitude. What made you hate the media so much?"

"The thing is, Eve, I don't. Because great people don't go away. Free thinkers will always find their outlets. People will seek out the anti-establishment line. That's why the best journalists won't hang around. We're going to see the emergence of alternative media where bright, articulate people unpick the narratives, research alternative explanations and explore new ways of publishing beyond the censors or self-censorship. Because, let me ask you, which mainstream journalists - working today - exposed Wall Street after the 2008 crash? Or questioned the justification for Bush's "War on Terror" after nine-eleven? Or questioned whether Jeffrey Epstein had, in fact, hanged himself in jail? Or how many progressives, like you, Eve, asked Bernie

Saunders, to his face, what companies were sponsoring him?"

"You're very aggressive, Mark? Why the very negative tone? I came here this evening to meet with you and perhaps write a story about you. I'm not sure why you're blaming me. You clearly have an axe to grind. I'm just not sure why you've chosen this moment to do it. Despite what you think, I just wanted to find out your motivations. Clearly there's a battle going on in geopolitical circles about energy and power. I thought you'd have an interesting perspective on those things. Sure, I come from a liberal perspective and my views on climate change are well known. But surely that means there's an opportunity to challenge me and provide insight through your answers, not just to hijack me and give me a tongue-lashing."

Mark was sitting uneasily in his seat at this point. Eve had made him very quiet with her defence. I must say, I was very impressed at her ability to disarm him. Sometimes, when he was on his soapbox, he could be very arrogant. So, I thought it might be time for me to intervene. Jenny gave the impression that she didn't really want to get involved. "Look, both of you, I think we have an opportunity here. Eve, from my perspective, I think that our business should be of interest to you. Clearly, neither Mark, nor I for that matter, believe that man-made carbon dioxide influences climate. But isn't it interesting that Mark, given his position, has created a business that allows a much greater percentage of energy to be produced that's carbon-free. It may be that we are not selling our technology solutions on their carbon reduction credentials. But we thought that you may be interested in the reasons why we think that decentralized nuclear power is important for reasons other than the ones you might think."

Eve looked at Mark. "So, what do you reckon Mark, is it time for us to start over? Maybe have a slightly more civil conversation? Perhaps we started on the wrong footing. Perhaps that's my fault. Shall I ask you a less antagonising question? The voice recorder is still on."

Mark leaned forward in his chair and put both hands on his knees. He looked at Eve directly. None of us knew what he was going to do or say. "You know what, Eve, I think you're right. But perhaps we need a drink. Would you like a very large glass of Irish whiskey?" Mark summoned a waitress and small talk ensued as we all sipped our drinks. "Okay, shoot, Eve. Ask me your first killer question."

Eve was clearly more relaxed. "Well let's start with, erm, this guy's point." Eve pointed at me. She'd clearly forgotten my name. "I happen to think that we should be creating much more sustainable energy in order to mitigate climate change. But you have other reasons for promoting nuclear generation. What are they?"

Mark was clearly more mellow. He'd now downed a very large glass of whiskey. "Well, first of all, I couldn't care less about sustainability. It's a buzzword. You ask about my motivations and reasons for pushing decentralised nuclear. It's very simple. It's cheap, it's clean and it should be available everywhere. This is incredible. I'm not a religious person but I happen to believe that nuclear power is almost God-given. Here we have vast amounts of energy waiting to be tapped. And it has the advantage of being carbon-free, as you might say. So what's not to love? But every attempt we make to make nuclear power available; it's scuppered. Why? Because it upsets the geopolitical order. And, increasingly, that geopolitical order is defined by energy - and America."

"So, are you suggesting that opposition to nuclear power is coming from the establishment? It's not a left/right issue?"

"That's precisely what I'm saying. Because just think of it. If pervasive, decentralised nuclear energy became available all our geopolitical problems would simply go away. The wars in the Middle East go away. The tensions between Russia and America disappear. Africa's economic development would be accelerated. At the heart of all of our conflicts is energy. There is an enormous amount of money to be made with energy. That's why the industrial revolution resulted in the greatest increases in our wealth. That's how Britain built its empire - on the back of its vast coal reserves and the power equipment revolution it produced. But since the discovery of nuclear power generation what have we done? The so-called developed nations have done little, if anything. The United Kingdom was one of the first nations in the world to develop nuclear power stations but over the past few decades it has been shutting them down. And what is being proposed instead of 'dirty' coal and gas power stations? Windmills. Or Chinese solar panels. Sure, there's a lot of money to be made peddling these ridiculous 'solutions. Or maintaining the fossil fuel hegemony. So, we have to ask ourselves who's challenging the status quo? And from where I am, it looks like just about no-one is. We need power. We love the advantages that technology brings. But currently, no-one is suggesting how we produce more power when all of the political parties seem to agree that fossil fuels aren't the way forward. And that leads me to conclude that there's a huge establishment vested interest in feeding us lies. Because if what I say is true, if energy became cheap and pervasive we'd have much less need for governments or defence or families controlling things through NGOs and controlled media."

Eve looked at Mark for a few moments before asking her next question. She seemed to be processing what he had just told her. "So, are you saying," she continued, "that everything we hear about man-made climate change, about CO_2, about conflict between Arab and Jew - all of these things - are all, ultimately, about energy power play?"

Mark let himself smile, for the first time, since the start of this conversation. "That's precisely what I'm saying, Eve."

Eve looked at him over the top of her reading glasses. "And how long will they allow you to keep saying these things?"

"Well, Eve, that remains to be seen. Unless you can do something about it, very few people will get to hear what I have to say about anything. So, I won't be much of a threat."

The conversation between Eve and Mark continued for about a further half an hour or so - but outside of my earshot and Jenny's. We wandered off to the bar when Eve had switched off her voice recorder and Mark suggested they have an off-the record chat. Jenny had a glass of Perrier while I sipped a Bombay Sapphire and Tonic.

"Do you drink those because you actually like it or is it because of the India reference in the Gin?" she asked.

"The British brought the G&T to India. It was supposedly invented there. Or tonic was - as an easy way to get quinine down among officers of the Raj. As you probably know, Britain and India are somewhat joined at the hip because of the empire and our mutual love of curries."

"Are you being funny now? I find it hard to tell if Mark is making fun of me sometimes. You clearly share his humour."

"No, I'm being serious. But, yes, you're right. Indians and Brits tend to have a good cultural understanding. But gin, for me, is a recent affectation. If I drink alcohol at home, it tends to be beer. But I do enjoy G&T. Do you not drink?"

"I do. But I'm being a good girl this evening. I'm new to this role and this is my first gig. I need to collar some more writers. What did you think of that little exchange between Mark and Eve?"

"Honestly, Jenny, I don't know. I love Mark's style. I love the fact that he is living out an anti-establishment fantasy and that the business is generating enough fee income to pay me. But there may well come a time when he prods the beast so much that he gets his head bitten off. But it'll be interesting to see him on his home turf. We're going to London in the New Year. I suspect 2020 is going to get interesting. And there'll be lots of London Dry Gins to taste."

Chapter 7: Anna Sussex

As you can probably imagine, I was a little bit conflicted after my meeting with Mark. I wasn't even absolutely sure what he was driving at. The whole bitcoin thing confused the hell out of me. On the one hand he'd clearly made a lot of money on the back of the thing - at the same time as believing it was some type of intelligence agency plot posing as a libertarian revolutionary currency. But now I had this bitcoin 'skin in the game' with my newly acquired 10 bitcoins lurking inside this box he'd gifted me.

I knew that to get on top of the head-frying ideas Mark was firing at me that I'd have to read. I'd have to read a lot. I also needed to get myself some credibility in bitcoin circles. Thankfully, 2019 saw quite a bull market for the currency and, no doubt, Mark was possibly walking with an extra spring in his step - probably around the time he met me - as a result of Bitcoin breaking the $10,000 barrier in July. Although just as I started doing my scouting for speakers for my show the price started edging away again - giving my producers the jitters.

Luckily, Mark had introduced me to a friend of his who ran a Hedge Fund in London. He was something of a secretive chap and was very reluctant at first to agree to an interview. In fact, he only agreed to the interview if he could wear a mask to disguise his identity and use a false name. In fact, he had quite a presence on social media using this pseudonym of the 'White Hodler'.

Alex had done quite a bit of work to my little studio in preparation for the 'Whiteyman' interview - as he called him. "Hey babes, I like this international vibe we're going for. Whiteyman sounds cool and fucking weird at the same time. I'm experimenting with this cool new tech that allows us to interview him on Zoom, live, and patch him to the studio feed. But we're gonna have to use a green screen."

"I've no idea what you just said Alex. What the fuck is Zoom?"

Seriously, I kid you not. This was the first time I'd come across Zoom. It is weird to look back on that time - just a few months before the Covid bullshit kicked-off - that video conferencing technology was so novel - especially in the broadcasting space. Conspiracy theorists could almost come to the conclusion that the Tech Bros had already fully tested the tech well in advance of lockdowns. Just to make sure it worked for when just about every keyboard warrior in the world would need it to.

Anyway, the interview was set up with Whiteyman. When the Zoom video conference connected, I could just about see him, in almost complete silhouette, against a window. Alex cut in. "Hey, I'm sorry Mr White, but you're going to have to angle your camera so that backlighting isn't throwing you into darkness."

But even as the camera was re-angled, I could see that my interviewee was, indeed, wearing a sheer - like 50 denier - balaclava affair. He looked utterly ridiculous. "Erm, Mr White, could we perhaps have a chat without the headgear? We haven't actually started recording yet."

"Could you just call me White Hodler?"

"Well, I could but it's a bit of a mouthful. What even is Hodler, out of interest?"

"Hold on for Dear Life. I hold on to bitcoin for dear life. But I do it for the best reasons. Hence White. I'd also prefer to keep my hood on, if you don't mind."

"Your call. And please don't get me wrong. I really appreciate the time with you, but I must admit it does look just a little bit creepy." I was trying to avoid looking at Alex…I knew he'd start me giggling.

"I can understand that. But I take my privacy very seriously. I have a wife and kids to consider. I don't want to be in an abduction situation. I just don't want to be recognised in the street, if you know what I mean."

"I do, of course. And I'm genuinely grateful for you doing this."

"No problem. Just start recording when you're ready. I presume you'll pay my fee in bitcoin as agreed."

"Yes, I think Alex is arranging for that to be done. Although, I must admit, it'll be a first for us. All a learning experience I suppose. Anyway, let's get started." Alex gave me the nod that we were recording. "Let me start by asking you to tell our viewers what exactly bitcoin is. Some of them will have more knowledge of it than others. And then you could perhaps expand on this and tell us why you think it is important to hold it."

"Of course. Happily." White Hodler's mask had the effect of making it impossible to see his lips moving. There was just an impression of movement from where his month was located. But the words emerged from an essentially black head. He obviously had quite a bit of hair - because the top of the 'helmet' was slightly asymmetrical and wrinkly.

"I like to refer to bitcoin as digital gold. But it's better even than that. Gold is actually being mined more than it used to be - the technology for locating it and extracting it has improved. So, the gold supply is growing more than it used to be. But bitcoin's supply is limited just like gold - but it has the advantage of being easily transmittable. It's just a string of digital characters, after all. Fiat currencies aren't like that. Dollars can just be printed when the treasury needs more money - so that means that the value of bitcoin will always go up against fiat currencies - all of which are inflationary."

"So hence your Nom de Bitcoin...you believe it's important to hang on to bitcoin because its value will always go up? Hang on for dear life...or HODL."

"Yes, indeed. Obviously, bitcoin isn't an island. There are other things for people to buy or speculate with. So, the price will fluctuate. But, if you look back in time, bitcoin's low prices are getting higher, and its highs are getting higher."

"I get that. But, as you, yourself, have admitted, it's not as though bitcoin is anything other than a few characters on a digital ledger. How can it be treated like a commodity or an asset?"

"Because that's how the network treats it. You or I could say that anything has value. But unless other people want that thing it will only have value for you or me."

"But the question is, who gave bitcoin its network? If I say something has value no-one ever gets to hear about it. Why did bitcoin become the go-to cryptocurrency in a sea of what you would presumably call shitcoins?"

"Probably because of Silk Road."

"You're referring to the dark web commerce site where people could buy drugs, AK47s and all sorts of dodgy goods and services, transacting in bitcoin?"

"Yes. Silk Road was the ultimate use case for the currency. Yes, there was lots of dodgy stuff going on. But people had skin in that network game. It showed the network effect. It showed the solidity of the currency for transactions."

"But wasn't Silk Road busted by the CIA - confiscating all the coins?"

"Yes, that's true. Well, the FBI operating in conjunction with the CIA and Europol, I believe."

"But presumably that means that, if it wanted to, the Feds could confiscate all your bitcoins if it wanted to?"

"But why would it want to? I'm not doing anything wrong. I'm just holding the coins as an investment."

"So are you saying, therefore, that because the Feds or Europol could bust the network any time it liked, that using bitcoin as a transactional currency became less important. That's why bitcoiners just hang on to the currency for dear life?"

"Yes, that's true. And the fact that it has become quite expensive to transact on the network. That's why most bitcoiners hold dollar stablecoins as well. It's an easier and cheaper way to transact."

I decided, at this point, that I was going to let the conversation with Whitey just ramble on. But watching him in his black hood, nodding in agreement with himself, arguing the merits of this digital currency - that meant he couldn't show his face in public - made me wonder if he might have unsuspectingly joined a cult. Or become the victim of a psychological operation.

I was keen to get Rahul's perspective on things, but he had been in New York with Mark. When he returned, he was keen to tell me about the meeting with Eve Lassiter and give me the low-down on the beautiful Jenny, Mark's new media person. I cooked some steaks, and we drank some Chianti. Rahul was shattered after the trip. But wanted to give me a full debrief. "Here's the thing I don't understand, Anna, what exactly is Mark's endgame? Don't get me wrong. I think he's a really great guy. I love my job. I'm sure what I'm doing exactly but it's very bloody enjoyable. But I just don't know what he's doing and why."

"I think he's just having fun," I answered while searing my strip steaks. He's collecting a harem, that's for sure. He employs you. He has bribed me. But he hasn't exactly made clear what he wants us to do for him. So, I know where you're coming from. But it doesn't exactly feel like we're slaves."

"I get you. I know what you mean. But before I tell you about New York, tell me how you're getting on down the bitcoin rabbit hole."

"It's interesting. I get the libertarian arguments for it. I could make them myself now, I've heard them so much. But the more I hear them the less I'm convinced that the entire thing isn't a stitch-up. The thing that I can't get my head round is the extent to which the community just emerged. The people who are into bitcoin aren't, for example, the people who were burned by the great crash. Techs tend not to be politically motivated. Well, they hadn't been prior to 2008. Now, I've read all the Reddit discussions about CIA involvement in the creation of the bitcoin protocol. They're quite easily debunked. Perhaps too easily. But if they were involved, what was the purpose? Have you any ideas?"

Rahul looked at me, frying the steaks. "God, you look hot this evening."

"Well, it's hot here at this cooker." I was aware that I was wearing a very tight pair of white jeans, and my arse looked rather good in them.

"Yes, well, aside from how lovely you look, I find your logical processes very alluring too. It's not just the jeans or your gorgeous bottom." I loved how he said 'bottom'. "But, as it happens, I do have some ideas. I have the advantage of having had many more conversations with Mark, and I think I may have a better idea of the roles he wants both of us to play. It's all about control. Everything is about control."

"What is?" I asked. "Do you mean us, or bitcoin or money or what?"

"No, it's more about the government. The nature of government. Specifically in the West. And it's about America and its role in the world. It's as though there's a new battle about to begin - big time. It won't be a cold war. It'll be a battle between governments and the people. Bitcoin is just one component part of a strategy that was probably hatched decades ago. The game has been playing for some time. And we're only allowed to - if we're free thinking enough - to see bits of it. They are essentially bombarding us with complexity, misinformation, controlled media and limited hangouts."

I wandered to the table with our two fully loaded plates. The steaks hadn't rested long enough. But I sensed that this was going to be an interesting dinner conversation. I sat down, took a glug of Chianti, and waited. "So, tell me then."

Rahul cut a sliver of strip steak and popped it in his mouth. "Tastes great, but a bit chewy."

"Oh, for God's sake Rahul, get to the point. I'm waiting. I'll chew; you talk."

"Well," he said. "On the subject of control, I think the media narratives are part of the process. The media is clearly being used as an agent of change. That's your role. I suspect. Your role is to scupper it to some extent. That can only really happen when you've built a big enough constituency. You're currently a bit niche. When you're less niche and more mainstream than you can have an impact."

"An impact on what?"

"I suspect it's about the lying. It's clear we're being lied-to."

"About bitcoin? Or other things?"

"I think we're possibly being lied-to about bitcoin. For me the jury's out as to whether bitcoin was a construct of the intelligence agencies. It might have been genuinely organic. But I sense it wasn't. Just as most of the Tech Bros were manufactured - or were certainly made successful by the establishment. As Ed Snowden said, 'and so the geek inherited the earth'. Bitcoin is a classic example of something that's highly complex - unfathomably complex for most people. Therefore, determining whether it's true or a lie is pretty much impossible. Therefore, does it really exist? How does it get its pricing? How, actually, is it mined? Is bitcoin mining a myth? But the same thing applies to the dollar. How can the dollar exist when it's backed by nothing? How are treasury stocks sold? Who holds them? What is national debt? No single person really understands the functioning of modern public finances. All we know is that, apparently, money seems to appear out of thin air. Treasury stocks are auctioned. People buy them. Debt and inflation increase. But the process is impenetrably difficult. All we know is that a relatively small number of people are controlling things. And, increasingly, they are operating across borders. And corporations are transideological and unaccountable. But these organisations own the media and, even, the alternative media."

"But what you're suggesting, Rahul, is that there's a conspiracy at play. I get that. But do you want to hear my theory - given that I've interviewed more geeks and bitcoin weirdos than you?"

"I'm all ears."

"Well, have you heard of this HODL thing?"

"I have, of course. Hold on for dear life?"

"Yes, that one. Exactly. Well, I think there's something of a weird symbolism behind it. I'm not suggesting that it's masonic or whatever. But the HODLers are frickin' weird. They consider themselves almost like Wizards or alchemists. They have an assurance that they can play the bulls and bears with complete confidence that in the long run they'll achieve positive returns. But here's the weird thing. The move towards holding the currency has happened since bitcoin became overtly a store of value and not really a true currency. In effect that means that bitcoin is always going to be, by definition, a hedge. A hedge against inflation. Hedge strategies are always created by people who bet against the system. The more I see of bitcoin the more I'm convinced that the establishment, itself, was created as a hedge against the world's reserve currency. The dollar. And let's face it. Most of these people holding bitcoin are kids with establishment knowledge -

or even hedge fund owners themselves. They also tend to be very close to government circles."

Rahul considered this for a few moments before replying. He looked at the ceiling, cogitating, before speaking. "Hmm, so let me get this straight in my head. You're saying that roughly coinciding with the end of the 2008 crash, the establishment itself created a hedging strategy for insiders - against the dollar. Initially the currency was positioned as a movement - creating private, digital money. But then, with the busting of the Silk Road it became obvious that the transactions could be traced. And the authorities were saying we know who you are. Don't fuck with us. But carry on hoarding the coins if you want. Just don't be buying dodgy shit with them."

"Exactly. But it also meant that they were giving the green light to a new industry. They were, in effect, saying that we'll turn a blind eye to you holding crypto because we know we're going to be kicking the shit out of the dollar for a good while. Just look at what's been happening to public debt under Trump. In fact, since the 2008 bank bailouts. It's as if they don't care. You could argue that crypto - but especially bitcoin - is a bit like the South Sea Company. Have you ever read Cato's Letters?"

"Anna, I'm Indian. I'm a coder. What the fuck?"

"Look, I hadn't heard of them either, until recently. One of my interviewees mentioned them. So, I looked into them. Because you know the old saying about history rhyming. So, I'm giving you a quick overview of my reading, from memory. So, this will be a very abbreviated account. But it's relevant for two reasons: tyranny and freedom of speech. But here's the deal. In the early 1700s these two dudes wrote a series of essays that were published in a literary journal in London. They were known as Cato's Letters because Cato was their penname. Cato was a Roman General who stood up to Julius Caesar. The essays were republished in the United States and had a huge impact. Because at the heart of the letters was the idea that lurking behind the scenes of the government tended to be corporations, corruption and wealthy interests manipulating things for their own ends. The letters exposed the extent of British government corruption and manipulation of the South Sea Company - essentially a latter-day Ponzi scheme. And anyone who spoke out against the obvious fraud was silenced or censored. Hence the importance of the Cato Letters in highlighting the government's tendency to get involved in asset-bubbles aided and abetted by the corrupt - and the suppression of free speech. The letters inspired the First Amendment to the US Constitution: the right to freedom of speech."

Rahul looked at me slightly blankly. "And this is relevant, how?"

"It's relevant, like obviously. We know that tyranny happens when people try to get in the way of get-rich-quick schemes. The government essentially weighed-in after the 2008 crash by bailing out the banks - or orchestrating mergers. The 2008 crash was a culmination of the biggest financial bubble we've seen in human history. But nothing really happened to reform the system. Clearly the central banks were in on the act. All of the players highlighted by Cato's Letters were active and are still active in the Ponzi scheme that's the fiat monetary system. Bitcoin has been created for a select few to hedge against a bubble that hasn't yet burst. They're up to something Rahul. And I suspect things are going to get a lot worse before they get better."

"But I get the impression, Anna, from what you're saying, that the system is so big now, and the governments are so corrupt that no-one is going to squeal anytime soon. It's like there's a land-grab going on and that the little people will ultimately suffer the most."

"I think that *is* what I'm saying. The media is lost. It has essentially been paid off. That's the nature of censorship these days. Oh, and political correctness. Or woke as I think it's being called. Create an environment where the media narrative can't be challenged. And create alternative media that has a very narrow frame of reference. And, of course, the alternative media can only be created by insiders who have enough money to pay people like me - young and dependent - or compromised in some way".

Rahul looked a bit stunned. "Is there any salvation, do you think?"

"There is, I think. I have faith in the human spirit, my lovely Indian boyfriend. I believe in free speech. I believe in Cato. You and I, Rahul, need to get through this war we're about to wage with a free conscience. We are going to be on the right side of history."

And at that point, I finally got to eat my steak. It was a bit cold by then but tasted wonderful. "But, anyway," I said, "tell me about Jenny."

"Well," Rahul said, I think there's a back story there.

Chapter 8: Mark Carlisle

When it started, I had no idea how epoch-defining 2020 would be. But the situation in China with the 'mystery disease' was spiralling out of control. According to the media, the Chinese government had, by the end of January, imposed lockdowns in Wuhan and other cities in Hubei. This was of mere academic interest, of course, because the crazy antics of the Chinese government were not, typically, copied by Western governments.

It was for this reason that my own travel schedule was hectic in the final two months of 2019 and the first two of 2020. We'd heard about these fake pandemics before, of course. So, Covid-19, as this new one was to be called, apparently, was yet another Bill Gates funded affair that could be ignored. No panic required. Or so I thought.

Rahul had been doing a great job spinning the story about AI requiring so much energy. It was for this reason that we were in hot demand by the British government. Artificial intelligence, it turned out, was becoming a major geopolitical hot potato. From my perspective AI was and is nonsense technology that underpins much of the technocracy argument that has permeated throughout the entire Western deep state. Globalists and technocrats need very simple premises. One that has been doing the rounds for decades is the idea that energy, in effect, is currency. In short, access to energy trumps everything else. It's part of the reason that I thought I'd build a nuclear power story as the basis of my own business endeavours. In effect, decentralised nuclear power is the ultimate antidote to all the posturing and politicking around energy. It ticks the carbon box. It ticks the low pollution box. It ticks the erosion of power-blocks box. And it's for all these reasons that technocrats hate it and I love it.

Nobody seemed to care that I had no real product offer. The fact was that we were tied up in knots as far as regulation was concerned. But that didn't stop the media being interested in what I had to say. And the establishment was quite keen for me to make the argument that the technology sector would need copious amounts of energy to make AI products - whatever they turned out to be. That seemed to be anyone's guess.

However, I had my own hedging strategy as well. It was handy that I was able to leverage my bitcoin holdings to fund several other business endeavours. During the course of 2018 and 2019 I managed to IPO three special purpose acquisition companies. These SPACs, as they are known, allowed me to acquire interests in manufacturing and data centre operations - two sectors that need copious amounts of energy. Our operations were across several countries in Asia, the United States and Europe. The market capitalisation of these companies had all increased markedly after the acquisitions - as a result of a significant amount of private sector investment in my new public companies. By 2020 the companies had a market capitalization of some two billion dollars.

Hence the interest that was shown to me by the UK Foreign Office and Trade Department. They asked if I would meet with potential investors in various parts of the world. It was obviously a great opportunity for me to increase my visibility - always liked by investors - as well as identify potential acquisition opportunities. I also quite enjoyed seeing some very beautiful embassies and consulates. I even got to stay in a few Ambassadors' residences.

Over the course of four months from November 2019 to the end of January 2020, I visited San Francisco, Seattle, Denver, London, Austin, New York, Sydney, Auckland and Helsinki.

It was after my Sydney and Auckland trips - when I returned to the UK in late January, around the time of the Wuhan lockdowns - that I fell ill. I have no idea what type of disease that I had contracted. I suspect it was possibly the result of total exhaustion - or perhaps just too much flying. I have no idea. However, I didn't even visit a doctor. I suffered, how can I put this politely, symptoms that could only be described as dysentery-like. I suffered the most horrific stomach cramps. I also had a high temperature. I was forced to spend two days in bed. But, by the third day, I had made a pretty much full recovery.

And then I was back to the same schedule. I attended a reception in the Italian embassy in London. And then I headed to Helsinki - at the invitation of the Embassy.

The visit was around three weeks after my bout of ill-health. Over those three weeks I was getting back to fitness again. And I was lucky that the weather, despite the time of year, was surprisingly warm and sunny in Helsinki.

I was advised that I was to present to around 50 guests - mostly local businesspeople in the Tech sector. So, to get myself ready for this I had packed my running gear and decided to have a run around this lovely city in the crisp morning air. The sun was just peeking across the horizon of a lake that featured in my run around the edge of Nuuksio National Park.

However, I felt strangely uneasy on the morning run. I hadn't visited Helsinki often, but the city felt distinctly odd. There were very few people out on the streets. I sensed I was one of the few guests in the hotel. I'd had a beer in one of the few bars that were open the night before and I was alone - apart from a barmaid who looked as though she wanted to go home rather than serve me.

Despite the morning air, and the low Winter sunshine, I didn't feel particularly positive about my day ahead.

When I arrived at the embassy at the appointed time I was greeted by a young woman who didn't really tell me who she was. As we walked to the Ambassador's residence stateroom, where the event was due to take place, she explained that she was part of the

Ambassador's team. The ambassador, she informed me, sent his apologies that he could not attend. "It's no problem," I said. I wasn't aware that I was important enough for the ambassador to attend my little event. However, I wasn't absolutely sure that my presence was entirely welcome. There was a coldness about her greeting. I wasn't sure if this was, in part, because of the Finnish 'way' or whether the Foreign Office was acting on new instructions from on high.

"We have around 30 people confirmed. They're all being held in the embassy building and will be escorted up in time for the meeting. We've had quite a few people drop out because of the Covid situation."

"Oh dear, that's a pity. Helsinki's not exactly easy to get to. I flew scheduled and had to stay over last night. I didn't want to hit you with excessive expenses. So, I flew Norwegian Air. I hear they are having financial difficulties." I wasn't absolutely sure why I was suddenly blabbing logistical details about my visit. The woman made me feel distinctly ill-at-ease. "But you can be sure that they'll be safe with me. I'm Covid immune now, I reckon."

She looked at me quizzically. By now we were in the stateroom and the catering staff were putting out trays of sandwiches and canapes for the buffet lunch that was to follow my talk. "You are immune? I don't understand. How are you immune?"

By this point I had committed myself. And my ill-at-ease blabbing continued. "Well, I have been travelling a lot and got quite unwell a few weeks ago. Perhaps it was the Covid thing that they're talking about in the news. I don't know. But the good news is that I recovered in just a few days. I feel fabulous now and am fully immune."

"You had Covid?"

"Well, I don't know what it was. It was pretty horrible for a few days. But I'm great now. That was a few weeks ago. I was out running this morning in the sunshine around Helsinki, so I'm fully fit again. Not that big a deal."

I wasn't entirely sure why I was telling her all this. But her face said it all. She was now displaying mild panic. She excused herself and made her way to the washrooms to wash her hands - tainted as they now were with contact with a recent plague victim.

On her return she advised me that I had an interview with the local TV news company. They asked me some questions about AI and how much power modern data centres needed. During the interview I could see that a group of two or three people were whispering to each other at a safe distance - all women, including my recently traumatised escort. When the interview finished one of the three made her way towards me. She was a big woman. Apparently, she was important - the Ambassador's chargé d'affaires. I offered her my hand. She refused to shake it. Instead, she offered an elbow bump. "Mr Carlisle, I'm afraid we cannot proceed with the meeting. I understand you were recently ill. With Covid."

I could see the catering staff looking nervously in our direction. Plates were being arranged, knives and forks being delivered. The smoked salmon open sandwiches looked fabulous. "I'm sorry, I don't understand. You're cancelling the meeting. You asked me to come here. I spent yesterday and today here because of this meeting. The meeting was your idea. As of yesterday, you wanted to avail of my knowledge and insight. And now you're using this ridiculous excuse to say that the meeting can't happen? What about those people waiting to attend?"

"Well, Mr Carlisle. You didn't make us aware of the full facts. You could have told us yesterday that you were unwell and potentially infectious."

I looked incredulously at this very large woman in her large serious suit. "I'm not sick and I'm not infectious. I told you the very opposite. I was out running this morning. I'm totally fit and very, very well. I have no idea what made me unwell a few weeks ago. It was probably my travel agenda. Are you seriously suggesting cancelling this meeting?"

"Yes. I've spoken to the Ambassador, and he has said that given your ill-health and the risk of infection that the meeting can't proceed. Please take your time to arrange your transport home. We've told the guests that the meeting has been cancelled."

And that was that. I was still somewhat dazed and fucking furious when I pulled my mobile phone out of my back pocket. I rang Jenny.

"Hey Mark, what's up. How's Helsinki?"

"You're not going to believe this Jenny. They've cancelled the meeting. I think the world may be going fucking insane. I don't want to fly back to London. Could you get me a flight to New York in the morning?"

"I can Mark. But, be warned, New York is going crazy too. I suspect they're going to put us into a Chinese style lockdown. And it's going to happen soon. I'd suggest you fly to London in the morning. I can cancel all of your New York meetings. All the big Tech conferences are being cancelled here - in fact, everything. The airlines are in panic mode. Getting a private jet flight charter is almost impossible. So, I'd really advise you to stay home. Go home to Alice. We can talk tomorrow."

"What the fuck is going on Jenny?"

"I honestly don't know, Mark. I suspect that Covid is going to be the biggest psychological operation we've ever seen. I've worked in the media for a while, and I've never seen anything like this. But the deepest state actors are spinning this. Your meeting was never going to happen. It looks like a co-ordinated plan has been put into action - probably over the last 24 hours. Trump and

Johnson are at the head of it. Imperial College is involved. But this disease is being used to put the whole world into full-scale panic. And they're spinning the fuck out of it."

No-one escorted me out of the Embassy. I was told by the security guy at the exit gate that a taxi had been ordered for me and would take me anywhere I wanted. I asked the taxi driver to take me to Helsinki airport. I called my wife from my hotel bedroom - the hotel was right inside the terminal building. "Hey, Alice, it's me."

And then I told her what had happened.
"Well, I suppose you have to see it from their point of view," she said.

"What the fuck, Alice. This is my second night here. They're paying me for my expenses, but I was doing this as a freebie. They didn't even fucking apologise."

"Well, Mark, everyone's paranoid. It's looking like the UK is going to go into lockdown. Probably all the ambassadors have been tipped off. They wanted you out of there. They only needed the tiniest excuse."

The evening in the airport was bizarre. The airport was near-empty. Only a few stragglers like me wandered the terminal building like we were citizens of an in-transit dystopia. The undead. I ordered myself a beer in the only bar I could find open. No-one else was there apart from two staffers, who used this as an opportunity to mop the floors and stack unused chairs. So I left my pint largely unfinished and wandered to my windowless bedroom.

When I returned to London the following morning it felt like everyone was getting prepared for a new era. On the 23rd of March 2020, Boris Johnson delivered a television address telling everyone to stay at home. To protect the NHS. I always thought that the National Health Service was there to protect us, not to protect itself. But people were in the streets applauding it. This was the lowest point in our history. Hitler had failed to reduce the United Kingdom to this - a cowering, scared and supine nation, hiding away from a media constructed enemy.

But, of course, the rest of the supposedly 'developed' world followed the lead of the UK and the US into lockdown.

At the time, of course, my thoughts were not that fully developed at all as to what was going on. The media's focus was clearly on the so-called 'disease'. I had been sick myself but none of my symptoms seemed to be the symptoms of what became known as Covid. Flu had apparently disappeared - to be replaced by this new-fangled disease that, frankly, became more and more like a media creation the more sensationalised they tried to make it.

At the time I was relatively well known in media circles and a go-to person to comment on government policy and business. Often, when I was in television studios prior to Covid, I'd be asked 'what side' of the debate I was on. The assumption was that I'd be a 'free trade' advocate keen to talk about the perils of government overspending. But now I found myself - like most businesspeople across the developed world - trying to make sense of why I was sitting at home, unable to travel to my businesses. Those businesses were, without doubt, in near panic mode. However, it seemed that the technology firms had lots of ready-made solutions just ready to run. Within a few days all of our units were operating virtually. We were holding board meetings over Zoom or Microsoft Teams. Our manufacturing operations seemed to run pretty much as normal - especially those in Asia. But, in the UK, the government was spending printed money to pay people on 'furlough' to stay at home. Millions of people were now being paid benefits to sit at home because of the existence of a 'virus' that didn't really seem to be that big a deal. Or any deal at all.

But eventually the call came. The BBC asked if I would appear on a national radio programme as a 'voice of business'.

The producer who'd booked me for the BBC many times before called me, ironically, on my first day back in our offices. My business didn't have a lot of staff, but we had a suite of offices in Belgravia, and I wanted to make a point of returning to the office. We'd been in lockdown for around 2 months. The government had now implemented 'test and trace' - a massive investment in surveillance and control - requiring people to submit to testing in order to do anything - particularly to travel. Hideous government-run test labs were being set-up all over the country and people were required to get tested in order to be able to return to work or to visit elderly relatives in care homes.

Companies were being given vast contracts to run these facilities and testing operations. Testing became a national obsession, and the media was then using positive test results to feed a narrative of rampant infection - even though most people who tested positive had little or no symptoms.

When the call came, I was sitting in my company boardroom, alone. "Hey, Mark," the producer said, "It's been a while. How are you doing? I hope the pandemic isn't having too big an impact on your business. I was wondering if you'd be free to take part in a discussion. The topic is broadly about Covid. We're going to interview the Chief Medical Officer first - give him a good big slot - and then bring you and a few others in. To talk about the impact of Covid on business."

"Yes, that sounds good. Where are you doing it? Bush House?"

"No, no, Mark. Everything is virtual now. No, we'll be using Zoom. Does that work okay for you?"

At the appointed time I joined the 'virtual studio'. The host was a BBC anchor that I'd met several times before. I could see the Chief Medical Officer on the screen waiting for his interview to start. The conversation with him lasted around 15 minutes and focused, as per normal, on testing, the growth in cases, the continued threat to the elderly, the impact of "Covid". My panel included three establishment sycophants and me. All three spoke before me. And around thirty minutes into the show the presenter came to me. "If I can turn now to Mark Carlisle. Mark, you're a very successful businessman. Can I ask, how is the pandemic affecting your business?"

Zoom makes eye contact difficult. It was hard for me to see the facial expressions of any of the participants. But, by the time I was asked the question was about the time I was reaching peak exasperation with the format. But I tried my best to remain calm. I sighed, then answered. "Pandemic? We're told there's a pandemic, of course. I really don't think there is. There's a pandemic of paid propaganda - like the litany of catastrophising we've just heard from the so-called Medical Officer. But from where I'm standing, or sitting in this particular case, it feels like the effects on business are all being imposed by a government that's running amok."

The presenter paused a moment before proceeding. I thought perhaps that the producer was shouting in his ear but perhaps my tone of voice, which was somewhat dead pan, didn't provoke much concern. BBC journalists are noted for not listening to answers. He then followed with a follow-up. "So, you're saying that the government needs to change its strategy to deal with Covid?"

"Well, it certainly needs to change its strategy, but not to deal with Covid. The government created this disaster. So, of course, it needs to change its strategy. Frankly, the last thing we need is a strategy - that we all pay for - to deal with this fakery."

The presenter was now getting more uneasy, and I could tell he was being shouted at to cut to another speaker. So, he switched to a "Professor" in business studies from some B-list university. "Professor, do you think the government is pursuing the right strategy?"

The professor chose to ignore the question. I seemed to recall that we'd met before in a TV studio. She didn't like me then. She seemed to like me less now. "Well, I'd just like to take issue with the nonsense that Mr Carlisle has just come out with. We are, of course, dealing with a crisis. This terrible disease is wreaking havoc across the world. People are dying and are on ventilators across the country."

I decided to interject. The presenter let me proceed - somewhat enjoying the type of confrontation he used to quite like on his shows. Although I sensed my interjection wouldn't be permitted much time. So, I decided to go very, very fast. "I'd suggest," I said, "that the reason people are dying on ventilators across the country is because they're on ventilators. If the learned professor would care to check, a sure way to induce death in patients suffering from the flu is to stick them on a ventilator. This 'disease' that we're confronting is a pandemic of propaganda and fear whipped up by organisations like the BBC."

The presenter then gave me something of a telling-off on air. I suspected that my time on this show was going to be limited. "Mark, I really must ask you not to engage in conspiracy theories. We have a duty of care to look at the government's performance in dealing with the pandemic. Our listeners don't want to hear this misinformation."

"Well, there's a surprise. For years the BBC has been inviting me onto your shows to take one of two sides in a debate. Is debate not permitted anymore? Is it the pandemic way or no other?"

I had, clearly, annoyed him with this retort. "Mark, you do what you always do. You claim to have some higher level of knowledge than the rest of us. But it looks to me that on this one you're among a tiny minority. Just about every public health professional in the world agrees that this is a killer virus."

"Yea," I said, knowing that my time was coming to an end. I figured I'd try nonchalant belligerence as long as I could. "The old consensus argument. Weren't all the scientists in Auschwitz agreed that trying out new drugs on the jews was a great idea? Wasn't the medical establishment pretty much agreed that it was a good idea to prescribe Oxycontin - an opiate based, and highly addictive narcotic - to people across America suffering from toothache? Wasn't there a scientific consensus that pregnant women really should take Thalidomide to treat their pesky morning sickness? Medical consensus really is a great thing."

The presenter, clearly, had to chip-in at this point. "Mark, that's enough. I'm going to move on." But remarkably, the show continued, and I still hadn't been kicked off. The programme rambled on. The rambling virus babble continued, and I could see from the Zoom clock that we were approaching the end of the show. And, remarkably, the presenter came back to me for a final comment. "Mark, what advice would you have to listeners facing this Covid crisis - particularly members of the business community?"

"Simple," I said. "Don't get tested. The test is a fraud. The government is a fraud. The virus is a fraud. Don't get tested. Don't download their nasty little NHS tracking app. Do what you always do. Rely on common sense and don't let these totalitarian thugs…"

"That's it, Mark. I've had enough. You're off air. I just won't sit listening to this nonsense. And I just want to apologise to my listeners for having to listen to that outburst. I can assure you that Mark will never be on this programme again and I'm pretty sure will never be on the BBC again."

And that was that. He was correct, of course. I was not invited back to the BBC again. I haven't appeared on it or any other mainstream media organisation since then.

The experience was very unsettling, of course. Until that point I, like just about everyone else I knew, was under the impression that I lived in a democracy that valued free speech. I couldn't quite believe how deluded I had been. I knew that my life, my career, and my relationships would never be the same again.

Chapter 9: Jenny McIvor

I first 'met' Mark Carlisle in a bar in Raleigh, North Carolina. I think it was 2009. Well, the meeting was assigned for me. It was an attempt at seduction, but Mark saw straight through me. The persona the Agency had assigned for me was that I was studying for the master's programme in public health at Duke University. And that I was working in Comms for a consulting firm that wanted to increase its fee income in the healthcare space. And, clearly, I made the moves on Mark.

The bar was very busy. It was a Friday evening. He was somewhat incongruous, in his business suit, in a bar packed with twenty-somethings. I guess he must have been in his early-40s back in 2009 and looked very, very proper and very English. I was wearing a very short dress that evening. I remember it well. And I was, apparently, in quite a party mood.

Mark was sitting at the bar, on a barstool. It was my turn to order drinks for me and my classmate. We were both, apparently, attending a weekend residential class on the Duke Campus. I walked to the bar and stood, very deliberately, beside Mark. He was drinking whiskey.

Now I wouldn't ever be so forward as to initiate a conversation with a guy at a bar. But, on this occasion, I made an exception. Mark smiled at me as I waited to be served. "It's crazy in here tonight," I said, I think. "What's that you're drinking?" He told me it was Irish whiskey. Jamesons, I think. He then asked me if I was proposing buying him another. "Jeez," I said. "What a cheap skate. I thought the protocol was that the gentleman bought the lady a drink." And at that point he ordered three drinks, for me, for him and my friend. I duly found my friend, handed her drink, and returned to the bar to join Mark at the adjacent barstool.

"My God," he said as I tried to tug my dress down so it didn't ride over my hips. "That's an extraordinarily short dress. Are you on the pull tonight?"

"I'm not entirely sure what you mean by that. Is that a British idiom?"

He smiled and sipped his Irish. I knew very well what it meant. "Hi, I'm Mark," he said and offered his hand. "Sorry, that was very rude. You look absolutely spectacular. You have incredible legs. The dress is perfect to show them off."

"Wow, so we get straight to the point. I've only met you and you're checking out my legs. I'm Jenny."

"Well, it's hard not to check them out in that dress. Anyway, isn't that the point? Clearly you wear a dress like that to get attention. Do you enjoy getting it?"

"Of course I do," I said. "You know what they say, if you got it…"

Jenny McIvor

"Yea, flaunt it. I get it. But it presents men sitting at bars sipping whiskey with a particular problem. Especially when you slide up right beside me here."

"Well, I'd expect you to concentrate on what I'm saying more than fixating on my body. We've only just met. I'm offering nothing but conversation. You have to prove to me that it's worth my time sitting on this barstool."

Mark, I remember, seemed slightly taken aback by this. I was definitely a bit drunk – or so I told him - and much cheekier than normal. He seemed somewhat confused. But it became pretty clear that he didn't want me to leave the barstool just yet. "Frankly," he said, "I can't believe my luck. But I suppose it's time for us to better understand each other. And why are we both here in this place chatting to each other."

"Dear God, man. Lighten-up. Bars are for fun, aren't they? To meet new people. To have a few laughs."

"Oh, I get that. But we have just started a relationship. We're no longer strangers. I know your name now and I've admitted that you're very attractive. But I know nothing about you."

"Well, I'm a student here. At Duke. I'm out with a girlfriend and I struck up a conversation with this British guy. Who now wants to know why I'm sitting beside him. We don't really ask ourselves, before striking up a conversation with a stranger, why we're doing it. What the nature of the relationship is that we want. Right now, my brain is firing loads of questions at me. Do you find him attractive, is he crazy, is he married, is he able to have an intelligent conversation?"

"I fully understand," he said. "But would you be curious to know the questions that my brain is firing at me?" I nodded and laughed. "Well, the obvious one, that is being fired at me right now, is why has this girl sat beside me rather than all the other younger, more handsome and more intelligent men in this bar? And I'm also asking myself if you might be working for someone. These are the inevitable questions that men ask themselves when apparently singled out by a beautiful woman. In short, why me?"

"Hmm… well it was definitely something to do with the British accent. I'm a bit drunk. You look intelligent. You look like you'd be an intellectual match for me. I don't want to marry you so I couldn't care less if you're married."

"Why wouldn't you want to marry me?"

"Because you're already married."

"How can you tell that from what I've told you?"

"Because of this conversation. An unmarried man wouldn't give a damn why I'd sat here. He'd have just gone for it. Would have his hand on my knee by now and would have ordered me another drink."

"Do you want another drink?"

"That's not the point I'm making, Mark"

"But you didn't answer that other question that my brain asked me?"

"Which one was that?"

"Are you working for someone?"

"Are you James Bond?"

And so, it continued. This was the nature of our conversation for the next half hour or so. It wasn't so much a mutual chat-up as a joust. I'll completely admit that I was unashamedly laying on the femme fatale schtick big-time. But he was straight back at me with his enigmatic Brit in America cosplay - with his sharp suit and wonderful vowels.

"Can I ask you something," he asked as we took delivery of two more drinks from the barman, "what is it that you want from life?"

"So, you go with the easy questions on a first date?"

"Seriously, it's an important question. We all have to ask ourselves what we want out of this life we have. We're born with certain attributes, or disadvantages. The advantages we have - or disadvantages - are accidents of fate. You have obvious advantages. You're beautiful.

You're intelligent. You're obviously the recipient of a good education because you had relatively wealthy parents. You probably went to an Ivy League school and now you're studying for a master's at Duke. But you're young. You're from the elite. What do you plan to do with the gifts that have been given to you."

Clearly this was not quite the question I was expecting to be asked by this strange guy I'd only just met. We were in a busy bar thronging with businessmen, students, rich kids, entrepreneurs, probably a few hookers, and maybe one or two spooks. The noise levels were going through the roof of the little bar. And the answer I gave him required a few false starts. He had difficulty hearing me over the din so he pulled his barstool closer and turned his head towards me so I could practically shout into his ear. That meeting with Mark was quite a bit of time ago. So, my actual answer, obviously, is paraphrased given the passage of time. Mark, would, no doubt, take issue with my reportage. But after a few faltering attempts it went something like this.

"You know something, Mark, you're probably the first person I've ever met who has asked me anything like this. I can't remember either of my parents asking me what I wanted from life. I'm not even sure that I've asked myself. I'm not sure that I'm even able to answer properly. As you say, our advantages are an accident of fate. I know I have had lots. But the conditioning starts early. We're not so much provided with an answer than put on rails. Our challenge, throughout life, is to decide if we want to be on those rails, going in the direction we are told to go. You say I've had a good education. Perhaps you're right. The British and the Americans have some great academic institutions. But do we get to debate the content? I'm not sure we do. Is it education or coding?"

I could feel myself getting more and more emotional as I tried to answer Mark's question. Not exactly the plan. He looked into my eyes, and I could see the emotion in his. I tried to continue speaking but he put his finger to my lips. And then he spoke.

"You know, Jenny, I've no idea why we met, or what brought us together this evening. Perhaps we're both on rails but our little choo-choos have collided. That's a good thing. To answer your question from earlier, yes, I am married. But I'm delighted to have met you and I'm so glad you chose this barstool. I'm going to give you my business card and I want you to keep in contact with me, regardless of where you are on your rail journey."

Mark and I didn't meet regularly after that first meeting. But every year or so we'd meet for drinks or lunch should I be in London or should he be in DC - where I ended-up working most of the time. Our conversations, over the years, were sometimes light-hearted but often very deep indeed. We both knew that we were on a quest for something, but we couldn't quite figure-out quite what it was.

Chapter 10: Anna Sussex

It seemed remarkable to me that my employers could have had such foresight well in advance of the Covid 'event' to make me fully remote. At the time I was installed in my little home with a fully integrated sound and vision studio it all seemed very odd. But by the time lockdown happened in 2020 it was a literal godsend. We were able to continue our output completely unaffected. At the time I didn't really question how this situation had come about. I didn't really ask myself why it was that my employers had installed my own production capability and the ability to build my own subscriber base without any real support on their part.

When lockdown happened, things did change somewhat subtly at first, but then more obviously. For one thing, Alex told me that we had to have twice-weekly meetings on Microsoft Teams with Xavier and a few additional team members in HQ who seemed to have no job titles. But they attended the meetings, saying very little, but occasionally typing little chat messages directly to Xavier mid-meeting. The weekly 'content' meetings tended to focus on my monologues and on my choice of studio guests.

I'll admit that in the early days of lockdown I didn't really know what to think. I suspected the China story about the origins of Covid. The video footage emerging from China about the gravity of the lockdown looked distinctly fake to me. But then we started getting reports about outbreaks in Italy where Chinese companies had sweat shops. Trump initiated travel bans from China in January 2020 - but these were then extended to Europe in March.

According to Rahul, Mark was literally furious about this. He had been, apparently, humiliated on a trip to Helsinki - when he was effectively sent home as a potential health risk. It was beginning to look like a panic was being orchestrated by the authorities, but the bureaucrats were as much in the dark as to what was happening than the general public. But by March 17 America was effectively in a Chinese style lockdown. Then just about the entire developed world followed the United States into a period of public health insanity.

Clearly, my circle of friends and colleagues were utterly appalled by what was going on. California's lockdown was particularly draconian. The governor seemed to want to ramp up the panic and threat at every opportunity. I had assumed, of course, that my supposedly libertarian circle would kick back against this state authoritarianism. But that simply didn't happen. Instead, all the supposedly 'free market' and 'human liberty' focused spokespeople seemed to coalesce around the 'public health' playbook. The flu, apparently, had disappeared. The common cold was nowhere to be seen. The only disease in town was the China one.

From my employer's point of view, they wanted me to focus on interviewing public health practitioners and doctors. I went along with this for a while, but we soon realised that every mainstream media channel and every podcast bro was pretty much doing the same thing. I started to seek out some alternative views.

I'd come across a new blogging and publishing platform in 2019 called Substack. The platform had started attracting a number of maverick voices - particularly in the cypher-punk community. It was probably for that reason that I was aware of it. I'd even started my own account and was heavily pushing it to my YouTube followers.

I started looking for some dissenting voices from the medical community. The only person I could find was a former hospital doctor who had decided to leave the world of so-called allopathic medicine and to become an 'alternative' practitioner.

Now, I have a confession to make. Prior to the Covid thing happening I was very sceptical of alternative health. I was scathing of homeopathy, acupuncture, herbal health and the associated tree-hugging world of new world oddness. But this woman (and most alternative health practitioners are women) - who had started her blog on Substack shortly after it opened for business - had already collected thousands of followers. When I contacted her, I could see why. I initially emailed her and told her that I'd like to chat, with a view to getting her on my show. She came back to me and asked me to come over to visit her. She lived in San Mateo. Her name was Susannah Garcia.

It was May 2020, and non-essential travel was essentially banned in California. My little Miata had been barely used since lockdown had been imposed. However, it started cheerily as usual, and I pulled out of my little suburban driveway in Santa Clara and headed towards San Mateo. It was a warm, sunny day and I'd pulled the roof down and had my shades on. I was wearing a white mini dress that Rahul had bought me just a few days before lockdown in Banana Republic in the Market Street Mall. And life felt pretty good. But the streets were deserted. Strip malls were closed. I could see signs for San Jose airport as I took the panhandle for Route 101 - but the usual air traffic was nowhere to be seen. Rahul had been working from home for nearly three months and was going slightly crazy. For the first time since I'd met him, he was talking about flying to India to see his parents as soon as the flights reopened. But there seemed no realistic prospect of that until a - erm - vaccine had been developed.

I was keen to discuss 'lockdown' and the urgent need for a vaccine with Dr Garcia. I called her a little ahead of our meeting time to tell her my ETA. She was keen to meet me on arrival and let me into her home as quickly as possible. She said her neighbours were incredibly nosey.

When I pulled into her drive in my little Convertible she was already pottering around in her small garden - inspecting a rosebush. She was a slim, very tanned woman. I guessed she was around late 50s. But she had an incredibly well toned body - especially her arms. Her hair was longish - shoulder length - and grey. She wore a loose-fitting linen dress and a pair of very well-worn leather sandals. She waved at me as I pulled up in her drive, holding a pair of pruning shears in her waving hand. "Am I glad to see another human being," she said as I stepped out of the Miata. "You must be Anna. And aren't you just beautiful? I've been watching some of your videos but, honestly, you're even more beautiful in the flesh."

It's clearly the Californian way for women to admire each other in this way. But this was very gratefully received on my part. Apart from Rahul and Alex, I'd barely interacted with anyone since the start of lockdown. This wasn't by choice, of course. The vast majority of Californians obeyed the stay-at-home orders without any question. While I was keen to break them, the opportunities were sorely missing. This meeting with an eccentric maverick doctor was a coming out party for me of sorts. So, I was very willing to receive these very nice compliments.

When I made my way towards her with my hand outstretched to meet her, she took it even further - clearly to make a point. She stepped towards me and gave me the tightest hug. And then she took my head in her hands and kissed me, very tenderly, on the mouth. I was very surprised, obviously. Such displays of friendliness, between two strangers, are rarely expected. But it was strangely poignant. After the kiss she continued to hold my head in her hands and looked at me. She had startling blue eyes. "My God, Anna, it's so lovely to meet you. You are so very welcome to my home. I can't wait to talk with you."

And then she ushered me into her home, her arm around my waist.

In setting up the meeting I'd had the chance to ask her about her career and her qualifications. But I could also see that behind her desk, on the wall, were her various medical qualifications. Her MD certificate was the largest and was in a grand glass-fronted frame. But she had liberally annotated the certificate, on the glass, using various coloured marker pens. There were so many I couldn't read them.

"Oh, *I* know what they mean. Most I scrawled over the last few months. Every time I heard a news report about a 'new variant' or new regulation to stop us being human or seeing our friends, I scrawled something else on it. Now I associate each scrawl with each event. You see that one...?"

She pointed at a "Go fuck yourselves" written in black in all capital letters. "Well, that was the start of it. That was the day they announced their stay-at-home crap. For me that was the day that I realised without any shadow of doubt that the entire medical establishment and the government are just one fucking pile of evil scum." She laughed at the frame with her hands on her hips. It was a big uncontrolled laugh. And then she held her fingers over her lips to indicate that she was somewhat shocked by her own profanity.

"Oh, don't hold back. I'm completely with you," I said, laughing at her lovely, uncontrolled outburst. "But I want to know more about that. About what you just said. You seem to be suggesting that there's an agency about the whole thing. That there is a cabal controlling the strings. Is that what you're suggesting? Is there no doubt in your mind that the whole Covid lockdown thing is not based on any genuine concern for our welfare?"

"Let's take a comfy seat away from all of these memorabilia," she said pointing nonchalantly at her graffiti-clad certificates. We walked to the kitchen, and she made us two cups of coffee. Then we settled on a sofa each and looked at each other over a very large coffee table stacked with books on yoga, alternative health and cookery. "So, I want to answer your question. Is what they are doing based on any concern for our welfare? Well, the answer is absolutely, categorically, 'No'. Now let me tell you why. First of all, we need to be aware that if the media is 'in' on anything - particularly a healthcare related issue - then it's effectively an 'op' - and probably a psyop. In my view, there is no disease. Covid-19 is, essentially, an intelligence agency manufactured media operation. Now, they've done this before, of course. But Covid is an epoch-changing operation. We've seen nothing like this before. I think it shows that we've reached a tipping point. It looks to me that they're pretty sure they can do anything now. They have essentially hollowed-out society - and the ability for people to think for themselves - to such an extent that they can literally play us. For years they - and I primarily mean big business buying the establishment, and especially the healthcare establishment - have been jerking us around. They feed us chemical junk. They pump-prime us for dependency - dependency on entertainment, junk food, drugs, sport, brands - and then they spook us that such things could be taken away if we don't behave. They monitor and control us with their gadgets. They make these little screens more addictive than real life. And then they tell us to stay at home and gorge on this shit that they call living. And God forbid that we might say, 'Fuck you, and fuck your internet of things'".

I'll be honest. I was relieved by this. After my experience in the UK during the Brexit referendum period I came to the view that the media was instructed how to behave and what to report. There was no appetite in media circles to adequately cover both sides of the argument. But a few shreds of journalistic integrity remained - possibly because there was money to be made on both sides of the outcome. But Covid was very different. Where there remained some journalistic room for manoeuvre around Brexit or even discussions about man-made global warming, Covid represented a sea-change. So, I asked Susanne why it was - in her view - this should be the case.

"I think it's because there are so many corporate interests that will make a fortune from this. Remember, they are literally playing hard ball with this one. Never before have they used totalitarianism on ordinary citizens to deliver their agendas. Whatever way you look at it there is no reason for them doing what they are doing. This disease they have mustered out of thin air doesn't represent a significant threat to anyone except in their heads. Because what they are describing is no different from what we used to call seasonal respiratory illness, or flu or the common cold. The symptoms are inconsistent. The test for it was conjured out of thin air. They apparently sequenced the virus in a matter of days and developed an approved test in a matter of weeks. This is totally batshit crazy. Remember that medical emergencies spook people. They create a feeling of emergency everywhere. They isolate the elderly - apparently for their benefit - and administer end of life regimens on people who aren't sick but who have tested positive based on their quack tests. Then they stick them on ventilators to finish them off. This is the sickest thing that has ever happened to humanity. But here's the thing. They have another card to play. Because they'll pay off everyone who's anybody in the medical establishment to reinforce the fucking bullshit. I'd bet that every so-called television doctor will parrot every government approved narrative. Because there's money in every part of this: the testing, the tracing, the tracking, the sanitisers, the testing reagents, and then the so-called shit-vaxes that they'll roll out in rapid time. I kid you not. They'll hit us with this fucking Ponzi scheme in rapid order with the othering of the unvaccinated. Lockdown is a big enough shit-show. But just wait until you see what they're gonna do to enforce vaccination."

"But what makes you think there's going to be a vaccine? Surely, it'll take years before one is developed.

It's not as though they've ever been able to come up with a cure for the common cold. What makes you think the vaccine will be developed that quickly?"

"Because just look at the mood music. The vaccine is being positioned as the get out of jail card. They developed the test rapidly. They supposedly sequenced the virus, rapidly, so that they could come up with the test. And now that Trump has essentially 'funded' the vaccine development with operation warp speed you can bet that the vaccine will come along in short order. But none of this could have happened without a vast amount of planning. Clearly the World Health Organisation is involved - it essentially just a lobbying organisation for the pharma industry. You gotta remember, this has happened before. It happened with AIDS and HIV. They create a new 'disease'. They create fear around it. Then they create a bunch of really expensive drugs that governments willingly buy. It happened with Zika. It happened with Thalidomide. It happened with Oxycontin. The entire healthcare industry is a fucking disgrace. They buy off every politician who may have enough sense to see through the bullshit - but most of them are too stupid or greedy or both."

"So, at what point did you decide that healthcare wasn't for you?"

"At no point. I believe that I still practise medicine but in a different way. The human body is immensely complex. It's not complicated. It's complex. But the allopathic healthcare industry works on the basis that there's nothing complex about it - there's a pill for every ill. They treat but they rarely determine the cause of the real pandemics such as obesity, premature chronic disease or drug addiction. Because there's a trillion-dollar industry riding on the treatment of all this stuff. There's now a shot to stop people eating. There's a pill for erectile dysfunction. Statins are routinely prescribed for no good reason - there's no clinical evidence that the consumption of cholesterol leads to heart disease. But by being an alternative practitioner, I help people reduce their dependency on an industry that's literally killing people under the guise of science. But, before I continue my rant, there's something else I'd like to say."

"Yes, please do, what is it?"

"Well, I'd like to give you a piece of advice. I'd try to avoid interviewing doctors about all of this. Even alternative doctors like me. In my view there's something much more sinister going on and Covid is just one manifestation of it. The thing that has struck me is the degree to which they have imposed control over the media. Dissent is literally being stifled. People are being cancelled from all the major social media platforms. The mainstream media is not challenging the narrative in any real sense. And there is mostly cross-party consensus. This implies that there's a vast amount of coordination going on but it's not the politicians who are doing it. They are low life. Covid is essentially a psychological operation which requires co-ordination. It's clear to me that the intelligence community is heavily involved in this. And given the degree of censoring going on, and the compliance of the media, they must be getting heavy handed in terms of using kompromat. Have you heard of this?"

"Kompromat? Yes, I have. It's the collection of compromising information in order to control or blackmail people."

"Exactly. I know for certain that doctors are being massively incentivised to push certain drugs. The Oxycontin scandal showed the extent to which so-called medical professionals could be bought. But this 'incentivising' approach doesn't tend to work if certain people don't play ball. For example, people like me. But it's simple to silence me. The media can ignore me. And they can cancel my social media accounts. But let's say they had allowed me to build a big profile. Let's say I was a TV doctor on NBC or CNN with huge amounts of influence. Well, I'd only be allowed to build such a presence if they 'owned' me. For example, I could be employed by the intelligence agencies. Or they could have kompromat on me which would enforce obedience."

"So how do they go about compromising? Surely, they couldn't do this systematically?"

"You think? I think they do. I think they do it systematically. And they have been doing it systematically for years. The thing is, I'm not the person to speak to about this. Clearly, we all know that Epstein was running a kompromat operation - probably for the

CIA and Mossad. Beyond that I'm not the person to give you what you'll need. But, for now, I think I'll have achieved my objective if I've convinced you that Covid is a psyop."

"Oh, yes indeed. In fact, I think I had already come to that conclusion myself. But I really want to know, why are they doing this? And who are *'they'*?"

"Hmm, that's obviously a question I've asked myself many, many times. I know there are many conspiracy theories. Some might have a degree of truth in them. But from my point of view there has been a hollowing-out of the nation. America has seen a slow decline in so many ways since it decided to take the global lead as a technology superpower. People have become bloated on success. And all businesses - especially healthcare businesses - became technology companies too. People became numbers with an associated revenue opportunity. Let's face it, just about everyone in the United States has grown fat - literally and metaphorically - on the corporatisation of America. At the top of the pyramid are the giant financial firms that own just about everything. They have essentially replaced the government and gorge on everything they see. There is no real antitrust law anymore. Financial corporations own all the major healthcare businesses, all the major pharmaceutical companies, most of the mortgages, the retail businesses - everything really. So, we have a population that has grown dependent, and fat, without the need to do much in particular. That's what I mean by hollowing-out. People just eat and watch sport and eat crap food and order from Amazon. Our education system is shit, our people don't really question, they just do what they are told. We don't have citizens anymore, we have consumers. Automata. And controlling everything are a few gargantuan corporations - with a revolving door between them and the government. So, the role of government is simply to partner with business and to create the policy agenda that the corporations need. We have the worst form of socialism - because it's operating under the guise of capitalism. We don't have a democracy because people are conditioned how to think and behave and consume from birth. And now they are told to stay at home because of a fake disease. So…to answer your question… *'they'* is really most everybody. Everyone is on the rails of dependency. You're probably too young to remember the Pink Floyd video for their song, 'We don't need no education'?"

"I've seen it." I sought to assure her that I was more in tune with baby boomer culture, but she didn't look absolutely convinced.

"Well, we're there now. So many are happy to be just another brick in the wall. But I'm not. I'm not prepared to be a tiny part of a vast edifice of rigid control. Brick-built walls are brittle. They look strong, and they are. But there's an innate fragility about them. But I know that many go along with the program because they have little choice. I'm lucky. Ironically, I was able to stay long enough inside to escape. My husband died - much too young - a few years ago and I inherited his wealth. I was also well paid when I was in the system. So, I can afford to live outside the wall. I can choose to ignore them as much as I choose. But they are NOT going to fucking tell me how, or where, I live my life or whether I wear a fucking mask or take one their quack-vaxes when they come along. They can, as you might say in England, jolly well go fuck themselves."

I'm not a person who is naturally demonstrative or huggy. But I felt I had, at this point, to join Suzanne on her sofa and give her a great big, long hug. "Thank goodness, Suzanne. Thank goodness. I just want to say that I'm with you. Fuck them, fuck them, jolly well fuck them."

As we wrapped-up our first meeting and conversation I asked Dr Garcia if she might be willing to appear on my show. But the answer she gave me was slightly perplexing.

"I'd be delighted to come onto your show, Anna. But something tells me that your team might have issues with it."

"What makes you think that?" I asked.

"Well, I gather that your ultimate employer is a hedge fund. I've done some poking around into them. Please forgive me. But it looks to me that they might take issue with you having such a maverick on your show. You'll be aware that you have built quite a following on YouTube. I used to be on the platform too but was rapidly deplatformed when I started sounding the alarm on the Covid scam. The thing is, I was never much of a threat. I only had a few thousand subscribers when they started censoring my videos - effectively delisting them - and then eventually banning me and taking down everything that I'd posted. But you have millions of subscribers now. You're an A-list property. They chose you because they can control you. They may permit you some latitude but having me on your channel will put you straight onto a watch list. Your platform would be rapidly demonetized and then your videos would be pulled. Have you heard of the Trusted News Initiative?"

"This is the BBC thing?"

"Yes, that's the one. I looked into it when I became deplatformed by YouTube. It was established in 2019 before they started deplatforming people. The timing is very suspicious in my view. Look, it came before Covid. It pre-dated Covid. Just look at the media releases they put out when they announced it. It was essentially a Western international censorship nexus specifically designed to remove people - mostly ordinary people who had a view. Or an axe to grind. The members of this 'initiative' made clear that they didn't want to support the spread of disinformation. Think of it. Here were some of the biggest media organisations in the world with billions of dollars of funding getting together to censor and silence ordinary members of the public doing what their own fucking journalists are supposed to be doing - asking questions. I mean, seriously, the BBC, YouTube, Facebook, Twitter - all of them getting together to determine what is acceptable. The sheer fucking audacity. Cunts, fucking cunts. Excuse my language. But be sure, Anna, your employers wouldn't permit me to be on your channel, much as I'd love to be. Because after YouTube pulling your stuff, you'd then be blacklisted by the entire international media industry. It's easy, you see. Everything is digital now. The censors are AI bots. And you would be unemployable, in the media anyway. And your employers would take a dim view of your disparaging companies into which they have heavily invested."

"I sometimes think I'm between a rock and a hard place though, Suzanne. Covid is the biggest story around. If I comment on it in the way I'd want to, I'll get de-platformed. And I'll probably lose my job. If I toe the line on the narrative, I'll lose all my journalistic integrity and I'm not sure I'll be able to tolerate myself."

I was becoming very aware that my situation was very fragile. Mark's bitcoin bung wasn't even providing much comfort. Bitcoin, like just about every so-called asset, had plunged in value. My 10 coins were worth less than my year's salary in early 2020. So, I knew that I needed to hang on to my job as long as possible. But it was dawning on me that I might need a side-hustle as well as my bitcoin 'hedge fund'.

Suzanne and I had walked outside, and we were standing by the Miata. Our conversation was still ongoing though. She kept uncovering new angles that she wanted to discuss, or air her views on. We both remarked, frequently, how incredible it was to be able to have a proper conversation face-to-face. I asked her, "Do you think that lockdown had a more deep-seated reason other than the one that was given? Do you get the impression that keeping us apart had something to do with stopping the plotting, suspending the cafe society?"

Suzanne beamed a great big smile at me. "Oh my God Anna you've lit the blue touchpaper. This is my rabbit hole topic. And, I have to admit, you have rounded out my thinking on the topic given what you've done on your channel. Many of the people you have interviewed talk about money being at the root of this new era we've been thrust into. It's always about money and people clawing as much of it for themselves as they can. I don't know about you, but I get the impression that this is all about getting us out of their hair for a while until they can decide where we go from here. But creating that level of firebreak, between us and them, would have required extensive use of covert operations and intelligence resources. But this nation - America - is the only one that could have delivered that. I'm older than you, so I know just how deep the state runs. The politicians all represent vested interests. But the number of those vested interests has dwindled over the years leaving only a few supremely powerful groups. In fact, I think there's probably only one group left to all intents and purposes. That group runs the intelligence community, provides the geopolitical analysis, controls the money, connects into the military industrial complex, funds the political actors, and tells the media what to say. Democracy is dead. Welcome to the Technocracy."

Chapter 11: Rahul Vaidya

Shortly before lockdown happened in 2019, Mark had asked me to make some investigations into nations that have large deposits of Thorium. You may not be aware that Thorium - assuming that nations can be convinced that nuclear is a future strategic energy resource - will become more in demand when reactors start using thorium fuel. I don't want to get too technical, but thorium is a naturally occurring element in nature. It can then be converted into fissile material (uranium-233) using neutron capture. But here's the big deal. Thorium reactors are breeders. That means that they create more fissile material than they consume. They also produce less waste.

Now I'm sure you'll agree with me that it's kinda cool that the nations that have more thorium are not necessarily the nations that have large indigenous supplies of hydrocarbon fuels like oil and gas. For me it was very gratifying to know that India has some of the largest thorium deposits in the world - about 25% of the world's deposits - and that a lot of those deposits are in the Monazite Sands in my home province of Kerala.

The thing is, we had been winning loads of consultancy projects with both various parts of the Indian government and some of India's biggest technology companies. Our strategy was to spin the fact that they needed to jump on the new energy bandwagon to help fuel their data centre capabilities. We had some insider intelligence that there was a brewing arms-race in artificial intelligence. OpenAI had become a for-profit company in 2019. But, meanwhile, all the big American tech firms were creating their own AI tech or collaborations. Meanwhile Nvidia - the company that was providing most of the incredibly power-hungry chips to power AI data centres - was seeing huge increases in its stock price. Our intention was to ride on this wave. We focused on fragility: how can you guys compete on a world stage for technology development capability - or bitcoin mining - if you are highly dependent on other nations for your energy needs? In short, our message was to start focusing on building thorium reactors. And we, obviously, could assemble the teams to do it.

But call me paranoid if you like, I was convinced that the 2020 lockdowns were conceived to fuck us up. However, in our case, I'm not sure how far this was from the truth.

Mark told me about his eve of lockdown experience in Helsinki. But it seemed to us that the whole scenario was rigged. It was clear that we had inadvertently found ourselves on the radar screens of the intelligence services.

The United Kingdom is a member - alongside the USA, Canada, Australia and New Zealand - of the so-called Five Eyes Network. Google it. Some people think that this network is more all-powerful than any government official, any politician. It was Mark's view -

and this was confirmed by his extensive reading of materials relating to Ed Snowden's and Wikileaks' documents that when push came to shove the Five Eyes network would always behave as one entity and with shared objectives, regardless of the flavour of governments in power. Mark was constantly referring to the failure to declassify the JFK files, the mysterious death of Epstein, the incarceration of Julian Assange and the failure to pardon Ed Snowden as collective evidence of how the nations always acted in cahoots. So, he figured, we must be annoying them - a little private company working with a BRIC nation and a nuclear power and some of the fastest growing tech firms in the world with some of the best talent.

But, meanwhile, I had an incredibly well-developed line-up of pitch meetings and project development meetings in India summarily cancelled. I'd planned to take Anna with me on a trip, and she was planning on conducting lots of interviews with some of India's leading Tech Bros. But, with lockdown, everything was suspended, and all the meetings had to be moved to video calls. It was very, very annoying.

But even more annoying was the amount of hassle we were getting from certain companies that seemed to believe that they had a God-given right to do whatever they wanted and to take issue with what we were doing. We knew that by operating in the energy and tech spaces we were potentially going to upset some vested interests. But the degree of upset didn't emanate so much from the energy companies as from certain technology firms that seemed to have very close relationships with the government and, more particularly, the intelligence community.

The problem seemed to be that we were being very successful opening up dialog with a lot of firms based in India that wanted to challenge the dominance of some of the Indian tech giants that had developed very cosy relationships with Silicon Valley 'partners'. These Californian companies were able to offer influence at the highest level to secure stupendously lucrative US government contracts. But that was simply a starting point. The fact was that there seemed to be a level of arrogance on the part of some of these companies that went well beyond securing government contracts. In fact, governments frustrated the ambitions of some of the fastest growing tech firms in both America and India. They wanted to govern directly. Governments were irritants.

Just think about it. If you were a tech titan and wanted to dominate a market, you aren't going to play fair. Let's say that you're selling cybersecurity or surveillance systems. It's going to be impossible to create a viable business model, and to invest resources in building a great product, if you're having to bid for government procurement. And, in fact, what government is going to put out an invitation to tender for a system clearly designed to monitor and control citizens? So, a great way to proceed is to go directly to the horse, so to speak. Just about every politician, bureaucrat, in every department or agency is controlled by a company or lobby group. Or both.

This means that at the upper reaches of government decisions are being taken that ordinary citizens have no idea about. These decisions typically involve budget allocations that are simply beyond belief. And the 'brotherhood' controls pretty much everything.

Mark and I were blown away by the extent of the stitch-up that was Covid-19. We have debated to what extent the whole thing was co-ordinated. And we have concluded that it was to some extent. But to be honest, it unfolded in ways that took even the 'fixers' by surprise. California, for example, became a dystopia almost overnight. San Francisco was cleared of office-workers almost by magic. People returned to local neighbourhoods where they lived - to work as well. The retail sector practically collapsed. Catering businesses cratered. The skies fell silent of planes. The new era had begun.

The Covid carve-up was largely co-ordinated by the Tech firms in cahoots with the pharma mafia. But the tech firms dominated the power-play. Handily, all the tools for home working had been developed and had massive cloud-based server capacity ready-built. Amazon flexed to deliver more products than it had ever delivered. Food delivery companies had their apps built and ready for a torrent of business. And, of course, people loved this. "Fuck the commute," they said. "We love lockdowns."

Meanwhile they were oblivious to the land-grab that was going on. America was being consumed by the corporates. Schools were closed in favour of 'remote teaching'. When teachers reluctantly returned to classrooms they insisted on facemasks for children and teachers alike. There was a vast educational setback for kids that would last for years. In a nation that was already dependent on foreign countries for better educated talent. Meanwhile, the cost of this de facto holiday for millions across the West was running at trillions of dollars. Trump oversaw one of the biggest hikes in public spending and borrowing ever seen in American history. And this punch to the head of Western economies resulted, effectively, in the end of the democratic period in the West. The oligarchs were firmly in control. The politicians were but actors on a stage.

Dr Garcia, Anna and I had many conversations over dinner in our places in Santa Clara and her place in San Mateo. We provided a mutual salvation for each other, and we all enjoyed breaking the so-called Covid 'rules. Separately, Dr Garcia had struck up a lockdown friendship with a retired Economist. Professor Ken Ivanov connected with Susannah via Substack. He subscribed to her newsletter - which was becoming a destination site for a group she nonchalantly referred-to as the Covcurious. After many exchanged emails and Zoom calls, she learned that he, too, lived in the Bay Area. Hence, they arranged to meet. The Professor had resigned from his position at Stanford's Economics

Department just a few months into lockdown. He claimed that he'd made a good enough living and had no need to put up with the bullshit anymore.

The first evening we met at our place we had dinner outside in our collective back yard. Anna and I had knocked down the dividing fence between both properties and installed quite a nice patio area and barbecue - with lots of twinkling fairy lights. It made a great venue for discussions about liberty and its removal. Ken, at our first meeting, was clearly using it as an opportunity to develop an argument relating to coercion and control. His specialism was health economics.

I knew he was itching to tell us more about his thinking about the origins of the lockdown. So, after a few glasses of Robert Mondavi Private Collection Chardonnay - he was good enough to arrive with a half case - I thought it was time to bypass the small talk and to allow him to get straight to the point.

"So, Ken, we're itching to know, I'm sure, your theory on what the hell is going on with this Covid business. You must have a theory."

"Well, that's the question, Rahul. Honestly, the only insight I have that is probably more detailed than yours relates to some of my analysis. I'm a Health Economist so I'm always quite keen to look at the numbers. Clearly the most relevant numbers are - sadly - the death numbers. I have looked at the models coming from all over the place - but especially the State level data coming out of the UK, here in California, New York and the EU. I've also looked in detail at the data, in particular, relating to Northern Italy - supposedly one of the epicenters of the so-called disease."

Anna jumped in at that point. "You say, so-called disease?"

"Yes, I do Anna. I have to. I know that you do too, because I've listened to several of your podcasts and it's clear that you don't accept the narrative being pushed by the media and organisations like the WHO or Gates. I have never come across an incident in modern history where a new disease has been described, symptomatically, then a so-called causal virus has been isolated, a test produced, and an entire disease response industry has emerged almost overnight. Susannah and I have discussed this at length and it's clear that everything is nudging us, pushing us, in the direction of acceptance of a novel disease causing a pandemic. But, in terms of the data, I've seen nothing to indicate that excess deaths are there in the numbers that would require such dramatic overreaction. It's clear that the very elderly with co-morbidities are dying and that those deaths are being attributed to Covid. But it seems to me that's more to do with the treatment protocols and attribution of deaths than to do with anything particularly sinister in terms of a new or novel pathogen."

I was first to respond, but Dr Garcia and Anna were beaming smiles and Mondavi-toasting the Professor at this point. "I'm pretty sure we all agree on that - and that explains why we're sitting here this evening breaking the social distancing nonsense. But you're an economist. I bet your view on the origins of the thing will be different from others. What are they?"

"Rahul, it's very hard to know where to start. And, I have to say, some of what I'm about to say makes me feel very uncomfortable. For decades I've been a sought-after expert from those on the right. I've always managed to avoid political sponsors. But I have advised politicians, and I have worked with some large corporations - advising on lobbying strategies and so-called free market economics. But the last few months have caused me to question some of my positions - and, certainly, my political affiliations."

"In what way?" I asked.

"Well," he looked up to the reddening sky, "I'm not sure that there is any such thing as left and right or Republican or Democrat or even party politics any longer. Or, indeed, if there ever was. As an Economist I have been concluding that Covid is a red herring. It's a big distraction. It's a distraction from what they have been doing for decades. It's a distraction from fundamental rules of economics and fairness. Because what Covid has shown us is that they work only in the domain of macroeconomics when it comes to human life. They literally will do anything to gain the economic upper hand. What they are engaged in is a land-grab to maintain their hegemony and they don't care a damn about anyone. And by 'they' I mean the oligarchs. I mean the energy giants, those with vast wealth and their puppet politicians. I also mean the tech titans. And the so-called green activists. Everything is a ruse to get us - or our thoroughly corrupt governments - to spend money on them. But the only means of creating money to be spent is to get governments to print more of it. They have become depraved junkies on debt. And there's a feeding frenzy going on at the top of the food chain."

Anna jumped in again. "So, are you seriously suggesting that they are doing what they are doing purely for money?"

"I am. Ultimately this is all about money. But it's also about America. Just think about it. We have the biggest corporations on the earth in terms of market capitalisation. But what do they actually do? Trump talks about making America great again but it's really too late for that. We ceased to be great decades ago. What we have been very good at is financialization. Our biggest companies don't really do anything but orchestrate production. All the difficult things go on elsewhere. But the money manipulation remains in-house. London and New York essentially own everything in the West. The banks and private equity businesses treat the central banks like serfs. The process of so-called wealth creation is, in fact, a process of debt creation. The process of globalisation needs a well-oiled financialization machine. And the usual-suspect corporations are always on hand to create new justifications for more debt.

"America has created the concept of bailout. In 2008, we bailed out the banks. With every war we fund we bail out the military industrial complex. With this new disease we're bailing out the pharmaceutical industry and health care companies. Fear is the motivator to get people to act. Fear of losing a job. Fear of a foreign aggressor. Fear of foreclosure. Fear of Islam. Fear of an invisible but insidious disease made by mad scientists in Wuhan. And the debt mountain grows to feed the corporate beast. It all flows from us. Because the more they print money the more the value of the dollar declines and the more people are impoverished while the oligarchs get richer.

Just look at how every Western government is getting more and more indebted to feed this Covid beast. But soon the calls will increase for us to feed the carbon reduction beast by buying battery cars and replacing super-efficient and extraordinarily reliable hydrocarbon-fuelled cars. Soon we'll be asked to support more wars in places most Americans will never have heard of. And the imperative for all these things will be sustained by poodle media organisations. There will be no discernible difference between the political parties' policies, except when campaigning. All populist policy commitments that they make will be dropped once elected. And they'll crank up the money printing once again. But with this velocity of financialization, inevitably we'll cross a Rubicon. In fact, with lockdowns, we have probably already crossed it."

Rahul Vaidya

At this point Dr Garcia chipped in. "Ken's spot on. We've never seen this degree of civilisational hatred before - or certainly not in the modern era - by governments for their people. Elderly people are being systematically euthanised in nursing homes. They're pumping them with end-of-life drugs if they test positive or show the slightest signs of so-called Covid infection. But that's not even close to being the sum-total of the evil that this lockdown represents. In fact, who came up with this term, lockdown? I mean, who the hell do they think they are? But just think about it. We're okay. We're all relatively rich. Like look at this place. You two have a house each and this outside space and you both do something in tech, so you're both well paid and live in a nice neighbourhood. So, do I. So does Ken. We all have money and cars and the ability to think freely because we're educated. But just imagine if, by accident of birth, you ended-up being one of 6 kids born to a single parent 'family' living in Hillside Apartments in Oakland. Or, Anna, I'm sure you know of many similar public housing shitholes in London. Imagine being a child trying to survive, months on end out of school. They closed the schools in March. When are they going to reopen? What the fuck are they doing? We have a pandemic of child abuse, child malnutrition, child injury, and horrific levels of child neglect in this state - never mind the rest of the supposedly developed world. Children who are at zero risk of their peddled 'virus' are now subject to the vastly greater risk of filicide."

Anna reached out for my hand under our garden table. I could see that she was very shaken by this. She tried to speak but was trying to stifle the emotion that was inhibiting her ability to. I squeezed her hand and tried to articulate what I suspected she wanted to say.

"What can we do, Susannah? Ken? What can we do?"

Ken was first to speak. "Look, Rahul, you…we…are not to blame. We are not elected to power. Nor are we seeking power. But we need to culture an entirely different mind-set in this new era than we had before. There's no doubt that we have been the subject of coercion and control in the past but perhaps we, secretly, knew that and it didn't really bother us too much because it didn't really affect our quality of life. But consider this. In the late 60s and early 70s young men aged 18 to 25 were required by law to register with the draft board. The Board operated a lottery system meaning that any one of those young men could be called to serve in a war that many people couldn't quite understand why we were fighting - in Vietnam. Many knew at the time that if they were called up, they would face death, or mutilation or humiliation if they tried to dodge the draft. Now they're locking us down, literally pillaging the economy on behalf of their corporate masters. The endgame is always theft. It's theft of the world's resources, or the enforcement of Pax Americana with war, or the pillaging of human rights. The manifestation of the government, increasingly, in all our lives, is - to put it as simply as possible - evil. It's evil. And the only thing we have available to us to fight it is truth.

Rahul Vaidya

"Don't get me wrong. I'm not a religious person. I'm not arguing - like many in the MAGA movement do - that truth is about pushing a particular religious narrative to counter one that we perceive as evil. Because arising out of that is sectarianism. Politicians love - more than anything else - the process of othering. They say that one particular group is evil and the source of all our woes. They'll say the Chinese were responsible for Covid. Or they'll say that Anthony Fauci was responsible by funding a germ warfare program. That's always the trajectory. They cause a problem. Then they seek a villain or a tribe of villains. Then they start a social media campaign. No doubt they'll be pushing a vaccine soon enough. It's their only way out of this mess. So, anyone who refuses the vaccine for their media manufactured disease will be vilified and othered.

"So, to answer your question, I think the only thing we can do is to say, 'No'. They are mobsters. They represent an organised crime syndicate - or several. The only thing we can do is to become conscientious objectors. We do not comply. We do not accept. We do not take their advice. We highlight their depravity. We show care and compassion to our fellow humanity being assaulted by their actions.

"And, I suppose, Anna, you might have a very particular role to play. You still have a platform. Your challenge is to consider how you use that. You clearly have significant influence. I suspect that most of your competitors - even those who might seem to be on our side - will be compromised in some way too. You might be as well. It might be true that if you push too hard or question too much your employers might weigh in. You could lose your job or your platform or both."

Anna was beginning to buckle a little under the pressure. I was guilty of putting pressure on her too. And Mark. She was still very young. When she accepted her new role, she thought she might one day become something in the media. But she didn't realise that the media was about to become the main purveyor of corporatist inspired state propaganda. "But what you're suggesting, Ken," she blurted, "is that we, I, become anarchists…that we do a sudden U-turn away from the globalism that has given us so much. Our lives are significantly richer as a result of global capitalism."

Ken smiled at her and touched her hand across the table. "Anna, I completely understand what you're saying. And the only reason I'm able to take the position I'm taking now is because the 'system' has given me such advantages in life. But that's only because the globalists chose to take advantage of people that we could safely ignore." He held his Apple iPhone aloft. "We have been fixated on getting the latest versions of these things: designed, apparently, in California but assembled in China. The anarchist movement - to the extent that it ever was a movement - emerged from the Ivy League campuses and demanded an end to war and specifically to American involvement in overseas wars. In that respect it was a libertarian movement, and a grassroots one at that. But one could almost have traced a line of ancestry from the Occupy Wall Street movement back to the Vietnam protests. I was very vocal in my criticism of those protests because I saw them as hypocritical. The protestors were mostly middle class and had all the advantages of the modern era - but were critical of the globalism that created it. But what they chose to highlight was the degree of exploitation that was going on. Wall Street was essentially funding American corporate imperialism and was willing to turn a blind eye to child exploitation, sweat shops and dependence. Those were laudable things to draw attention to. In creating a them and us society the American corporate elite showed that it couldn't care less about human rights or decency. And now they have turned their attention to us. The land grab continues, but the Anarchists are saying nothing or have been bought by corporate lobbying firms. The Anarchists have simply gone away - to be replaced by the coerced, the supine, the compliant.

"And my concern is that the lockdown phase is just the start of a new level of compliance. Lockdown has crystallized compliance. When they roll out their 'vaccines' in short order the anarchists will be at the front of the line to get them."

"But Ken," Anna interjected, "you started this conversation from an Economist's perspective. You mentioned debt. How does this fit with your coercion narrative? I mean, how does debt work towards creating the new world order that is coercive and compliant in the way that you have outlined?"

"Well, that's the absolute core of the issue Anna. Debt is the ultimate instrument of control. Debt creates dependency and alters free will. Let's say I make a loan to you on condition that you meet the repayment terms. But then you lose your job. So, your ability to repay the loan becomes impossible. Let's say you had children who you were sending to private school on the strength of the loan advance. You may have to stop them going to such a school in order to make your loan repayment. Therefore, your decision-making has been altered by your dependence and repayment commitments. You may also be forced to sell assets or remortgage your property in order to meet your commitments. In short, your entire focus switches from doing the best for your family and your security in order to meet your obligations to a creditor - that is, me.

"But just think what happens when your government gets into huge amounts of debt. In order to meet its obligations, it is obliged to focus on meeting the needs of its creditors - that is, organisations that hold its treasury debt or bonds. The government of America now owes trillions of dollars to corporations - financial institutions, custodians, pension funds, private equity firms and investment banks. So, you have to ask the question, "Is my government doing its best for the citizens of this nation or is it totally fixated on the needs and wants and instructions of its big creditors."

Dr Garcia intervened at this point and said, "Jeez, Ken, let's lighten-up this conversation." At that point he apologised, and we moved on to have dinner and play cards and drink lots more wine. But I could see that Anna was strangely affected by this. It was as though she had some type of awakening as to what was going on and why the lockdowns and public health crisis were absolutely related to what Ken had outlined. She wasn't convinced that this was the full answer. But it was part of it. The following morning, we reprised some of the discussions from the night before. As we sipped our coffees across each other at Anna's kitchen table she pointed her finger in the air. "You know something, Rahul, Ken made me consider something that I had missed before. About Mark, and that weird gesture he made - giving me that little magic gadget containing my own little stash of bitcoin."

"Yea it was very generous of Mark."

"It was. But it was more than that. There's a particular reason why Mark gifted that to me. It was nothing to do with the value of bitcoin or that he was giving me something that he considered a valuable asset. Mark was teaching me something in doing what he did. He wasn't advancing me a loan or giving me any debt that had to be repaid. He was in fact doing the opposite. He was giving me the right to free speech. And I see that now. But he has also given me a task to perform. And a challenge. I now know what the challenge is."

"Would you care to tell me what that is?"

"You'll know in good time, Rahul. All in good time."

Chapter 12: Alice Carlisle

Mark made something of a habit of employing the people he'd later have relationships with. Sometimes these were personal relationships, sometimes business. But they were relationships all the same. He often admitted to me that he wasn't absolutely clear what line of business he was in. He had been fortunate enough to make money relatively easily - often just using gut instinct or common sense. He also admitted to having some 'insider' knowledge that helped him along the way. But he admitted to me, quite early in our relationship, that the greatest benefit he saw from business was the people he worked with.

I met Mark because he employed me as his personal assistant and then Chief of Staff. I'd followed him through various businesses and acquisitions. We didn't so much fall in love as we became inseparable. I knew everything about him. I could predict, pretty much, how he'd react to just about every business situation. I was his right-hand woman. And we ended-up loving each other just because we trusted each other so much. When we married in 2007, we both came to the conclusion that I couldn't carry on as his employee and wife. But I wanted him to promise me that whenever he appointed a replacement that he'd not appoint anyone like me. I didn't come out and say that he shouldn't appoint a woman. But I'm pretty sure he knew what I meant.

As it turned out he didn't really appoint anyone as my replacement. I remained his confidante, his muse and grew into the role of wife. His business reputation was such that he needed more and more specialists rather than someone like me. But he made me a non-Executive Director and Board member and shareholder in the business. So, to all intents and purposes, I was very involved - I just didn't come to the office.

The irony was, though, that as his wife I spent less time with him than when I was in the office or joining him on business trips. I couldn't quite get my head around some of the changes in direction of the business. It was as though Mark knew exactly the direction, he and the business were taking were absolutely the right directions. But his opportunity to discuss these fundamentals didn't really involve any conversations with me - like they used to. They just happened. And because they seemed to be very successful strategies I felt, strangely, sidelined.

There were, of course, compensations. Mark knew that the role of dutiful wife wouldn't quite cut it for me or give me the fulfilment of a job in business. We were building a property portfolio and had quite a few investments in early-stage businesses so he suggested to me that I should run a 'family office' - an investment business. And, associated with this, I became moderately successful in my own right. The financial media took an interest in me and, before long, I was giving Mark a run for his money in terms of media visibility.

Sadly, we weren't able to have children. It just didn't happen and then we tried to make it appear that we didn't really want to have any because we were too focused on business. We had some fleeting conversations about adopting or IVF but both of us were almost too busy to do anything about it and the conversations eventually petered out.

But I threw myself into business, possibly to compensate. And as my personal reputation grew - possibly because I was one of only a very few women running family offices - the investment community wanted to work with me. And eager startups wanted to be my friends.

It's odd though. I found myself being almost as busy as Mark. The social side was fabulous. Some of our investments were wildly successful and, as a result, I was being invited to sit on various advisory panels and government bodies and 'women in business' organisations. I know that many of these organisations just wanted to be seen to be important by association. But I have to admit, I was enjoying every minute.

Clearly, Mark was coming against the establishment a bit given his outspokenness on Covid. I just wasn't so sure. The irony was that had I been Mark's Chief of Staff, rather than his wife, I probably would have understood his perspectives better. I was sure that some of Mark's business motivations to take the directions he was taking also influenced his positions on things like Covid. But he had very little time to articulate his thinking, so I suppose I just defaulted to the establishment line on things.

Alice Carlisle

I was spending a lot of time with tech firms that were vying to offer new gene therapies or were developing the technologies to support mRNA - the technology that was being touted as being the route to a rapid Covid vaccination. I didn't really understand Mark's perspective that there was no need for these technologies because the disease that was being described as Covid didn't really represent a threat. Because, every person I spoke to, every co-investor, every journalist, saw Covid as one of the biggest threats to humanity. I suppose I just hadn't thought things through enough to come to Mark's point of view. Or perhaps he was wrong. I just wasn't sure.

There's no doubt, however, that, from an investment point of view, it was clear that there were significant opportunities emerging from Covid. I can tell you, it was like the Klondike, the Covid years. Until the end of 2019 we were very focused on what I'd describe as quite boring technology businesses. These were companies that Mark mostly introduced to me. So, we were offering money to companies that were in banking, financial services, online retailing or enterprise software. But during the Covid years all of the outstanding investment offers (we call them term sheets) were pulled. Because, suddenly, there were fortunes to be made offering technology solutions for lockdown, tracking and tracing technologies, digital ID. Governments were falling over themselves to spend money on these technologies. So, we were willing to oblige by providing seed funding to eager teams of engineers keen to take just some of this government largesse.

I'll admit that I got caught up in the gold rush madness.

Mark, of course, didn't agree with the directions I was taking. And, I'll admit, this caused certain frictions in our relationship. Perhaps if he'd taken more time to explain his thinking, I wouldn't have been so keen to make the decisions I was taking. But to be honest, many of the companies I was backing needed very little. It was more about credibility. By investing relatively small amounts we were able to give our investee companies everything they needed to hit the ground running. Many were literally negotiating contracts weeks after incorporation and seed funding. As I said. It was a goldrush being fed by public money.

And, of course, the focus very quickly turned to the development of the vaccines. At that point there was only one investment game in town.

Ironically, when Mark tried to explain why we shouldn't touch this with a barge pole, I got more engaged. I'll be honest, there was a degree of competition involved. I knew that if I only even got a few crumbs off the table, I could make a serious amount of money for our relatively small office. I suppose I wanted to show that I could become a serious player rather than a novelty item.

I had a feeling that perhaps I was a bit late to the party though when Trump launched Operation Warp Speed. Mark had - indirectly - made me aware that researchers at Penn's Leonard Davis Institute were working with both Pfizer and Moderna and had licensed a technology called mRNA to both companies. It became obvious that both companies were being gifted golden calves by the state. I'd heard on the grapevine that our very own Chancellor of the Exchequer, Rishi Sunak, had previously been employed by a hedge fund that was an early investor in Moderna. So, they had made a serious amount of money when Moderna went public in 2018. Impeccable timing.

Mark was incensed by this, of course. His interest in all things healthcare had peaked after the lockdowns were announced. Everything about lockdown annoyed Mark. He saw it as a major interruption to his personal and professional growth - particularly the travel restrictions that were implemented. But honestly, I really enjoyed lockdown. The Spring weather was lovely, I was able to spend time in the garden, get really fit, and even go to Soho House and visit the pool on the roof level.

When Mark returned from his BBC interview - where they cut him off-air - he was incensed. I listened to the programme from the kitchen as he did the Zoom broadcast in his study.

Now, I had every sympathy for him when he was sent home from Helsinki. I thought the way he was treated was terrible. But I'll be honest, I thought he handled the BBC interview very badly. In my view he should have been much more diplomatic.

When the interview finished, he wandered into the kitchen to get my opinion. He was furious. He ran to the coffee machine and punched the keypad for a double macchiato.

"Be easy, Mark. I'm not sure how we'd fix that if you mess with its Italian brain."

"Oh, fuck its Italian brain." The coffee machine launched its boot-up mode. "Fucking thing. How much was this?"

"A lot. The swearing won't make the thing go any faster."

"So, what did you think of that?" he snapped.

"The interview? Well, you didn't get much chance to put your side of the argument. But perhaps you could have been a bit more diplomatic."

"Diplomatic? Seriously? It was a total mess. Did you hear those people? Like, seriously, what is it with the BBC? They're totally up Boris Johnson's arse. What the actual fuck?"

By now the coffee machine had decided to dispense Mark's coffee - admittedly with some odd-sounding clunks. It obviously sensed the tension. It seemed to be taking an establishment position given Mark's petulance.

"Look," I said. I agree you were outnumbered but you need to be aware that you're massively outnumbered on this. Most people are scared shitless about Covid. Everyone in the government and in the opposition are at one that this is some type of international pandemic emergency. Look at Trump. He has announced a multi-billion programme to fund the vaccine development."

This statement seemed to put Mark back into a state of apoplexy.

"Holy shit, Alice. What is happening to you? Can't you see that you are being played every which way? There is no deadly virus. It's so fucking obvious that they are lying to us. There's no virus."

"But they've sequenced it, Mark. They have sequenced it. In China. Penn State is already working with Moderna and Pfizer and that other German lot whose name I can't remember to develop a vaccine. Why would they be doing that if there wasn't a virus? Why?"

"Because there's money in it Alice. Not just a bit of money. Billions of dollars. Trillions even. They'll be peddling this crap to everybody. Everybody. Moderna has only just IPOed. They conveniently do deals with the Chinese, with Penn State, with anybody. They're creating vaccine candidates as we speak. But why?

There's no fucking disease. The only people who are dying are people with co-morbidities or the elderly who they're sticking on ventilators."

"Jesus, Mark, you sure are swallowing the conspiracy theory Kool-Aid. Like I knew you'd gone a bit cookie because you couldn't fly to New York and your business was being affected, but this really is beyond belief. So, you accept none of it? Oh, and while we're at it, you don't think we should be looking into this Operation Warp Speed to see what positions we might be able to take - if this turns out to be the trillion-dollar opportunity they think it is?"

"No, I fucking don't, Alice. I want no part of it."

At that point Mark stormed off. And then went for a drive. In his big car.

Since I'd started working separately from Mark, I certainly spent less time with him. But with lockdown we were suddenly thrown together again and, only then, realised that we'd actually grown apart. Sometimes he quipped that I'd become a member of the establishment - an establishment that he seemed to thoroughly detest.

I knew Mark well enough to know that I'd have to meet him half-way on some of his positions. But on this issue, he appeared not to come anywhere near my position. So, I mentally resolved - for the sake of our marriage - that I just wouldn't engage on this topic. It was tricky. For months on end the BBC and all the media would publish daily infection reports. Social distancing rules meant that we were constantly reminded of the rules and regulations that - I had to admit - seemed ridiculous, or made up on the spur of the moment, or both.

As it turned out I didn't invest in Moderna or Pfizer or any of their supply-chain companies. Instead, I started buying into the travel and hospitality sector. There were serious bargains to be had. And Mark gave me full support in buying a small portfolio of hotels knowing that they would thrive again after lockdown. I hoped it was a good decision.

As it happened, this was the common ground that we found that saved our marriage. Mark knew that I'd never be convinced about his arguments. I knew that he'd never be convinced about mine. The fact that he was willing to accept that I didn't have to agree with him all the time in order to continue loving me made me love him even more. I trusted him implicitly. But that wasn't to say that I always agreed with him - if you know what I mean.

Chapter 13: Rahul Vaidya

Who is Mark Carlisle? That was a question that people kept asking me on Zoom calls when I was pitching for business. Mark's photograph was all over our website. He was the face of the company. As an investor he had a considerable reputation. His YouTube videos had millions of views. But as 2020 progressed he became more and more invisible. He still attended board meetings. But his social media presence was frozen in time. His last post was on the day of his fateful interview with the BBC.

He told me that Alice had made her own decision to get the Covid vaccination. He wasn't even with her when she visited the vaccination centre. They were planning to make their first international trip since lockdown - to Greece. They had their honeymoon there in 2007. On the island of Santorini. They planned to visit again in May 2021.

The irony was that the Greek authorities never made it a requirement for tourists to be vaccinated. However, Alice had managed to survive Covid-free, as she put it, for all of 2020 so wanted to be vaccinated as soon as she could - for the sake of others, she insisted. She attended a special 'vaccine centre' in central London in April 2021. But she became seriously ill and died as a result of blood clots and cerebral bleeding - according to the autopsy report. Mark had called the ambulance when she fell very ill on her return from London. She was unconscious by the time she reached hospital and died shortly afterwards.

Mark and I had managed - against the odds - to keep the business momentum going, despite Covid. With ever greater reliance on tech, since lockdowns, businesses - and especially data centres - were putting in place more energy resilience measures. Small nuclear as a concept was gaining traction everywhere. But everything was falling on my shoulders. Mark had asked me to take over as CEO even before Alice's death. But when she died, he fell into a spiral of depression.

In order to see him I had to charter a private jet. I used this as a wonderful excuse to take Anna with me to London. Don't get me wrong. The circumstances were awful. And the trip wasn't as easy as we thought it would be. The plane had to refuel in North Carolina before crossing the Atlantic. We were travelling with fake UK and American vaccine certificates. Although, thankfully, no-one asked to see them. And although security and immigration were light-touch we were very jittery - as were the airline staff on both sides of the Atlantic.

But the flying hours were wonderful. We asked the cabin crew to dispense with their silly masks. The champagne was cold. And Anna looked more beautiful than I'd seen her - especially as she walked across the tarmac from the private jet centre in Raleigh-Durham International Airport after our refuelling had finished. The late Spring sunset bathed her in shimmery bronze light. We were only on the ground for half an hour or so, but it was enough time to get a shower and freshen-up prior to our transatlantic flight to London.

Both of us dreaded meeting Mark, given the circumstances. We were unable to attend the funeral which took place under social distancing rules anyway - with the crematorium insisting on everyone wearing masks. Mark, we gather, refused.

We touched down in the early morning in Luton Airport and made our way to Mark's apartment in London. He'd bought what he called a live and work apartment quite close to Liverpool Street Station and within walking distance of Shoreditch in East London. It was a tall building of about 20 floors, and his apartment was one of a few penthouses right at the top.

When we arrived the apartment had an abiding smell of burnt coffee and Mark was flapping around trying to mop up coffee that had spilt from what looked like a very new Italian style stove-top espresso pot. "Guys I'm so sorry. I'm in a flap. I got this stupid coffee-pot rather than buy a coffee machine. I've only just started using this apartment and it is not really properly equipped with all the gadgets needed for modern life."

"Don't worry Mark. Come and sit down and talk to us." I then gave him a hug, and he hugged me back very tightly and seemed not to want to let go. He then spotted Anna and broke away from me to hug her too."

"It's great to see you guys. I genuinely can't tell you how incredibly glad I am to see you both. Really. Incredibly glad. Honestly, guys, I'm really not coping very well at all."

Anna stepped forward and put her hands on his shoulders and looked at him. "Mark, you're not supposed to be coping. No-one expects you to cope. What has happened is horrific. Utterly horrific. But we're here with you now. Let us look after you for a while." And then they hugged again, and Mark sobbed on Anna's shoulder for several minutes. It seemed like an incredible release - as though this was his first semi-public show of the pain he was suffering.

Anna and I had resolved that we didn't want to talk about Alice or their relationship or his loss. We'd listen, of course, if he wanted to talk about her. But our being there was all that he needed at this particular time. We knew that he viewed us as his surrogate children - or at least his proteges. So we knew that he wanted us to provide a diversion and relief from the grief. We were left in no doubt that our roles were to allow him the time to recover and come back. But we were surprised just how much thinking and planning he'd managed to do.

I managed to make us a few cups of coffee using his espresso contraption and he praised me for the quality of my brewing. Then he managed to speak.

"I want you both to know, although it's probably no surprise to you both, that you are very special to me.

Both of you. And your being here - admittedly as a result of a not exactly cheap flight - is simply wonderful. What has happened, with Alice, has obviously changed my life. And I want to explain to you both that while I had severe reservations about lockdown and Covid - and resolved never to receive the bloody vaccines - that I never expected them to be so thoroughly evil as they have proven to be. But do you know something? I never cautioned Alice against taking their shots. She and I didn't agree about the so-called pandemic. She gave them the benefit of the doubt. That's why she eagerly accepted the shot. I suspected she might. But never, ever, did I assume that it would be as devastating as it proved to be.

"Alice's death has been widely reported, of course. And the cause of death has been attributed to the shot. Just one, by the way. She only had one. That was enough to kill her. But nearly all the news reports state that the horrific side effects of the shot that resulted in her death were extremely rare. But, of course, they weren't rare for Alice. As you both know, there was no need for Alice to get that shot. The myth that they manufactured around this so-called disease was that in order to recover our freedom as many as possible had to get the thing. But there was no disease that ever represented a threat to Alice. The only threat - that Alice knew nothing about - was from them and their vaccine.

"I have come to live in this flat because it has nothing whatsoever to do with my life with Alice. It's nothing to do with evading memories or escaping my life with her.

If so, it hasn't worked. Because the grief that I'm feeling is literally the most horrific thing I have experienced in a life that, until a couple of weeks ago, was blessed. In fact, Alice bought this flat. The plan was that she was going to furnish it and rent it out - with a few others she'd bought in the area - at very expensive rents to executives visiting London on short term gigs. Little did she know that I'd end up living in it and she'd be dead.

"Why am I telling you this? Because, frankly, I'm faced with a dilemma. I'm just not sure what to do. I mean, I'm not intending to jump out the window to splat myself all over the pavement. Although I must admit I did consider that briefly. No. I'm pretty sure that I want to do something. But I want to do some things that get to the bottom of why what has happened has happened. I'm not just referring to Alice. I'm pretty sure she is one of thousands - probably millions globally - who have been terribly injured by them. Or killed. No, I'm talking about something much more fundamental.

"Since Alice died, I've been facing a very particular dilemma of who I am…who is Mark Carlisle? And, at this particular time I have no idea. But I know that this is going to put a particular burden on you, Rahul. And by placing a burden on Rahul, Anna, it's going to affect you."

Anna looked at Mark carefully and took a moment to respond. Her eyes had filled with tears, and she shifted uncomfortably on the sofa beside me. "Mark, you need to take your time. You've had no time to grieve. You don't want to be making any rash decisions."

"No, I get that Anna. I totally do. And, please, don't get me wrong, I'm not going away. I need to take time to focus on what's important. They're overstepping. And I think it's going to get much worse. I will never forgive them for what they did to Alice and what they've done to me. And I appreciate I'm just one man. There's a limit to what I can do. But they've silenced me. So, I'll remain silent. They've taken my wife, and I can't get her back. So, I'll take myself out of the way for a while until they want me back. But they must want me back. I won't come back, I won't participate in their system, until they plead with me to come back."

I was slightly taken aback by all of this. I was also a bit confused. Mark clearly knew what he meant but Anna and I were confused. He looked at us and smiled.

"Look guys, don't panic. For you two I'll always be here. But I need to get creative again. Because here is where we are. Biden took over as President in January. He's clearly not making any decisions. Nor was Trump when he was in office. Biden is running with the same policy positions as Trump. Biden is clearly a very bad actor playing the part of a senile President. Trump played the part of a President who was going to 'drain the swamp' but then did nothing but terrible autocue reading. But his handlers gave us Covid, Operation Warp Speed Fauci and stablecoins. Oh, and bitcoin as a store of value. Biden will give us all of these things too but also "woke" and brilliant character acting of a President with dementia. And globalism."

"Listen, Mark," I interjected, "this isn't really making any sense to me."

"It will, Rahul, it will. And I appreciate that I'm in grief and you have probably awful jetlag and would prefer to be in bed with Anna right now. But, please, bear with me. And things will become clearer. But, Anna, I have a particular request to make of you. I want you to interview me. For your show. Here in London. All will become much clearer after that interview. Would you do that for me?"

Anna and I said little to each other as we made our way to our hotel having met with Mark. We sat in the back seat of a London black cab, staring out at the remarkably empty streets. It was early May 2021 and more than a year since Boris Johnson locked-down the United Kingdom - in lockstep with the rest of the developed world. There were rumours circulating on social media that the UK would finally 'open up' after the success of the vaccine roll-out.

"My God this is sad," Anna said as the taxi made its way round Trafalgar Square, then down Northumberland Avenue to our hotel near Whitehall.

"It is," I said. "What the hell are they doing? What has happened to the world?"

As we walked into the hotel lobby the masked concierge asked us if we could wear a face covering. As a consideration for the other guests. We both ignored him. The check-in staff were more accommodating and quickly issued our room-keys and we made our way to our room.

In the elevator Anna looked at me. "What does he want to say, Rahul? Why does he want to do an interview?"

"Honestly, Anna, I have no idea. I suppose he just needs to get certain things off his chest. He must be incredibly angry, incredibly hurt, by what has happened."

"I'm not so sure. I think there's more to it than this. I get the feeling that things are never going to be the same with Mark. It's not just about Alice. Mark is up to something. I'm just not sure that I'm up to the task. I'm young. I have limited reach. I'm not in the mainstream media. I'm not sure I can give him any type of platform. And I'm not even sure what he's going to be platforming."

"That's the least of your worries, Anna. He has asked you to do this. He has chosen you. He chose you years ago anyway. He sees that something special in you. This is the way Mark operates. He has that unique ability to choose people that he sees the universal in. He isn't asking anything more from you than being a listening ear. He doesn't see you as a grand inquisitor. He sees you as someone who values life, who loves life. That's why, when you interview him, you'll provide an insight into what it means to be ourselves. Mark wants you to be you. Nothing more. And I suspect that if the interview touches even just you it'll have been a success."

As we entered our hotel room Anna wrapped her arms around me and squeezed me hard. "You know something, Rahul? Outside there's so much pain. We both know that these last two years have been horrific. What is being done to people in the name of 'health' is utterly barbaric. But it has taught me a lesson. We need to grab this life we have with a passion we never knew we had within us. I love you. I want to spend the rest of my life with you. I want you because you make me feel wonderful and I know I make you feel the same way."

"Well, thankfully, you do. We're going to get through this together, babes." Then we turned and looked at our hotel room. "But, holy shit, look at this room. I think it's time to have some fun."

And at that point we both leapt onto our emperor size bed.

The following morning, we picked up a rental car and drove to Hertfordshire to meet with Anna's parents. This was my first meeting with them in-person since meeting their wonderful daughter.

Chapter 14: Anna Sussex

Rahul was very formal, and very nervous, when he asked my parents if he might marry their daughter…me. It was very sweet. And my parents were genuinely delighted. But Rahul was very, very nervous when he asked if he might meet with them both, privately, while I was sent off to Tesco to get some Chapel Down sparkles in anticipation of a positive response. The positive response came, and we collectively toasted our impending marriage.

We had no idea when the marriage would be, of course, but whenever, it would be in Tellicherry. I made my opinion very well known about that. My parents eagerly anticipated the trip to India and to Kerala. Rahul said he was very humbled that we all wanted it to take place in his hometown, rather than the bride's hometown in England.

"Well, you've really bigged it up, Rahul, there's no going back now," I said when he expressed any doubt about the location. "Also, what bride wouldn't want to be married in India? Oh, and I want your Mum to ensure we have the best wedding feast, with the very best Biriyani."

"My God, no pressure then," he answered with a gorgeous smile.

But despite the joy of our engagement and being with my parents I couldn't stop from thinking about Mark. In fact, it wasn't even Mark. It was everything. It was the enveloping pall of sadness that hung over everybody. My parents felt it too.

I never had any doubt that their response to the dystopia we were witnessing would be any different from mine. My Dad, while he occasionally had a dalliance with Conservative Party politics was, fundamentally, a libertarian in the English tradition. He detested governments of all hues. My mother was slightly more left-leaning and rarely expressed any political opinions except when watching the BBC News. It represented everything she most despised about the British liberal lefty establishment. And this political nihilism gave me a great start in life. My Dad, who wasn't one for dishing out much advice, tended to repeat his defining philosophy: "Listen more than talk, Anna. That's the best way to know whether people are worth your company."

I took his advice, of course, certainly in terms of my career choice. But now I faced, with some trepidation, that interview with Mark. I had no real idea what to expect. I hadn't really figured out in my head what he wanted to say. But I knew that if he used it as an opportunity to seek vengeance against the vaccine manufacturers or to call on the government to reverse its Covid policy that the interview would go nowhere.

Mark wasn't helping. He said he wanted the conversation to just 'develop'. He wanted this to be an opportunity for both of us to learn from each other. He said that the semi-formal format of a media interview would allow us to perhaps help nudge events along. But none of this left me any wiser as to what to ask him.

Alex suggested that I set up a call with Mark's PR, Jenny McIvor. I was hoping that she might give me some tips, and I presumed that she had talked with Mark or had even suggested the interview in the first place. According to Alex she had been in contact with Mark several times since the death of Alice. We knew that much. So perhaps she might give us some insights. Rahul didn't want to be involved at all, so I asked Alex to coordinate things and to join me in the Zoom call with Jenny. She agreed to the call but insisted we use Signal.

Jenny appeared on the call impeccably dressed and beautifully lit, as always. She was in DC. I wondered, as we were chatting, if she might be AI-generated, her make-up was so perfect.

I kicked-off. "Hey Jenny. Alex and I are so grateful that you could make the time for this call. As you know, Mark has asked that we do an interview for my weekly interview slot. So, we're planning to shoot it here in London tomorrow for live streaming."

"What's your feeling about it, Anna? Are you comfortable being the owner of this particular scoop?"

"It doesn't feel like a scoop, Jenny. The circumstances are terrible."

"They are, indeed. And that's why I don't think you should refer to the circumstances. Or certainly not at length. This is not a story about Alice or even Mark's grief. And this is certainly not a story about vaccines or big pharma. I sense that Mark is going to go much deeper than that, Anna. Much deeper. As you know, he's effectively been cancelled on mainstream media. Now we only have alternative media. But I've been doing my work on them - certainly most of the podcast bros who have considerable reach. They're nearly all compromised, Anna. All of them."

I asked her to elaborate.

"Do you know anything about my background, Anna? Do you know why I'm working with Mark now?"

"Not really, I must admit. I hear, from Rahul, that you can work a room and have incredible contacts. I hear that you have the ears of some of the most influential journalists on The Hill and in the Westminster village."

"Hmm. Perhaps that used to be the case. But, believe me, everything is turning to shit. It's true that I used to be a player. But there's no real game to play anymore. All of the mainstream media, pretty much, is totally compromised. They were always stenographers but now they're just lost souls. They're dead behind the eyes. They just take the pay checks. My role was to place the stories. But now every story has been placed.

"Thankfully we're not on Zoom. But there's still a limit as to what I can say. But my background - prior to jumping ship into commercial PR - was to put it mildly, from the establishment. I'm ashamed to admit it but early in my career I was involved in some pretty nasty little kompromat programs mostly focused on people that were on low-grade watch lists. These tended to be foreign nationals that were deemed to have an excessive interest in potentially sensitive markets or posed a potential threat to American corporate interests.

"I was a perfect fit for them. I had wealthy parents, and I had the benefit of an Ivy-league education. The red-brick colleges tend to produce academics, tech entrepreneurs, politicians or spooks. Or combinations thereof. It's the same in the UK. We copied your system. So, I ended-up being a spook. That's how I first met Mark."

My mouth had fallen open. "So, what, you were what, CIA?"

"Indeed, I was. You gotta remember that I was young and it all seemed very glamorous, and I was very flattered that they wanted me. So to speak. But the actual work wasn't exactly what I had in mind. The MO was the same every time. I, in effect, used my feminine wiles to target men - who we knew to be married - and get them into compromising positions. So to speak. Mark was deemed to be potentially useful. But he figured-out pretty quickly what I was up to. And then he gave me his business card before leaving me sitting by myself on a barstool wearing a very short dress with nowhere to go, so to speak. It was very demeaning. He was very loyal to his wife and his moral standing.

"Anyway, I didn't contact him for 2 years after that meeting. I knew I had to get out of the profession. It was beginning to dawn on me that there wasn't even much of a fine line between being a hooker and being a low-grade spook. So I managed to get out and say bye to Langley. I met Mark in London when I was working client-side. He made it clear that one day he'd have a perfect role for me - but it would have to be the right time for us both. So here we are. The irony is that he's no longer got a wife. But that, I assure you, was nothing to do with me."

I was having difficulty taking this all in. It wasn't exactly the conversation I was expecting to be having. "Can I ask, then, Jenny. What role are you playing now? I mean, what exactly are you doing for Mark?"

"Oh, that's a good question. And the answer is not as simple as you might think. My relationship with Mark was always rather synergistic. We found ourselves strangely close to each other in terms of our world views. I was, clearly, a product of the intelligence services but was too lowly to be secreted away, like Epstein. My role was never considered that important. Often, I was given very little information. Little to no back story. But my experience was enough to know that the operations I was engaged in were about control. I knew that further up the chain of command that similar operations were being co-ordinated that were targeting journalists, judges, politicians, businesspeople. The idea that America was a functioning democracy quickly evaporated. In fact, the machine had consumed everything. Next to no-one in the establishment achieved any position of influence without Langley's approval. They were, and are, pretty much running everyone. They and the Brits, and the Israelis.

"But I digress. I'm not really answering your question. What role do I play? Well, I suppose the role I play is to keep Mark safe. He is very, very ambitious. And I share his ambition. He doesn't want power, nor money, particularly. He knows he needs money to be a player and to get his way in certain things. But I suspect, when you interview him, he might give you a better idea of what his ambition is. My role is to ensure that we have a channel, of sorts, to get the information out. That's really not easy these days. And we know that this might be a long game. But we need to start somewhere. And we're good at picking winners and losers. You have managed to break through, against the odds. Except that's not really true. Because we know more about your employers than you do. So, the dice were always loaded in your favour, possibly without your knowledge."

"So, are you saying, Jenny, that this interview might be somewhat problematic as far as my employers are concerned?"

"Yes, we think so. We also think it might be problematic with others too. Just don't expect as many Christmas cards this year."

If I was confused before my meeting with Jenny, after I was slightly terrified. But it was good to be distracted with the impending interview. We arranged for a video crew to set up in Mark's apartment. When I arrived his open plan living area had been transformed into an interview set complete with a lighting rig and sound engineer.

"What are they doing to my house, Anna? Isn't this a bit of overkill?"

"Not really," I answered. "We want this to look professional. On a par with the networks' productions. Or Hollywood's. Although the video guy is a friend of Rahul's so it might be more Bollywood. How are you feeling about this, Mark?"

"I'm feeling good Anna. Just remember that there's no pressure on you. Whatever happens, you'll be fine. I'll make sure of that. But don't let me get away with anything. If anything I say makes no sense to you, please be assured that I'll take no offense if you challenge me. That's why you're doing this."

The production team needed about another 30 minutes before they gave me the thumbs-up to start the interview. Mark and I hadn't discussed any type of running order or questions in advance. He hadn't even hinted at what he wanted to cover. But just as I was about to ask the first question he said, "You look lovely Anna."

I could feel myself flushing slightly at the compliment and knowing we were being recorded. I looked down at my notes and then lifted my eyes and asked the first question. "Mark, I know many people in the business community on both sides of the Atlantic know you. But I suspect many people will be watching this interview who don't. What would you like them to know about you?"

Mark looked into my eyes for what seemed like an eternity. He didn't look like he was thinking. He wanted to find a metre, a form of words, to begin. And then he spoke.

"No-one watching this needs to know much about me. The people who will get to see this and hear this will be the type of people, I'd imagine, who are a bit like me. They love their lives. They value their freedom, and they love the people closest to them. That's the type of person I am. I love my life. I've been blessed with good fortune. But I've never wanted to tell others how their lives should be lived."

"You say that you have been blessed with good fortune. But just a few weeks ago you lost your wife. The coroner's report stated that she had died directly as a result of the Covid vaccine…"

"I loved my wife. Her loss has been the worst experience of my life. But my wife made the decision to take that injection. The decision was hers alone. Some people say that she was coerced into taking it. That the government, effectively, mandated it. But that's not what happened, of course. We live in a society where people make decisions that go against their own best interests. My wife knew what I thought about the so-called pandemic. She also knew what I thought about the so-called vaccine. But clearly, my arguments were less convincing to her than the arguments she heard others make that there was some type of moral imperative for people to take the vaccine for the sake of others. I find that argument both spurious and offensive. But my wife didn't. She took the decision that she took, took the drug, and paid the ultimate price: her life."

"But they argue that the drug was safe and effective for the vast majority who took it. Is that not a valid argument?"

"I'm not sure what you mean by valid. Because just think of that argument from my wife's perspective. Clearly her decision to be injected benefitted neither herself nor society. The vaccine acted like a virus that killed its host. As you know, governments claim that by intervening in our collective lives they seek to do so in a way that benefits most people. But, based on a survey of Alice it's clear that the vaccine was a toxic killer. The fact remains that an argument was used to convince my wife to take a medical intervention that killed her. Therefore, that was an argument that resulted in my wife voluntarily taking a drug that nearly instantly killed her. In acting for the public interest, she acted against her personal interest. In my view no-one should ever take a decision that has the potential to ruin their lives in order to protect the lives of others. I love my life too much to make such a decision. And it makes me very sad that my wife made a decision that she didn't think about enough."

"You said 'argument' Mark. What do you mean?"

"Well, it's quite obvious. Millions of people have been subject to an argument. The argument was everywhere. Except it wasn't, of course. Because arguments tend to have two sides. But that didn't stop the governments, the media, the establishment, the corporations engaging in a nasty, never-ending, one-sided argument. What I mean is that they used the emotional heat of an argument but gave us no opportunity to state an opposing view. It felt, immediately, like there was total, universal consensus. The one opportunity I had to take a counter position to this view; I was shut down. Which seemed odd. I mean, up until that point the media wanted me to take a side. You know the idea. The two sides will be featured in a debate. Left versus right. Black versus white. Christian versus Muslim. Capitalist versus Socialist. Whatever. But there was no indication coming from anyone in media circles - when they were making their argument - that there was anything other than consensus. But there wasn't, of course. The political parties were in unison. The media was - and is - a united front. So, the only conclusion we can come to is that the so-called pandemic marked a turning point in human history. They were no longer taking part in the charade that there were two sides to an argument. We entered a new era in March 2020."

"But that implies, Mark, that there was collusion or planning. Who are you saying colluded and planned this?"

"I don't think it's as simple as this. We tend to think of cause and effect. We have been conditioned, to some degree, to believe that if something happens, it's as a result of central planning or control. And there's clearly some truth to that. But there's a widely accepted myth that we elect governments which then frame policy. We also believe that governments get together to plan and shape foreign policy or trade or public health policy. But we have to suspend this belief system in order to fully understand what's happening.

"So-called Western democratic governments long ago ceased being democracies. In fact, it's questionable if they ever were. Just look at history. Just about every form of government typically results in a small elite pulling the levers of power. But this elite doesn't just emerge. Typically, it's a power syndicate with vast amounts of intergenerational wealth. The syndicates - let's call them that - invariably emerged from organised crime. All of the world's richest power-players are beneficiaries of organised crime. Over generations they can accumulate considerable wealth - particularly in the form of tangible assets. And we're not necessarily talking about just very rich families - but also corporate dynasties that continue across generations."

I wasn't sure, at this point, how to continue the conversation. It sounded like Mark was suggesting that there was a huge globalist conspiracy going on. And that, in some way, he was caught up in it. And that Alice had been a victim of this. I decided to probe a little deeper.

"You say that democracy is dead. Can you elaborate?"

"Well, let's assume, for a minute, that the concept of government that we have been told exists, doesn't. What we need to do, therefore, is assume that the idea of government is a myth backed up by propaganda. But part of the myth is that there are competing political agendas competing for our attention and, ultimately, our votes. That's what we have been led to believe. This creates the impression that with every election new leaders come in to change things. But they don't, of course. Nothing ever really changes. Because nothing of any importance can be changed. Our social structures, networks, businesses, logistics operations, financial systems, are immensely complex and have evolved over decades, centuries even. The modern society we live in requires us to suppress our individual agency as much as possible. We're given the impression that working for a company or the government will ultimately benefit us and benefit society. By working, we're creating wealth and providing for our families. But the fabric that sustains the system is one that benefits others much more than it benefits ourselves. But for the system to be maintained they must give us the impression that we have free will, or agency, within the system. So, in the West, and particularly in America and the UK, we are forced to define ourselves as Capitalist or Socialist. And we're encouraged to align ourselves with people who espouse Capitalist or Socialist values. Our news media broadcasts non-stop about the battles between the Republican Party and the Democratic Party in America or the Conservative Party and Labour Party in the United Kingdom. But all the political parties are answerable - not to the people - but to their handlers."

"So, who are the handlers?"

"Ah that's the big question. But before I answer that question, I just want to focus a little bit on the so-called pandemic we've all been subjected to. In my view, of course, this was not a pandemic in the true sense of the word. Rather it was an over-played hand. It succeeded in busting the central myth of the handlers. It exposed the system's dark secret. For the first time in human history the handlers tried to impose their will using the united forces of all the political and social structures they have created. It may have been a test. But, if it was, it showed the extent of compliance that they could expect. It was nearly successful. But their central problem was, and is, that they have created a cohort that no longer believes in the system. The myth has been broken. Perhaps it's because a lot of us implicitly knew it was a myth even before March 2020."

"So, what is - or was - the myth?"

"The central myth is the idea that we need governments. In fact, it's even more fundamental than that. It's the idea that others should be able to tell us how we should behave and what decisions we should take. It's the idea - the central myth - that we can't make our own decisions without the support of people who know better than us."

"But don't we need experts? Don't we need specialists?"

"Yes, of course, we do. Some people build up huge amounts of knowledge. But this knowledge, of course, is based on an accumulation of learning, innovation and breakthrough. As our technology gets better, we can also mine knowledge in ways that can help us get better at things. But no man, no government, no expert, has the right to tell any man, or woman, how they should live their lives or what decisions they should take. All the myths that we are fed suggest that we have a duty of care to society to take certain actions that might, ultimately, require us to live for the sake of other men, or ask other men to live for us. But ultimately, we have to make decisions that are for our own benefit. We have to question everything - but, especially, demands from others that we take certain decisions that could result in our own demise."

"And do you think, Mark, that governments demanded that we take decisions that resulted in our demise? Are you seriously suggesting that?"

"I am, most certainly. Let's take America's greatest city, New York. In 2019 over eleven thousand people died there. It sounds like a big number but then it's a big city with millions of people. People die. Babies are born. And 2019 was an unremarkable year. But just a few weeks after the end of that year - in March and April 2020 - tens of thousands of people in New York perished. Most of them - that's over thirty thousand people in just a few weeks - died in hospital or at home having been sent home from hospital. America's greatest, most prosperous city killed thousands of its own people in the places where they are supposed to receive the greatest compassion and care."

"But the Mayor of New York, at the time, claimed that it was a virus that killed all of those people. Not the public health system."

"But we know that to be definitively nonsense. New Yorkers were getting tested for the so-called virus at the time and nearly everyone was testing positive. New York has millions of people. But the only people who were dying were people going to hospital. The public health system became the killing fields of New York.

"And that's the point Anna. New Yorkers were terrorised by the government. They were told not to panic about the Wuhan Flu - and promptly panicked. They were told to trust health-care professionals as they were put onto ventilators. They were - at the end of 2010 - told to take a series of toxic injections to protect them from a so-called virus when the virus is, in fact, the government and its media."

I was wearing an earpiece that allowed the team to communicate with me as the interview was happening. Alex was connected via a Zoom link and could also talk with me as the interview progressed. It was Alex who told me that YouTube had pulled the feed. We were offline. I told Mark.

"Mark, I've just been informed via the production desk that the live stream of this interview has been pulled off-air by YouTube. We haven't been given any reasons as yet. But I presume they will use their 'community guidelines' or something to justify this. But obviously, I want to continue the conversation, and we'll get it out as a recording as soon as possible. But I just thought you'd like to know."

"Well, clearly, I'm not surprised. I'm sure you're not either. It's a very neat way of making my point for me. The media firms are there to allow the parroting of government approved lines only. I suppose we have to get used to this. But I think, Anna, that we need to look at what's happening more fundamentally. We have to consider the possibility that if the Covid period was a psychological operation - organised on an international basis and involving co-ordinated government and public health actions - that it's only the beginning of something even more sinister. If we are to consider that possibility, we need to consider the real possibility that we're at war."

I could feel that we had reached a turning point in the conversation. Mark was aware that the live feed had ended. He knew that what he was about to say was, until such time that the piece was edited and made available at a future date, was largely for my ears. He paused momentarily and fixed his eyes on me. There was an added poignancy in that moment. He had lost his wife. His business was in suspended animation. He knew that the interview would almost certainly result in the end of my current employment status. Everything was in flux and hanging in an unresolved balance. I looked down at my notes. But that word, 'war', hung in the air. "Who will be at war, Mark? Who will be waging the war?"

"Well, we can be sure that the war mongers will have no skin in the game - apart from their equity stakes in the war machine. Wars, invariably, are paid-for through debt - debt incurred without our approval. Wars, invariably, are about maintaining scarcity and market rigging. That's what mobsters do, remember? They seek to maintain limited supply, but also to maximise price. That depends on permanent scarcity. We used to be taught about democratic systems being fundamentally different to command-based societies. But this is just a myth. In the West the mobsters realised that the easiest way to keep people in check was to feed them the idea that they participated in society through the democratic process -

and that everyone, regardless of background or wealth, could aspire to achieve the highest political office in the land. Nothing could be further from the truth. Because the endgame is always to control, in order to maintain scarcity.

"The United Kingdom and the United States, to all intents and purposes, are the same nation under the rule of a small number of crime syndicates. The pre-eminent syndicate - more powerful than any other - is the one that maintains energy wealth and ownership in just a few families, funds and corporations. But others play their part too. Drug syndicates - operating under the guise of legal pharmaceutical companies - can trace their roots back to the British or Dutch East India Company. Drug and energy cartels have pretty much defined our democracies and our social structures for decades.

"Western oligarchs predate the oligarchs who emerged in Russia at the end of the cold war. Our Western variety have pretty much wrapped things up to ensure that their lines of succession are protected. Their money has built the Ivy League colleges, the investment banks, the political institutions, the Military Industrial Complex and the Public Health Industry. The vast imbalance of asset wealth at the heart of our civil society ensures that no-one outside of their control will ever get near the reins of power. And the primary function of this internecine network of crime is to ensure scarcity and asset wealth. And until around 2008, the system worked, and we were given no real insight into how it almost exclusively benefitted just a very few extraordinarily powerful people."

"But isn't that too neat a solution, Mark? Surely, you're just hijacking the 'masonic orders are behind it all' conspiracy theories?

"I have a humble attitude to knowledge, Anna. For years I just went along with the comfort of making money relatively easily. I didn't get the feeling that there was a "them and us" type of society. Or, if there was, it was working pretty well for me. I had all the baubles of success. I could see people making bad decisions all around me, but I chose not to make those same decisions. I knew instinctively that they were poor decisions. I have no idea why I was less accepting of the advice of those who called themselves experts. I never really believed that the government had my best interests at heart. But I could choose to decline. I could choose to avoid hospitals. I could choose to avoid drugs. But let me ask you. Have you ever been on prescription medication or had any type of drug habit at any point in your life?"

"Thankfully not," I replied with some degree of pride.

"Nor me. But, believe me Anna, we're in a tiny minority. Most adults - especially in the West - are dependent on drugs to some extent. Most Americans - about 70% - are on prescription drugs. Anti-cholesterol drugs are among the most prescribed. Nearly 40 million

Americans are on anti-depressant drugs like Prozac. Millions of Americans are addicted to Fentanyl - with most initially receiving it on prescription. But what most people don't realise is that the modern drug industry is a huge spin-off from the petrochemical industry. Prozac is synthesized using petrochemical-derived intermediates. Fentanyl, a synthetic opioid, is entirely synthesized in laboratories, relying heavily on petrochemical products. And I have no intention of boring you with a list of the other drugs that are dependent on the petrochemical supply chain. I've made my point. But the pharmaceutical industry is worth around $2 trillion a year. And many of the drugs that it peddles are neither safe nor effective. But many are highly addictive. My suggestion is that if the control of these industries - petrochemical and pharmaceutical - feels like the work of organised crime cartels, with such market valuations involved, it probably is.

"But, like you, I'm looking in on this. This is a world that has nothing to do with me. I choose not to use the products. But just look at what's going on. It's not difficult. These drugs are being manufactured at industrial scale using tons and tons of chemicals for distribution all over the world. The top 10 companies - mostly American or European - make hundreds of billions of dollars of revenue. The scale of operations is vast. And the results are there for all to see: dependence, addiction, lawlessness, dead or dying cities."

"But this is corporatism, not capitalism. And it's ruled by an oligarchy that doesn't exactly respect humanity or human agency. There's no getting away from the fact that corporations are manufacturing and selling products to people that are readily consumed and destroy lives. It's clear that the food industry is also culpable - with food additives in manufactured foods making people sick or causing cancer or dementia. But the corporations behind these practices are employing lobbyists that buy support from most politicians. And industry funded NGOs work for the interests of corporations, not for the benefit of humanity."

"But this state of affairs, Anna, leaves us - the minority that stands aside and looks in - with a problem. We are facing a situation where globalism, as it's known, is hijacking the idea of international trade to peddle products that are destroying our species. Meanwhile the self-appointed saviours are essentially a death cult: the technocrats."

I wasn't sure where Mark intended to go with this. But he sounded excessively nihilistic. He sounded a little defeated too. I needed to get him out of this spiral and focused on his vision - his belief in humanity. It was clear that Alice's death had affected him profoundly. It felt to me that his confidence, his hope, his belief in truth was ebbing away. I decided that I needed to get him a little angry to pull him out of this defeatist rut he'd put himself into.

"Oh, come on Mark," I said after letting his reference to the technocrats hang in the air for a while. "You're beginning to sound like you've accepted defeat - that they are winning. If you believe that they are selling us lies, spinning us lies, putting lies into the mouths of politicians, then surely, we can have the upper hand. We have access to truth. It's up to us to tell the truth. It's up to us to say 'No' - to switch off their controlled media, to opt out of their social control systems, to get out and walk on a mountain or to make love on a beach. Isn't that our moral duty, to take care of ourselves?"

"It is Anna. But the difficulty we have is that each and every person has to reach that conclusion for themselves. We cannot impose our world view - even if we had the wherewithal to do it. You're right, though, that this is a battle for truth. I have no religious faith, but over the last few years I've come to appreciate the battle that is also being waged on those who do. We all arrive at our understanding of what it is to be human from a variety of different directions. In my case I benefitted from parents who cared for me and loved me. For me that made me - for want of a better word - good. The rules of life that my parents gave to me were good rules. They encouraged me to be kind, because, they said, kindness is always rewarded. They encouraged me to travel, because, they said, travel enriches the mind and allows us to meet strangers who teach us things. They encouraged me to love my life with people who loved me in turn. These were the things that they held as their basic, fundamental laws of life. Good laws.

"Now we all know that the 'powers that be' won't allow us to decide how we should govern our own lives with such good laws. They believe they have a better way - and their corporate string-pullers feed them the lines, and the laws. As a secularist, I can object to such laws. I have objected to the mask-wearing, the destruction of our small businesses, and the vaccine coercion. But so have many of my friends who believe that their cherished truths have been handed down from their god. Many of them have been abandoned by their churches - most of which closed during lockdown. Their church leaders have adorned their altars with their belief in vaccines rather than belief in fundamental truths and good laws.

"But I'm curious, Anna. What's your view? Do you think that Covid represented a massive awakening? A sea-change? A new epoch? Am I over-egging it?"

"I don't think you are. But remember, I'm younger than you. I suspect your generation is less respectful of authority. If you consider most young people who have just started on their career - if they work for a corporation then they've had to button their lips about many issues. The woke agenda, DEI, climate emergency nonsense. And now, pandemics, lockdowns and vaccines. If they challenge the agreed narrative, then they won't have their jobs. And their jobs mean being able to pay the rent, or the mortgage - and all the other trappings of young professional life. More than ever, my generation is a slave class. We can't challenge anything, or we'll be unemployable. The result is that we forgo our privacy, we're obsessed with Instagram or TikTok - because those are the places in which we live our lives.

The real world is just too expensive - just try buying a beer in central London.

"As to whether I agree with you that Covid represented a major sea-change? I'm not sure. Woke culture was working to reduce freedom of speech well before people like you started to be cancelled on social media. I sense that this was orchestrated. It seemed to come from nowhere. I can see the logic of your argument, but I sense that we've had much less freedom in our youth than you had in yours."

Mark seemed to be considering this. He took a few moments before responding. He suddenly looked tired. I could see him looking at the cameras and lights and production team. I asked him if he wanted to take a break. To collect his thoughts. But then he seemed to connect with an idea. He started speaking again.

"I think you're right. I can see why younger people might have taken a different path. But you didn't. I think it's less about generational differences that it is about the way people deal with authority. It's why totalitarianism works - for a while at least. But you're right that this thing has been, or is, a work in progress. I think the Covid era will ultimately be seen as the point at which they over-played their hand. Prior to Covid we were given the impression that major geopolitical fuckups were the responsibility of governments or rogues within government. But Covid, I think, will come to be recognised as the first time they tried to manipulate us, coerce us, harm us, on a global scale. It represented the first time that some of us realised that the nation-state was effectively dead - in the West, at least. And that some form of one-world corporatist government had arrived.

"Prior to 2020, however, it was clear that much of the groundwork was being done. Not just in terms of woke. Which was, essentially, a side-show. It seems to me that they need to create trivial culture wars or identity politics in order to give politicians something to do, so that they could appear relevant. But fundamentally, the new world order is a globalist one. And Covid showed that they had already achieved something that is critically important in the achievement of global totalitarianism. They have managed to get most people to outsource their thinking.

"Let me explain. Thinking requires us to observe in order to learn. The process of observation doesn't just involve our eyes. We use all our senses. But as soon as we're born, we start the process of collecting information to determine the natural order of things. We work out causality for ourselves. We know that by doing something results in an effect. It's this process of observation that allows us to develop skills. Like riding a bicycle. Or painting. Or playing music. Or just living and developing relationships. We learn how to pick up subtle visual clues from other people too. This we could probably describe as emotional intelligence. Some of it is innate. Some of it is learned. But emotional intelligence isn't totally rational or even explainable. But it's universal. Regardless of our cultural background we can get very good at understanding the world by just getting out there and appreciating it. The more experiences we have, the more we observe, the more causes and effects we see, the more we think. Thinking is essential for us to thrive.

"But it's clear that the media - and especially electronic media - can bypass our need to think - by, in effect, thinking for us. The media feeds us answers that could be wrong. Our process of emotional intelligence building can be hijacked. In effect we're being given duff answers, constantly, in order to fool us into thinking we've arrived at our own conclusions - thoughts - that have, in fact, been pre-programmed for us.

"In short, we're living in a society that is increasingly defined by media-driven stupidity.

"It used to be that we were able to tell the difference between paid advertisements and all the other content that was supposed to inform us or entertain us. But that was part of the trick - to give us the idea that the news was unbiased or that there was a social obligation to provide us with wholesome entertainment. I take it, Anna, that you've read Brave New World?"

"Yes, of course."

"You're probably aware that there has been some debate as to which world Huxley seemed to prefer. He presented two worlds. One was a world of primitives, who lived on the outside and didn't have the advantage of the technocratic state of the brave new world. In particular, they didn't have soma. You'll remember that soma provided a near-constant euphoric state, allowing everyone to be happy despite living in a totally immoral and controlled world. In my view we're living in that world because we're given the choice between thinking for ourselves or outsourcing our thinking to the controllers. By accepting the entertainment, the propaganda, the state provided free drugs and entertainment, we accept to submit our will to the will of the state god. But the state isn't democratic or even paternalistic. It's simply the state provided by soma."

"Isn't it ironic," I mused, "that the SOMA district of San Francisco is full of fentanyl addicts."

"I think it's even more ironic that it's where Twitter has its headquarters.

"This reminds me of an anecdote, Anna. Back in 2019, just a year before the Covid event, I was invited to speak at a small conference in San Francisco. The organisers decided to hold the event in a quirky little venue in South of Market, SOMA. I think it's still there. It's a small museum and conference centre called the American Bookbinders Museum. Inside the museum are several artefacts associated with bookbinding. Tools used to make books are on show, from the 17th century. Also, more recent innovations in automating the process of binding books.

"I was asked by the organisers to arrive early so that they could show me around the venue and also do sound checks and meet with the other speakers. But I arrived super-early at around 8am. The event wasn't due to start until 9:00am. As it happened, I arrived at the same time as the Museum Manager who was about to open-up the premises. But this task was not easily accomplished. Because, lying in the doorway of the premises, was a very large man in a sleeping bag. He was, probably as a result of the use of certain chemicals, comatose or asleep, we weren't quite sure which. But it presented us both with a moral dilemma. Should we waken this guy from his sleep - something that he clearly needed - so we could get into the premises? We decided to dither and delay the confrontation. I went off and got us two coffees from a nearby barista place. And the Manager and I allowed the guy an extra half hour of sleep. We engaged in some chit chat, and she told me a few facts about bookbinding and the origins of the museum. But then, at around 8:30am, she decided that enough was enough and she prodded him with her foot and told him to move on.

"Now, I can't remember much about the conference at all. But for some reason that event has stuck in my head. When the conference ended, I walked from Clementina Street to Market Street and walked past Twitter's headquarters.

"I've asked myself, over and over, why it was that Twitter was located there in SOMA? I'd walked past many times. But this time it just seemed very odd. Why was it not located in Santa Clara or San Mateo? Why so close to the city centre? And why in this particular part of the city?

"If you think about it, the Tech Bros who essentially run the world these days, have an aura about them. They have created a new screen-obsessed underclass of addicts. The drug addicts are a lost cause. They'll eventually die in doorways or on the street. The city of San Francisco and the State of California no longer cares much where they die. But there in SOMA is a social media HQ that's feeding the new beast of addiction, to nonsense parading as media. It's no accident that 'social' media is what it's called. Because it's all about the social pervasiveness of lies and propaganda and scientism - while giving the impression it's about letting everyone have a voice.

"But just a few blocks away from Twitter is a museum dedicated to the bookbinders' art and craft. The production of printed words in books. The condensation of knowledge. Presented in a way that just one person at a time can discover their treasures. The antithesis of social. But the purity of freedom.

"In effect the emergence of social media is the creation of an abundance of data but with no concomitant increase in knowledge. By creating this abundance, we can't see the wood for the trees. When books were the work of great scholars and bookbinders, knowledge was scarce. Relatively few people could read in the 17th Century. And the books were expensive.

Education was, therefore, mostly unaffordable or impossible for the masses.

"The modern solution for this pervasiveness of data is to offer the means to synthesise it all using artificial intelligence. This is the ultimate outsourcing of thinking. Now, we no longer even need to bother encouraging people to read the source material. All the work of 'thinking' is undertaken by a server farm in Texas. The 'intelligence' of course, is canned like the music the AI users pipe into their ears via their buds. The conditioning is relentless. Welcome to modern soma and the brave new world.

"Now I don't know about you, but I'd prefer to live in a world where people come to their own conclusions by asking questions - not accepting answers from whoever or whatever offers certainty. I prefer nuance, argument, dissent. That, in my view, is life."

I found myself agreeing, intuitively. But I was at a loss. There had to be an endgame or strategy - but my difficulty was knowing who was at the top of the chain doing the manipulation.

"So I go along with your analysis, Mark. I can see that the more compliant people are, the more they can be told what to do, to comply with the wishes of the Alpha Plus class, as Huxley described it. But who are the World Controllers in your analysis?"

"I don't think the answer is as simple as you'd like it to be, or I'd like it to be. But it's clear that there have been a variety of eugenicists who have been highly influential in our recent history. Where totalitarianism emerges, it tends to be highly identitarian as well. One group is favoured above all others and lower castes or classes or religions are 'othered'. That's why, in my view, it's best not to identify with any group. In effect the individual must be sovereign. But, over time, there is no safety to be found in any particular caste or identity. Indeed, the tendency for people to identify with groups is used to isolate and ostracise them.

"But the thing to be aware of is that the controllers are primarily interested in power through the accumulation of wealth and assets. They're on a land-grab. These include global organisations of all sorts, including corporations, NGOs, hedge funds and private equity firms. The motivation for such organisations is survival. Their apparatchiks are senior executives and lobbying firms. The method of working is largely to argue the case for so-called shareholder value - that is maintaining their hegemony for the benefit of their owners. But they'll rarely admit that this is the case. Typically, they'll jump on 'social good' bandwagons as proxies for their real aspirations to survive and keep their share prices up.

"But lurking within this community are intelligence agency actors. I call them that because, often, they are, indeed, actors. These are people who are placed in positions of power and are the chief social change agents. They rarely display much in the way of independent thought. However, they are kept in check because, often, they have been conditioned and trained to do what they do. Sometimes they'll be members of enormously wealthy families - typically families who have derived vast intergenerational wealth as a result of previous waves of land-grab. As I mentioned earlier, some of the largest and most influential corporations are merely the public faces of family wealth. And, typically, these families work hand in glove with the intelligence agencies.

"But don't think that the CIA, for example, has any duty of care to the American people or to world peace. No. It's a hired militia unit that uses psychological operations, media manipulation, kompromat, thuggery and terrorism to get its way.

"At the heart of the 'system' if I could call it that, is the creation of an impression of scarcity and peril. The system always creates false narratives that give the impression that things that we depend on - or think that we depend on - are scarce and getting more scarce as a result of circumstances that the system manipulates into being.

"So, for example, drugs. Illicit drugs are being seized. Dealers are subject to terrible legal sanctions - including death - if found smuggling. But remember, just about all illegal drugs have a legally available equivalent.

"Or think of oil and gas. We're told that the use of such products is damaging the environment - creating greenhouse gases. We're implored to avoid using the products and they are increasingly taxed because, supposedly, they are so damaging. But, of course, the alternative - so-called sustainable energy - doesn't really work and is, itself, hugely damaging. Meanwhile, keeping supply channels for oil and gas open is becoming increasingly difficult as war and geopolitical tensions tear apart the Middle East.

"And, given the strategic importance of energy, weapons and instruments of war are in constant short supply. The big war companies, supported by politicians, get to supply their weapons into war zones that are clearly orchestrated into being because they also threaten supply chains for energy - thereby creating more scarcity and elevated prices. And the more war zones proliferate the scarcer the instruments of war become.

"Which brings me to the so-called pandemic. This was, in fact, the first attempt to create the circumstances where health itself was deemed to be scarce. In asking people to demand their health in a world ravaged by a 'virus' they created the circumstances whereby people would willingly subject themselves to the will of experts doling out scarce health.

"Dissenters were deemed to be purveyors of the plague. The unvaccinated were called out as jeopardising the health that was suddenly in such short supply. The media othered anyone that dared to object. Twitter and

Facebook banned alternative views. Google put disclaimers on pages that were deemed to be spreading misinformation - at a time when truth was in such short supply. Jacinda Ardern, the Prime Minister of New Zealand, argued that the government was the single source of truth.

"The people who turned out in droves to queue for their jabs believed that they were acquiring health again. The obese, the diseased, the chronically ill, all got in line and stretched out their arms to be given the elixir of rare, precious and health-giving promise. But, of course, many paid the ultimate price for accepting that promise that turned out to be a lie.

"We give up our ability to think, to ask questions, Anna, at our peril. We must love life. I'm not sure if it's God-given or not. But we must live our lives like it is."

Mark, at that point, unclipped his lapel mic and made clear to me that he was done. He walked over to me as I stood up and hugged me very, very tight.

Chapter 15: Jenny McIvor

It was May 2023 before I was able to meet Mark face-to-face again - about 18 months after he had completed the interview with Anna. I met him in Greece on the island of Poros.

I'd never been to Greece before, but Mark had taken to practically living there. It wasn't as though Greece had been particularly lenient on its citizens or implemented a 'light' lockdown. Quite the opposite. Many Greeks were very reluctant to obey the rules, and the regime used financial coercion, in particular, to encourage the local population to take the vaccine. But, for foreigners, Greece never made vaccination a requirement for entry.

The United States was another matter. Although both Anna and Rahul had returned to the States shortly after the interview, they had to do so using forged vaccination certificates. But much to their amazement, neither the airlines nor the immigration officials were that fussed about checking them.

But Mark was of the view that he could not take the chance. And he had ethical objections to being refused entry to a country on the basis of his medical choices.

And so it was that he started exploring Greece, alone. And had chosen the island of Poros as his 'base'. He said it gave him everything he needed, with the added advantage of much more sun than he was used to seeing in London.

The interview that Mark had done frustrated him. It wasn't because we were unable to place it. In fact, clips were used extensively all-over social media and Anna was able to publish it in full on her Substack blog. It also made Mark one of the most popular, and in-demand, commentators on the so-called 'alternative' media. But what frustrated him was that he hadn't referred to the central idea that he wanted to in the interview.

It was for this reason that I was in Greece - so that we could discuss a strategy to change the focus of the conversation (as he called it) away from just the Covid coercion and towards the creep towards totalitarianism. Now, as I'm sure you'll appreciate, I could think of lighter topics of conversation that I would have preferred over a plate of moussaka in a taverna on the beach on a Greek island. But beggars and choosers etc.

I arrived at the Port of Piraeus early in the morning in order to catch a fast ferry to Poros. It was late May, so the Sun was already warm. I was absurdly early. I found my departure gate and bought a ubiquitous Cappuccino Freddo. I regretted wearing so many clothes. Numerous tourists were already wandering around - most wearing shorts and t-shirts, but with many younger kids weighed-down with huge rucksacks. It was comforting to see so many young people eager to catch up on lost time. This was Piraeus and out there, on the edges of that sea, were so many beaches to be discovered. I intended to find some myself on this trip.

I pulled the hem of my skirt above my knees, noting their need for a tan. But they were now enveloped by that copper-coloured early morning sunshine, getting brighter and more intense by the second. I closed my eyes and felt the sun on my face. And, my God, this was bliss. Until it wasn't.

"Your first time to Greece?" someone said, so close to my left ear that I knew the question was for me. Mark had warned me that the likelihood was that I'd be chatted up a lot, travelling alone. I opened one eye and peered out of the slit. Beside me was an astonishingly handsome man, probably aged in his mid-50s. As he proceeded to speak, I realised that he was not Greek. "Are you American?"

"That's two questions. Which one do you want answered first?"

"Well, I gather that you are American from your accent. So that answers that one. This your first trip to Greece?"

"You're very forward. Why should I be talking with you?"

"I'm sorry. You're right. I just thought that you might like to meet a fellow traveller. From spending a lot of time travelling I know that it can be lonely sometimes without an occasional person to chat to."

"You're right. I'm sorry, my name's Jenny," I said as I reached out my hand. He shook it gently.

"I'm glad that we're still shaking hands. I thought for a while that all personal contact was to be outlawed. Was it bad where you were? My name's Gordon, by the way. I know, it's a really silly name but my parents thought it was a good idea."

"I think it was bad everywhere, Gordon. What's your theory on what happened?"

"My goodness, Jenny. That's quite the question. And we've only got half an hour until this ferry arrives. It may require us to continue this conversation when the ferry gets here. Are you going to Hydra?"

"No, Poros. But we can chat until your stop. But you've got time to get started."

"Okay. What happened? Well, clearly this is all speculation on my part. But it's informed speculation. I'm a former medical doctor you see. I no longer practice. I decided to get out and travel again when the bastards allowed me to. So that's why I'm here, chatting to you. You're very beautiful, by the way. But I presume you know that already."

"I do know. Yes. But I could do with a tan."

"You could. But that won't take long. Just don't use sun cream and don't burn. Anyway, as I was saying. In fact, no. What's *your* theory?"

"I'm not sure you'll want to hear it. In fact, part of the reason I'm here is to meet my boss. He has become something of a conspiracy theorist as far as Covid is concerned. But he lost his wife as a result of vaccine injury, so I suppose he's allowed to be as conspiratorial as he wants."

"Your boss, did you say? That wouldn't be Mark Carlisle by any chance?"

I was taken aback. "You've heard of him? You know Mark?"

"I know of him. I heard the interview. I've also watched him on a few podcasts with some of the podcast bros since. But I can't believe this. My God. How weird is this? Honestly, I have to say that you guys are doing a great job. It's so good to know that there are people like Mark in the world. What happened with his wife was utterly horrific. But it's not just that. The way he responded was superb and his analysis was spot on. But I so wanted him to talk more, to say more, in that interview. I can understand why he didn't, he was clearly in grief. But I hope that he gets the chance to do and say more."

"I'm astonished that I just met you and that you heard the interview and that you know Mark. I'm his media person. I know I did a good enough job getting the interview out there. But I'm a realist. There aren't that many people in the world who know him or know the argument."

"I appreciate that. But don't be spooked Jenny. People who are and have been travelling - even now that most of the restrictions have been lifted - are not typical. Travelling, for me, was almost the most inalienable right. It made me very angry when they grounded the aircraft. But Greece, for me, represented freedom. Yes, they did do some nasty things to their people. But they always let us in - to bask in the sunshine. The tavernas never really closed. But it means that the people you meet here in this crazy, busy port, are, truly, fellow travellers."

"Okay, I get that. And I'm delighted you know of Mark. But I'm not going to let you off that easily. You started chatting me up. I didn't give you your marching orders for interrupting my me-time. So tell me what you think. You don't necessarily agree with everything Mark says. Do you?"

"In his analysis of what was going on, I can say that I agree with just about everything. I think I'd go a little further. I'm a former medical doctor so I'd go further than Mark in debunking virology. I think it's nothing more than pseudoscience. But they need this as the basis for all the bullshit they heaped on us. There has to be a virus in their playbook. If it's not one that spreads from pangolins, then it was made in a lab. But this is utter drivel.

"It used to be that when I was a General Practitioner up in Dumfries in Scotland, I rarely saw any patients during the Winter with flu symptoms. It was accepted wisdom that during the Winter people tended to get seasonal colds or flu or whatever we want to call those conditions. It didn't require me to see them. If they did come to see me, it was normally because they'd developed chest infections or throat infections. In those circumstances I'd prescribe antibiotics.

"But Covid was a game changer. And it was because of the testing. The testing. The tracking and tracing. The vaccine apps. The digital incursion on our lives. They created a matrix. And they created the precedent for surveillance. They destroyed the doctor/patient relationship and the Hippocratic oath.

"But none of that will surprise you. What is likely to surprise you more is that the medical argument is a slam dunk now. I don't think anyone with an ounce of intelligence can believe that Covid was a novel virus or that the vaccines were needed. So, it's for this reason that I was disappointed by two things. Firstly, Mark didn't really explain his thinking around scarcity and how they use the idea of scarcity to manipulate. And second, Mark should not have chosen to be interviewed by the podcast bros. Because many of them are part of the problem."

As he made this point our ferry started boarding. So, we joined the line. Gordon graciously helped me stow my trundle-bag in the luggage area marked 'Poros' and we made our way to the top deck so that we could sit in the sun.

"I have to say Gordon, you're the first man who has tried the old scarcity line as part of his chat-up routine."

"Ah, you can blame your boss for that. I hadn't even considered the idea until he mentioned it. But here's my idea. You'll remember that in his interview he talked about how they created the idea that there was scarcity of oil and gas - even though they are plentiful. But the whole idea of fossil fuels was to give the impression that they were in short supply and time limited. The Net Zero argument has gone even further and suggested that we shouldn't even use them because they are polluting the atmosphere with carbon dioxide - the trace gas that helps plants grow.

"But let me add something else into the mix. For a while I thought - like quite a few other Libertarians - that cryptocurrency might present an opportunity to get out of the system and to allow the creation of a decentralised society. Bitcoin, in particular, represented - for me - currency nirvana.

"Now, I know what you're thinking. This guy is a doctor. So what the actual fuck is he talking about."

"Well, yes, the thought had crossed my mind."

"Well, then, let me elaborate. It wasn't just me, by the way. If you attend meetings with bitcoiners many are libertarian freedom warriors. They want to get rich, but they want to do it outside of a system that they see as rigged. But the captivating thing about bitcoin that they all get excited about is its scarcity. Only 21 million bitcoins will ever be mined. So, if everyone wants bitcoin then the price can only go up.

"But then I attended a big bitcoin conference. And something dawned on me. Like Mark, and you, no doubt, I tend to question things. But I arrived at this conference, and no-one seemed to be questioning anything. No-one seemed to want to question why it was that we were required to worship the bitcoin god. No-one really questioned why we didn't know who Satoshi was or is. And, almost instantaneously, it occurred to me that this was a cult. And I don't like cults.

"But then, when I watched Mark's interview with Anna, it just hit me. If you think of it, the way to get people to do something en-masse is to suggest that they need to act quickly or they'll miss the boat. Forgive the pun. But think about every cult. They peddle the scarcity idea. And this is the stock in trade for the major psyop masters. The intelligence agencies. They peddle scarcity. They scare people with scarcity.

"The central scarcity argument that they use is that democracy and freedom are in short supply. And they are under attack. So, they use this argument to wage war against people who threaten the limited supply of freedom. Have you ever considered that paradox? They essentially murder people who challenge their definition of democracy and freedom. For example, the Israelis argue that they have to kill Arabs who are attacking their single-religion, democratic state that was won by force.

"The Nazis argued that the jews were threatening their Aryan cult. Or cult-ure. Same thing. They were overrunning the place, they argued, like pests. And taking stuff that was rightfully theirs. Right at the heart of the cult argument is this idea of scarcity and others claiming more than their fair share. Land grabbing. Turf wars. Gold rushes. But, behind all of these, are people whispering to others that the precious is being grabbed.

"And they do this even when it's self-evident that there's plenty. We're running out of water. Over-exposure to the sun is bad for you, so limit its supply with a sunscreen. But, for me, bitcoin has to be the greatest example of how scarcity can literally be plucked out of thin air. Remember, there is no such thing as bitcoin. Just as there was no such thing as the Covid virus. But do you remember just how scarce the vaccine was in the early days? Or how toilet roll was in short supply during lockdown?"

"I think, Gordon, that he's familiar with these arguments. However, I can see a flaw right away. I get what you're saying about scarcity being the control method. But you haven't really gotten me any closer to the answer as to who the controllers are. I think my view, and Mark's, is that Langley is just an enforcer organisation, it's not defining the strategy. The strategy, to the extent that it exists, is much further up the food chain.

"I think there's a good case for me introducing you to Mark though. I think he'd like to meet you. And until such time I'd suggest that you tell me a bit more about yourself and why you're travelling to Hydra - and chatting up strange women."

"Oh, please, Jenny, you're not strange. You're very beautiful, extraordinarily intelligent and work with a very inspiring person. But I take your hint. I think it's time for us to lap up this sun and take in these views. And if you could give me the chance to meet Mark some time, that would be simply fabulous."

Gordon departed the ship at Hydra, and I sailed on to Poros. Mark was at the quayside waiting for me when I arrived. He gave me a huge hug when I finally managed to trundle my bag off the big catamaran.

"Mark, before we go anywhere, I just need to let you know that a guy chatted me up at Piraeus. Scottish. Coincidentally, he seemed to be a big fan of yours. I sat with him on the ferry. A spook do you think? Just wondered if we might be under some type of surveillance."

"Hmm. Possibly. Did he have access to your bag?"

"He helped me on with it. But he couldn't have had access to it on the boat. Tracker, you mean?"

"Yes. But it's a bit old-school these days. The likelihood is that he'll have your cell phone number now if you sat next to him. He probably had a stingray device. Suggest you power off the phone. I'll give you a Greek SIM. Also, we should get out of Poros. Let's get over to Spetses. It's not far and we can stay in a hotel that I think you'll like."

"Dear God, Mark. I've only just arrived. And I like the look of this island."

"Just wait until you see the Poseidonian Hotel. But, okay, I'll take you to a little taverna I know on the beach. Then I'll get my friend Nikos to sail us to Spetses. But I'll take you home first and you can get changed. I presume you'll want to slip into something a little more comfortable."

Mark's villa was remarkably understated. I was slightly relieved that we were going to be staying in a hotel. "It's adequate for my needs," he said, "but I presume you'd like somewhere more salubrious to show off your handbag collection."

"As it happens, I'm done with the handbag thing. I just have one - fake Birkin as it happens - with me on this trip. But this place is understated but totally gorgeous. But, sorry to change the subject, but what I don't understand is why he went on so much about how right you were and how he could improve your argument."

"The spook guy? Maybe it was just a coincidence. Maybe he was genuine."

"Nope. If he was genuine, he wouldn't have let me go without fixing a date or asking for my phone number."

"You have a point. Anyway, here's the room you would have been staying in. Feel free to get changed and I'll drive us over to that place for lunch. I'd suggest a bikini and something to cover your modesty while in the restaurant."

I sat on the side of the bed and pondered how completely bizarre this situation was. It wasn't totally clear to me who anyone was anymore. Or why I was in Greece, and why I was having to choose a bikini to wear to a beach restaurant with my boss. And a man I wasn't entirely sure I knew anymore. In fact, did I ever know him? What were we going to talk about? Who was Gordon? And would he end up in Spetses? But of one thing I was certain. I needed a drink.

So, I popped on a yellow string bikini. I was appalled at how pale I was. I needed a tan too. So, I quickly threw on an oversized shirt to, as Mark suggested, cover my modesty.

Mark drove us to the beach restaurant in a Wrangler Jeep that he'd hired. The roof was off and my hair whiplashed my face for the five-minute journey. As he parked-up a giant flying bug crashed into my forehead. "What the fuck is that?" I yelled, trying to get out of the jeep without looking too American.

"Don't worry. It's just a Cicada. They're harmless. Although some people think they're surveillance drones."

We giggled as we walked the few steps to the restaurant in the warm sand.

It wasn't exactly a taverna. It was more of a beach restaurant and Mark ordered my lunch for me - as he was a regular and knew the best dishes. He also ordered a bottle of Assyrtiko that he claimed was the very best in all of Greece.

"My God, Mark, do I *need* this glass of wine."

"And you deserve it Jenny. There'll be no work talk today. So, enjoy. And later I have an idea as to how you can get your tan topped up."

"You're a cheeky bastard," I said as I stretched out my very white legs out for him to see.

"So, what was his name?"

"Who?"

"The spook guy."

"Oh, um…Gordon. He was, apparently, a doctor in Scotland. But he saw the light. You were a big influence."

"Out of interest, what was his angle?"

"He wanted to put you right on your analysis of scarcity. He put forth a pretty good argument. He was good. They gave him some very convincing material."

"But what is their strategy? What are they planning to do?"

"I think they're almost certainly planning to whack you."

"Yes, I'm unfortunately coming to the same conclusion. But why now? What's changed?"

"The business. We're getting too successful. You know better than I what this business is about. It's ultimately about taking away their monopolies. And Rahul is doing such a good job. He's proving that we can decentralise power - literally - because our technology is better than anything else. This challenges everything. It challenges their carbon nonsense. It can power their silly battery cars. It can power factories all over Africa. The guys are getting the price points down to such a level that even farms and small villages can take our units to power everything."

"Indeed. If we could get the fuel. They still have a stranglehold over everything. They don't really need to whack me when they've got their hands round my throat anyway. All we're selling at the minute are pipedreams."

"You're being excessively negative, Mark. Rahul's building a huge amount of interest in India given the Thorium supplies there. Indian tech is all over it. Have you seen our latest quarterly numbers? Our consulting fees are off the scale."

"I have. And here we are talking business. After I said we'd stay off the subject."

"Unfortunately, though, Mark, the business is the reason why we're hiding in this taverna. Your vision for ubiquitous energy is the reason why you may be running from them for the rest of your life."

"I have no intention of doing that. Well, perhaps today. We need to run from them today, because you're here with me. I want to make sure you're safe. That's for my own benefit. I have been lonely these last few weeks."

The light twinkling off the bay was dazzling. I shut down the conversation about the business and sipped on the chilled wine, closed my eyes and let the heat of the Sun on my body dissipate some of the fear I felt. When I left the Agency, I thought I'd left these types of feelings behind. But at least I knew, now, what I was up against.

"I can see why you've chosen this place to hide."

"Just wait 'til you taste the tuna carpaccio."

"I thought Greek tavernas just served stifado and moussaka."

"Not this one, Jenny. Not this one."

After lunch we lay for a while in the sun and I, at last, started to develop a sun-kissed look rather than my post-Winter in DC pallor. We then made our way back to the port and boarded a motor-yacht to take the short journey to Spetses. Mainland Greece, the Peloponnese, was practically within touching distance.

On the plane from the States I'd read Henry Miller's book, The Colossus of Maroussi. In it he describes how the narrowness of the straight between Poros and the mainland gives the illusion of sailing on land. But we found the egress and soon we were sailing - never too far from the mainland - past the island of Hydra towards Spetses.

The hotel - the Poseidonian - was clearly visible as we approached the island. That such a grand hotel should exist on such a tiny Greek island was tricky to comprehend.

One of my disappointments about many supposed great hotels is that, once inside, corporatism takes over and destroys the illusion. Not so here. Although it helped that the hotel staff were impeccable actors, playing their parts. For one thing they knew not to refer to Mark by name at reception or in any of the public areas. It was always "Sir," never Mr Carlisle.

The three-bedroomed suite that was to be our refuge had, no doubt, harboured many very wealthy people - possibly on the run. We felt that we were probably the first to be fleeing an MI6 operative called Gordon. Or was he just a nice chap with a novel chat-up patter? We weren't absolutely sure. But we were taking no chances and had the benefit of being in the Presidential Suite of the Poseidonian as some form of consolation.

I'll be honest, it was bliss being on the island. Spetses was possibly even more beautiful than Poros. Mark suggested that I spend my first full day just cycling around the island on an electric bicycle that the hotel kindly provided. That was Mark's suggested method for getting a tan. A cooling breeze, and frequent beach and taverna stops, made it one of the most euphoric experiences I'd ever had.

Cycling around that island, alone, with only my thoughts, made me contemplate what life in America - in the West - was all about. I was in my forties now. I'd never married. I had been fixated on success. But here I was, on a bicycle, in the sunshine, drinking cheap Greek taverna wine, and with the sun on my body. And I realised that this was all that was important. Living. Living and embracing life and the sun and wanting nothing more. In fact, it almost felt like it was the first time I'd lived.

When I returned to the hotel I was covered in dust, distinctly sunburnt, and my hat had developed a sweat tidemark. I made my way up to the suite hoping that Mark wasn't there to see me in this state. But he was in the sitting room sipping a Negroni. "Dear God, look at you."

"I know. I'm sorry. I'm a fucking mess. Look at me."

"I'm looking at you. And, honestly Jenny, you are more beautiful than I've ever seen you. Did you have a good day?"

"I hate to admit it. But honestly, I had the best day. I'm a bit sunburned though. Let me go and get changed. I take it we've a dinner reservation. I think it's about time that I earned my stay here. We need to talk business tonight."

"Oh, indeed we shall, Jenny. We have much to talk about."

"I like the look of that Negroni, by the way, any chance you could be a darling and order me one?"

With a cool shower and lots of body butter I managed to look slightly less sun ravaged than I had. Some make-up helped my nose look less like Rudolf's. And I slid into a black mini-dress and donned some heels. I started to feel a bit more DC again. It made me slightly sad. But it was probably the right frame of mind for the conversation I was about to have. I knew - and perhaps I was evading it up to now - that I was about to embark on something. It just felt that a battle was about to commence, and I was part of it. I just didn't know who I was fighting or if I had any hope of winning. I wanted Mark to assure me I would.

The hotel terrace restaurant was already buzzing and noisy when we arrived. The men were mostly dressed in long shorts with Gucci loafers and white shirts. Most of the younger women were just enjoying being out and enjoying doing what they should never have been prevented from doing. Having dinner, flirting, and showing off their tanned limbs.

As we sat down at our table, I had the opportunity to look at Mark, properly, for the first time. He had aged since I last saw him, but in a good way. His hair was now more grey than dark. But with his Grecian tan it suited him. I looked at his hands and noted he was still wearing his wedding ring. I'd noticed that he was wearing it when he did the podcast with Anna. But I was a little surprised that nearly two years after Alice had died that he was still wearing it. But I made no comment.

"How are you, Mark? This is the first time I've sat with you face-to-face in…how long?"

"Far too long. But what would I have done without you? I'm so grateful that you have come."

"Well, I work for you. And the working conditions aren't so bad," I said as I waved my hand out to the sun setting over the Aegean.

"Yes, it's a special place. I have been so angry so often over the last three years. I needed Greece and it saved me. It showed me that despite all they did to us people have not changed. They weren't prepared to give up their humanity. We're in a grand hotel. But you saw how modestly I live here. Part of it is remaining inconspicuous. But another part is that most Greeks aren't wealthy. But they get to eat great food and live the lives that most wealthy people couldn't even comprehend as being blessed. Family and community are everything here.

"I now have a routine of visiting a farmer's market every Saturday morning. I buy organically produced vegetables, fish that's been landed in the local harbour, and honey from bees that fly around the island. And olive oil from trees that have been here for centuries. Before Trump, Biden, possibly even Washington."

"Ugh, you have to introduce politics and spoil the evening already."

"I know. My apologies. But you know why you're here, really, don't you?"

"I think I do. I think it's to decide what it is that we stand for."

"Indeed. Jenny, you know me better than most people. And I know you. I know your secrets, literally. You know mine. And you know that I love you. I'm not your employer. You're not my employee. We're kindred spirits. We're travellers. We're the resistance. And the reason we're here is because we need to do something and it needs to be done. But what I need to know from you is what you think our task is. I need to know that you and I are as one."

"I think I preferred Gordon's company. At least he told me how beautiful I am."

Mark smiled but remained silent. I tinkled the ice in my Negroni.

"I'm at a slight disadvantage here, because I've had two Negronis."

"Just one. You haven't even sipped that one yet. You're just playing with it."

"Okay. So here goes. The conspiracy theorists have been proven correct. The world is not as it seems. Much of what we're told by the media is lies. Most of our so-called leaders are puppets or actors. The West, in particular, is stitched-up by an elite that's largely Anglo-American and comprises hugely wealthy families that own most global corporations and organised crime syndicates - through a myriad of NGOs and the British, American and Israeli intelligence agencies. Those agencies also run or are associated with the biggest crime syndicates.

"Democracy is an illusion. And party politics, a scam. The purpose of the media is largely to perpetuate the illusion of choice and agency.

"The elite's main focus is to own just about everything. They regard humanity with contempt and use wars, the military industrial complex, and toxin warfare to keep the population in check. Public health systems are there, largely, to prescribe toxic 'medicine' and to provide medical interventions that supposedly fix the effects of the toxins they prescribe. Health systems are also major purveyors of pseudoscience - such as virology.

"How am I doing?"

"You're doing well. I presume you have some more?"

"How's this? The elite's primary method of control is to create fear and division. Often this fear relates to loss or losing out. They create fear about scarcity. They create fear narratives about identity, religion, and gender. And they create narratives that humanity is responsible for threats to our existence - like the so-called climate emergency. These narratives, therefore, are used to justify centralised control and surveillance by an all-powerful state."

"You put it beautifully," Mark said, with a smile. "But there's a problem, of course."

"There is. Most people, having been conditioned all their lives to outsource their thinking to others will think we're bat-shit crazy if they ever get to hear any of this articulated like this. And, of course, there's the issue that we have very, very limited reach. So, we don't even get to sound bat-shit except on the fringe media which specialises in bat-shit."

"But there's another problem. Who the hell are *we*?"

"You're right. The only reason we're here discussing this, Mark, is because you're wealthy. And your business relates to the very thing on which they fixate: energy."

"The technocrats have always made a feature of energy as the unit of exchange. Energy credits. They also argue that experts, rather than elected officials, should rule the world. That's why I saw energy - particularly decentralised energy - as a means of annoying them or breaking them in some way. Many businesspeople are dependent on state handouts so can't say anything. They might contract for government work. Or they might sub-contract to corporations that are part of the technocratic ecosystem. So, speaking out isn't really an option. The system requires compliance.

"I appreciate that I'm somewhat unique in that I don't really care if my entire business comes crashing down. I have money stashed in various forms and I have collected assets that will allow me to lead a pleasant life. But I derive a certain utility in making fun of them. They're cultists. And their days are numbered. But what I'd like to start contemplating is what things might be like once we return to some form of normalcy. My role, to the extent that I have one, is simply to say that humanity is the endgame. Each individual must have agency - but they can't currently have that if they're inside the control grid that the technocrats have - very successfully - created."

"So, what you're saying is that we make your story the universal story that as many people as possible get to hear?"

"I think so. I see myself as a universal soldier to a degree. I do not matter. Well, I matter just to me and the people I love but not to the people who get to hear about me. I simply describe their predicament."

"And what is their predicament?"

"Lack of agency is enslavement. It's not being able to make any decisions. In fact, it's even worse than that. It's not even knowing the choices that are made available are chosen by someone else. It's false hope. False agency. It's like being told that the prison compound, rather than solitary confinement, is freedom.

"Western society has become a more sophisticated version of The Truman Show. But few people know they are living in a set. The illusion is constantly being reinforced. We need to go to work. We need to behave appropriately at work so as not to be fired. We take vacations maybe twice a year. We need to celebrate secular versions of religious holidays. We need to eat processed shit. We need to keep up to date with the 'news'. We need to act for the common good. We need to heed the advice of experts. We need to take an interest in the lives of the celebrity class and royal families. We really should start using ChatGPT to write because it's much better than humans at expressing things well."

"But is there a real possibility that if we shatter the illusion the reality will be much worse than what they currently have? As you've said, you're okay. You have played the system well and you've done well for yourself. But are we at risk of red-pilling people and the alternative is simply isolation and loss of hope?"

Mark looked at me and smiled a little before answering.

"I don't think so. I might have to get a little Zen to answer this. And it's an odd answer. I apologise in advance. But I find that once I'm settled here, in Greece, a few days after the stress of travel and bureaucracy has worn off, I get to sleep really well. Especially at this time of year. Perhaps it's the heady mix of blossom in the air, or the warm Spring breezes. But I sleep, and I dream. And a few mornings ago, I woke up very early.

Jenny McIvor

The Sun was just peeping over the horizon, but my bedroom was filled with light because I'd forgotten to close the shutters before going to bed. So, I remembered what I had been dreaming.

"In the dream I was giving a speech. I was younger and a bit stressed about the speech I was giving. So, I had notes. But I had mislaid them. And in the notes were the words of a poem I wanted to read, as part of my speech. And all I could remember was the poem was called *The Bowl*. But I couldn't remember the words.

"Then I woke up. And I thought to myself, how odd. How weird that I wanted to read a poem called, *The Bowl*, in my dream. So, I googled it. Still lying in bed, fiddling with my phone, I found a poem by a poet called Jane Hirshfield. It's an odd poem. The bowl, essentially, is our daily life. It's filled with stuff. But each day it's back to being 'spotless and hungry' as she says in the poem. And it fits exactly in two human hands.

"I can't recall the poem in full. But I also found, in my Google search, some thoughts by the poet about the poem. And she discusses life. And the fact that we've been given it. And that we must find a way to live in this world. We can't refuse it. But, as she says, along with the difficult is the radiant and the beautiful.

"We, each of us, has a bowl that's clean each day but quickly filled. I suppose it means that we need to decide, from day to day, how we might change our futures."

"I think I like the Zen version of you, Mark. I think you're saying that your way of changing your future is what *you* want to do. It's not really about society or their salvation - but rather your decisions about your future might be of some value. But everyone needs to make similar decisions."

"Absolutely. Decisions are decisions. All we can do - in living outside the system and shining a light on the stitch-up - we might make people more aware of stuff that should be in their bowls and stuff that shouldn't. It's up to them to decide.

"But I do sense that, for many, the bowl is a begging bowl. Like Oliver Twist, people seem to think it's the responsibility of others to fill their bowls. And I'm going to drop this fucking metaphor here. You see what happens when I over-egg the Zen."

"Yes. Time to stop with the bowl. But on the subject of futures, is this your future, do you think? Here in Greece? Rahul is running the business well. But how many times do you need to find yourself? How ridiculously tanned do you need to be?"

"The tan does help. Although no matter how tanned I get, the Greeks still assume I'm a Brit."

"Maybe it's because the Greeks know that only mad dogs and Englishmen go out in the midday sun."

"That is true. But to answer your question, I don't think it matters where I am. At the minute I'm pretty safe because they can choose to ignore me. I've bought into the bitcoin 'store of value' nonsense because I might as well profiteer from their schemes. I'm arguing the merits of alternative energy using nuclear power. Although that doesn't conform to the Net Zero narrative - because that's all about replacing reliable power with unreliable power and blackouts.

"And I have no skeletons in my cupboard. So, they've nothing on me to take me down. But this means that they might want to shut me up more permanently. The irony is that I'd like you to help me get back into the mainstream media again. I'm probably blacklisted. But I want you to do everything to get me back."

"There's no possibility of that Mark. You know as well as I do how they work. You'll never have a shot at mainstream media again. You challenge their conventions too much and too eloquently. The only possibility is that you try to do a Tucker Carlson. But the problem is, no offence, you're not a former anchor on a primetime news network owned by Murdoch. You're not Tucker and you're not Piers Morgan."

"Dear God, Jenny, never say that again."

"Well, you get my drift. Okay, your podcast with Anna got a pretty good audience. Maybe the clips were viewed by two or three million people. Tucker Carlson's audience was in the tens of millions on X when he launched his own channel. But, do you know what, it'll ebb. He, too, will be ignored in time. People will grow bored with the B-list guests he's able to attract. Or the nutritional supplements he'll be peddling so he can pay the production team. And, anyway, what is it you want to achieve? Why do you want to be in the media? You've just said that this is all about your bowl, your agency. So why the fuck are you trying to influence everyone? Are you an influencer now?"

"You're my Head of Comms. I thought we were meeting to discuss comms."

"In case you hadn't noticed, Mark, you run a very successful business and employ quite a few people. I think you need to start thinking a bit more strategically. I sense you want to be John Galt. But he was a fictional character. And he wasn't dependent on a 24-hour news cycle stitched up by the media and tech bros.

"I prefer you when you're being Zen."

I could see him flinching a little at that comment.

"Look, Mark, I get it. You're a marvellous communicator and a freedom fighter and want to be seen to be part of the resistance. But, seriously, do you really think that the media wants any perspectives that will show them for what they are? Do you seriously believe that if I pitched you to the BBC or NBC that they'd welcome you with open arms - and value your alternative views?

Jenny McIvor

"You're a contrarian. You're a free thinker. You believe that bitcoin is stitched up by the CIA. Your wife was killed because she took the vaccine. Your business was created so that you could take the piss out of the climate emergency lobby. And you're on record as saying that the mainstream media is a propaganda network. So, tell me again to whom I should pitch you?"

"Okay. Hurtful. But okay."

"Listen, here we are in paradise. Just look at this. Okay, perhaps there are a few too many Gucci loafers here but look at that sunset, that sea. How can you, in all seriousness, think about strutting around TV studios like Bill Gates? Seriously, that's the calibre of actor the studios want to interview. And you're literally sitting in one of the most beautiful places on earth with, let's face it, a very hot date."

"You are very hot. Especially your nose. It's very red."

"Only because you insisted I ride around the island on a bicycle with no SPF."

"Hopefully you used coconut oil, like I suggested."

"Mark, seriously, I don't want to be your Head of Comms anymore."

"What do you want to be then?"

"Your wife?"

"Okay then. I like the sound of that."

"That just slipped out Mark."

"Yes, but it was kinda Freudian. Are you serious? Would you really want to be my wife even though I refused to be seduced by you all those years ago?"

"Seduction wasn't on offer. I was just planning to get you naked. I had no intention of getting naked with you."

"But now you want to be my wife?"

"I thought you'd like that too. I think you just proposed, or were you joking?"

"No, I wasn't joking. You know I wasn't. I can't imagine anything I'd want more. My days might be numbered though."

"You mean Gordon?"

"Well, Gordon's people. I'm sure he has people to do the whacking."

"I don't think you're important enough to whack."

"You did earlier. Anyway, are you going to be my Dagny Taggart?"

"I don't think John Galt married Dagny. Anyway, I preferred Hank Reardon."

"Okay let's just say I'm Hank. Will you marry me?"

"Okay then. But there may be a condition attached. I may want to stay on as your Head of Comms."

"I thought you wanted to resign."

"I did, earlier. But things changed. Listen, I share your ambition. Liberty is being assaulted everywhere we look. I thought I'd escaped when I managed to get out of Langley. But that's nonsense. We're being stitched up. And maybe Ayn Rand was totally wrong. Maybe, in each of us, there is a shared desire for freedom. This may not be altruism. But I know that I feel your pain too when I see how supremely evil it's possible for the collective to be. And, as an individual, as a woman, I want to do something about it. Perhaps it's the mother in me. I don't know. But there comes a time when we need to stand up for what we know to be true. And the only standing up I can do is to use my particular talent to do everything to unravel their stitch-up.

"This morning, I watched a clip from a morning TV show that was posted on Twitter. It was a TV doctor being interviewed about the Covid shots and making clear that everybody should get them. For the benefit of everyone. You get the drift. The nodding dog interviewer just let the shill talk, and talk. Platitudinous bollocks as *you* might say. On and on. They make us fucking gorge on their nonsense and expect us to say nothing. But I'm going to say something. *We're* going to say something.

"I know that Alice let you down. You two had grown apart and, in parting, she had joined them, accepted the baubles, the accolades, the riches. Perhaps Ayn Rand would have applauded her for accepting the riches afforded by capitalism. But I suspect not. I suspect that she too would have seen through the corporatism acting under the guise of the entrepreneur.

"Like you, Mark, I love life. But only one thing threatens this - *them*. When lies are paraded as truths by people with grand titles and power we know that there is a real possibility that people might try to take away the things we love.

"There are too many people like Gordon who are willing to play the parts assigned for them in order to have a life of sorts. But it's not a life. A life is not worth living if it means suppressing the spirit, suppressing the soul, letting whatever shit that's flying this way plop into our bowls. We're gonna fucking fight them until we cease to draw breath. Are you with me?"

Mark walked round the table to me and eased me up so that I stood looking into his eyes. "I'm with you," he said, as he kissed my sunburnt nose.

Jenny McIvor

He returned to his seat at the table, opposite me. And he ordered some champagne.

We had no idea when we might actually get married. Both of us knew that it might be some time. Neither of us knew how things were going to pan out. The shit-show we'd just come out of was just a precursor to galloping madness. But it was clear that only a very few people grasped the fact that we'd just come through the first truly audacious social control event that was the harbinger of some flavour of globalist shit.

Over the next few days in Spetses and then driving around the Mani Peninsula on the Peloponnese, we discussed how there was no going back. That everything had changed. Our circumstances were fortunate. And we had each other, and we had a really strong company and a really incredible team. But we both knew that if the company went down the tubes and all Mark's investments went South, we could never have our old lives back again. We were unemployable. And we no longer had the ability to bite our lips or not to proffer our opinions.

But this was totally different from what had come before. I'll give you an example. I had dated, for quite a long time, a British Conservative politician, on and off, for around three years. He visited DC quite a bit because he was, for a while, a Junior Minister in the Foreign Office. And then he just looked for any excuse to get trips to DC to, well, see me.

Politically, we thought we were aligned. And we had some great conversations about the gossip around The Hill. Or in the Westminster village. He was a very lovely man. Although he was married, of course.

I had no desire to break his marriage. He provided what I thought to be some intellectual stimulus. And he bought me some fabulous meals and very lovely wine in the best restaurants in Georgetown and Alexandria.

But, as it turned out, we weren't really that well aligned. Something started to bother me about him. He was always kind, courteous and gentlemanly. He provided a listening ear. But he once admonished me for being too strident in my views. Not because he didn't agree with my views but because he said I sounded a little ideologically fanatical. I asked him what he meant. And he responded, "ideologies are dead, Jenny…we just don't do ideologies anymore."

I asked him to clarify what he meant. "You said, 'we', just now. We don't do ideologies anymore. Who did you mean? Who were you referring to?"

But he didn't really answer. And I knew that I wouldn't see him again.

Mark and I discussed this at length as we whizzed around some very scary mountain roads in West Mani. I told him the story about my Conservative Party friend who gave up on Conservatism.

Jenny McIvor

"It's a maxim of the New World Order. The global government conspiracy theory. Well, there are several. But there's a clear strand of 'end of ideology' that has emerged from the British elite that regards ideologies as a means of controlling the masses. Therefore, they don't 'do' them. Ideologies I mean. It was a clear slip of the tongue in his case.

"Have you ever noticed how very senior, very polished, politicians never seem to have any real political passion. They'll talk about issues. Often, they'll directly contradict themselves, speech to speech. They U-turn frequently, if they have to. It gives rise to another theory that politicians don't really emerge from the people. They're selected, chosen, grown."

"Anyway, let's return to this conversation later. We're here. This is Limeni. You thought we'd done paradise in Spetses. Wait until you see this place."

We walked from where Mark had parked the car into a village built around a tiny harbour. On one side of the harbour was a taverna clinging on at the sea's edge and we sat down and looked to the harbour where around fifteen or twenty people were swimming. Most were quite elderly and most were women. Just ordinary women, cooling off in the azure sea or bobbing about chatting to their friends in rapid-fire Greek. We drank Ouzo and orange juice before wandering down to the water ourselves, stripping down to our underwear and depositing our clothes in two untidy little piles either side of ancient, rickety stone steps leading into the sea.

Soon we were in the middle of the bobbing ladies who shouted 'Kalimera' at us - clearly flattered to be joined by two non-locals. And then they ignored us to return to their water-based village gossip.

"I like this ideology," said Mark as he paddled himself into an odd backstroke and glided past me, grinning. "This is the ideology of life. These people know that the best way to live is to love."

"True that," I said, as I submerged myself into the water and pondered in the relative silence of my personal underwater world how life might get any better than this.

Our hotel, just outside the village, had been finished just before lockdown. It was stone-built, and the bedrooms were little individual stone-houses scattered across a campus that wrapped itself around a cliff edge.

"The guy who built this put everything he had into it," Mark said as we threw our bags onto the bed in our very opulent room. "The problem is that it was due to open in the high season in 2020. But he's had just about no paying guests. Lockdown has been financially crippling for him."

"My God, how sad. But what a beautiful place."

"Indeed. You'll get to meet him at dinner. He was quite a successful businessman and had done a few much more modest developments in the area. But this place has almost finished him. Of course, all the usual suspect vulture funds have wanted to take the problem off his hands, but he told them all to 'fuck off'.

"If you think about it, telling people to stay at home and closing all the airlines for months on end was a brilliant way to distress lots and lots of very successful businesses and the people who ran them. People who had never had any difficulties in the past - who were reliable and hard-working - literally had the rugs pulled from under them.

"Bizarrely, this was another one of Alice's investments. She took a minority position in the business and gave him the working capital he needed to survive and to stop the bank foreclosing. She could easily have taken the whole business. But, instead, she accepted his valuation and gave him the money."

"She was a good person, Jenny. I'll admit, we did grow apart. But she wanted to do her own thing, to be her own woman. I can't fault her for that. In fact, I was very proud of her. And this will be one of her better investments. I'm sure of that. But I'm left with that distinct feeling that the psychological operation that we were all subjected to was designed to take advantage of people like Alice - people with good intentions, who wanted to do their bit, who wanted to be seen to help out."

"My God," I said, "I seriously did not see that one coming. You own some of this? Because of Alice? She was a dark horse indeed."

"She was, Jenny. But she's also, weirdly, representative of the old world. The world before the end of ideology that your Tory friend alluded to. I knew that Alice was a bit inclined towards a worldview that I didn't agree with. But in the West, we all took the view that capitalism could do some social good. The paternalistic textile entrepreneurs of the British industrial revolution gave their workers free homes and decent sewage systems and schools for their children. The state couldn't be relied-upon to raise people out of poverty. We had to rely on the wealth creators. The social contract was between the workers and their employers. The state didn't really get a look-in."

"But the problem, and you know this as well as I, Mark, is that my Tory friend hit the nail on the head. The state - and that's not just the government - pretty much calls all the shots. That's why, regardless of the political party in office, the same policies are implemented, the same wars are supported, the same foreign policy positions are taken, and the same pandemics are peddled."

"I get that, Jenny. But here's my question for you. Their so-called pandemic marked a turning point. This was a whole new order of magnitude of control. You worked for the intelligence agencies. You know that the extent of global coordination was like nothing we've ever seen before. Langley was never really noted for the slickness of its operations. This feels to me like it was organised by something much more sinister.

"Some have gone all spiritual and suggested that the scamdemic was satanic in its nature. It, and all the other geopolitical tendrils that have emerged from it, feels clinically evil. But I don't buy that.

"We've all assumed, Jenny, that artificial intelligence is an attempt to create human-like intelligence in a machine. There's much talk of the singularity and the Turing test. But has it ever occurred to you that artificial intelligence actually refers to an operation, carried out by the intelligence agencies. And they're performing the operation on us?"

"Hmm, interesting. Like a control grid? The timing looks like it's right. They keep the AI models under wraps and use them to organise the op - pulling all the necessary agencies, media organisations and information portals together. The ultimate large language model. The ultimate communications programme. The psyop to end all psyops.

"But you know what the consequence of what you're saying is? The program is still being run. Now that they've played their hand they can't stop playing it. Everything, all media, all news agendas are slaves to the model."

"Exactly, Jenny, exactly. So, does it scare you?"

"Not really, Mark. I'm not scared. But I think we may now be at war with them. You reckon we'll survive it?"

"We will, I think, for a while. But the resources we have are miniscule compared to theirs. The opportunity, though, is this. If we are right, and I think we are, it's clear that everyone who's a slave to the model, is essentially an actor. So that includes all of the big-name journalists, the networks, the celebrities, the politicians, even the supposed opposition. The only way we can succeed is to be ignored. Our mission is to creep. To hide behind the scenes. To plant doubt and uncertainty. But I sense we may need to have a chat with our comrades in arms."

Chapter 16: Anna Sussex

There was no shortage of alternative media commentators questioning the so-called pandemic narrative - certainly by the end of 2023. But the yawning gulf between the supposedly mainstream media and the media that I was seen to represent made me a little suspicious.

For one thing I didn't want to be lumped into a group known simply as vaccine sceptics or Covid deniers. I'll be honest, some of the podcasters and commentators who were supposedly on 'my side' held views that I didn't agree with. And, I'll admit, sometimes I was downright confused.

The source of my problem lay in the fact that if the pandemic was a hoax the media was right at the centre of the hoax-making. But to make things more difficult, I was at the centre of another problem: I was being bankrolled by people who wanted to popularise alternative narratives. And, when they got the impression that I was popularising ideas with which they did not agree, it created a problem for them.

There was considerable interest in my interview with Mark. Although YouTube took it down and I ended-up having to host it myself on my own website. My employers took a dim view of this. But they also made clear that they needed me to get closer to some of the narratives *they* were keen to popularise.

South of Market

I'll be honest. It wasn't clear to me what these narratives were. I was having to second-guess their thinking and their objectives. With Covid and all the social control that went with it I couldn't quite understand how I was expected to make the case for some ill-defined libertarianism without, at the same time, making clear my thoughts about the assault on liberty that the Covid era represented.

As a result of this crisis of conscience I felt it was time for me to get a meeting with the CEO of the Hedge Fund that essentially owned me, and my ability to say the things I wanted to say. And securing this meeting wasn't exactly easy. I had to work my way through various HR teams at various levels of the company. But eventually, I received an email that I had to fly to New York to meet with him. But the strange thing is that the guy I was due to meet wasn't the guy I thought was our CEO. It was someone else entirely. Someone I'd never heard of before. His name was Jacob Stapelberg.

Admittedly, I was able to find him on our corporate website. But there was nothing about him on Wikipedia.

On our corporate website he was described as being CTO of our media and analysis division. Although his PA's job title was 'Personal Assistant to the CEO'. So, I presumed that his page just hadn't been updated.

The day that I received the email confirming the meeting was the same day I received a call from Jenny - who was in Greece at the time, seeing Mark.

She was a bit vague on the phone. But she told me that Mark wanted to arrange some type of meeting with people he trusted to 'chew the fat'. I'd no idea what this meant. But I could tell that she, and Mark, wanted my perspectives on 'things'. She mentioned that they were of the view that I had particular insights that they'd find valuable. It was in this context that I mentioned - largely because it was top of mind - that I was to meet Stapelberg.

"*Jacob* Stapelberg," Jenny said on the phone.

"Have you heard of him?"

"Yes, Anna, I've heard of Jacob Stapelberg. Are you telling me that you're meeting him face-to-face? I mean you're physically meeting him?"

"Yes, I've just received an email from his personal assistant."

Jenny terminated the call pretty quickly at that point leaving me totally bewildered.

However, I received a Signal message from her shortly after the conversation to tell her that she and Mark would provide a briefing prior to my meeting. To give me the inside track. However, they didn't want to provide me too much background in case it might skew my thinking or disadvantage me in the meeting.

South of Market

The meeting, as it happened, was brought forward somewhat. I had a call from Stapelberg's PA the following day asking me to come to New York immediately - not allowing any time for Jenny's briefing.

I flew into New York the following day and overnighted in the Algonquin Hotel. The meeting was to take place over breakfast in the hotel. Stapelberg was already at the breakfast table when I arrived, slightly earlier than the appointed time of 7am. The restaurant was largely empty, although an adjoining table was occupied by his 'driver' and a big guy who looked like a minder.

As I walked to the table I stretched out my hand to shake hands. He provided a limp and sweaty hand but refused to stand.

"I do apologise for not getting up, Anna. My knees aren't great. Please, do sit down. Can I order you some coffee or tea?"

He was a big man but was clearly not in the best of health. His knees were clearly suffering as a result of his upper body bulk. He wasn't obese exactly although he was flabby and sweaty. He had a stubbly beard, dark wiry hair and was going a little bald on top. He wore thick black rimmed glasses. Put it this way, he was not endowed with beauty. Although I had already checked out a huge gold Rolex and a big, vulgar sonority ring.

When coffee arrived, and a basket of Viennoiserie, he started the conversation.

"Anna, what do you know about us?"

"I'm not sure I know what you mean."

"I mean, how much do you know about the organisation you work for? I know we haven't been very proactive in getting you up to speed on the group structure, but I thought it might be helpful."

"It would be helpful, yes. But I'll be honest with you, I haven't really sought to find out. I suppose I'm old-guard - in that I think journalists shouldn't know too much about who's paying them."

"I have huge respect for that. Believe me. Huge respect. But I'm sure you're aware that we don't really do altruism. You've been working through Xavier and his team since you joined us. Isn't that right?"

"That's right. Although the brief was always that I was to deliver you eyeballs and subscribers in big numbers. I think I've delivered that."

"Indeed you have Anna. But you always need to be cognizant of the endgame. This was never about you, so to speak. It was always about building a particular worldview. And you, I'll be honest, are our most successful project. You have exceeded expectations. But we have certain concerns. Do you remember the earliest conversations you had with us and with Sebastian, even, before you joined."

"The head-hunter guy? Goodness, that's some time ago. I'll confess that a lot of water has passed under the bridge since then."

"I agree. But what Sebastion told you when he first met you was absolutely correct. We needed you to create a rich seam of editorial content to redress the balance that we saw. We needed to create a narrative around freedom and liberty. To counter the liberal woke agenda."

"Didn't I do that?"

"You did, in the early days, yes. But we detect that your direction of travel has changed. What might help is that you outline for me why things changed. Why have you, perhaps, gone a little off message?"

"Off message? I'm a little intrigued by that. I thought I was in the business of producing long form content based on interviews with thought leaders who could broadly be described as 'Libertarian'. I think I achieved that. But then some things happened."

"What happened, exactly?"

"Goodness, Jacob, you know what happened. 2020 happened. We had the greatest intervention in human liberty that we've ever seen in our lifetimes. And the so-called libertarians that you wanted me to interview and seek opinions from didn't want to talk about that. They wanted to talk about woke or about Joe Biden's dementia but not about the fact that no-one in the mainstream media was prepared to address the problem: the loss of freedom, the loss of free will and the destruction of the free press."

"Look, Anna, we get this. And we were willing to give you quite a bit of latitude. We had concerns about lockdown too. But our view was that there was a need for a vaccine and that's why we supported the rapid vaccine development. It was a great way to showcase the ability of the drug companies to fix a very significant global crisis.

"So, we were quite keen to support your criticism of lockdown, but we felt that your focus on vaccine critics was a step too far. It, therefore, leads me to my most fundamental question. Why do you think we do what we do?"

"Well, perhaps you can clarify that for me. But I presume, given that I'm meeting you here today, it's clear that you want me to focus on messaging that better meets your clients' needs. So, to answer your question, I presume you want to maximise the return from your investment portfolio."

"Yes, that's true to an extent. But perhaps you think that in order to do that we respond to the news in ways that would reflect well on our clients. That's not really what we try to do. We're much further up the food chain than that. Or to put it another way, we don't find anything that governments do surprising. Because our clients often tell them their expectations. In effect, our clients, and our government partners, tend to make the news rather than respond to it. And I'm sure you'll agree, that puts you in a very enviable position."

He ended this statement with something of a self-satisfied smile as he took a gulp of coffee and then ate a mini croissant in one bite.

"So, are you saying that you make the news?"

"We don't make it as such. But I'm sure you are aware that if any news story makes headlines it tends to be about some corporate agenda or other?"

"Indeed, I'm rapidly learning that. But I want to come back to what you said earlier about lockdown. You were happy with me taking a position against lockdowns - because that's almost required for a libertarian-leaning media organisation. But taking a position against the vaccines - themselves touted as being the route out of lockdown - was a step too far. Is that what you're saying your position is and was?"

"In a nutshell, yes. I know it may seem contradictory, but you have to be aware that sometimes it makes good business sense to adopt what might seem to be contradictory positions."

"So, you're all for human liberty, except when it comes to your portfolio companies peddling drugs that kill people."

"So, Anna, now you're getting fucking cheeky. We require of you that you do nothing to undermine our positions. Perhaps our definition of liberty is slightly different to yours. But remember, you wouldn't have any liberty to do the things that you do or to have the lifestyle that you have if it weren't for us. I need to remind you of that. I appreciate that you have achieved a level of visibility that we hadn't fully expected. You have exceeded our expectations in that regard. But that puts you in a position that makes us slightly uncomfortable. So, it's for this reason that we wish to terminate your employment contract. And, incidentally, I hadn't reached that conclusion before this meeting. But I detect an attitude from you that makes me feel very uneasy indeed. Therefore, I'm terminating your contract with immediate effect.

"You're terminating my contract because I was too successful?"

No, we're terminating it because your success was built on a worldview that we don't share. For us, libertarianism is not about human liberty, it's about American liberty and values and the American dream. I'm older than you. I lived through the cold war, and we won it. We won it on the back of American innovation and enterprise."

"But that would primarily be American innovation and enterprise in instruments of war and pharmaceutical poisons."

"You're simply confirming that my decision is the right one, Anna. Your interview with your friend, Mark Carlisle, was an embarrassment, Anna. There was no way we could have been associated with this worldview."

"But another problem for you is that Mark can't be bought. He is too wealthy, too independent, too fond of drawing attention to the damage that your portfolio companies are doing. And your sponsor nation."

"What do you mean by that…sponsor nation? We're a US headquartered company. Our loyalty is primarily to this nation."

"And Israel. I've done my research. I'm a journalist, after all. I've known about the strategic partnerships with Israeli cyber-security companies, Israeli research institutes, and American elected officials who, in turn, are paid off by Israel."

"You're beginning to sound very antisemitic, Anna. I'm going to terminate this conversation as well as your employment. However, I should remind you that you signed an NDA when you accepted our offer of employment."

"Listen, Jacob, I just want to say one last thing before I leave your employment. No NDA is going to stop me drawing attention to every company you work with, every CIA or Mossad funded organisation that has made its way into your portfolios or every intelligence agency asset that is in your employ. I'll expose every so-called think-tank that you fund, every shill that you pay off, every politician actor that you own. And at every opportunity, through the media visibility that I create, I'll remind you that you can't get away with killing people or using them as lab rats or robbing them of their liberty because you claim that the holocaust justifies it. Corporatism, and especially your Zionist version of it, is fascism. I'll not let you forget that. So fuck you and fuck your job."

Before I had time to finish my closing sentence - which, I'll admit, was not exactly lady-like - Stapelberg's big goon was helping his bulky boss out of his breakfast-table chair and out of earshot.

I sat-on at the breakfast table, somewhat in a daze at being unemployed for the first time after graduating and not exactly knowing what to do. I could feel my heart racing and had an overwhelming feeling that I may not be safe. I called Jenny on Signal after taking a few deep breaths and sipping on some tepid hotel water. She answered almost immediately.

"Hi Anna," she answered, "where are you?"

"I'm in New York. My meeting with Stapelberg was brought forward. Sorry I didn't have time to have that briefing with you. It might have been a good idea."

"Why? What happened?"

"Well, I'm unemployed. He fired me."

"Anna, listen, get yourself to DC. I'm back from Greece. I know you're probably shaken by this. But Stapelberg is very, very bad news. He's very dangerous in fact. This represents a great new start for you. We need to have a long conversation. Get a flight to Dulles today. For one thing you and I need to drink some martinis. Are you on your way?"

"I'm on my way. I'll see you later."

Chapter 17: Mark Carlisle

When Jenny returned to DC I decided to return to Hydra. I had come to the conclusion that it was highly unlikely that Jenny's ferry-friend, Gordon, was anything other than a smooth-talking lothario. In any case, I figured that if he was, in fact, a spook that he'd have long since left the island in his search for me. Frankly, Greece is a great place in which to get lost.

In truth, I hadn't spent much time on Hydra, and I wanted to get to know it a little better. For one thing, I wanted to visit the house that Leonard Cohen had bought on the island and had lived-in on and off until his death - and that was still owned by his family. I was aware that it wasn't open to the public, but I wanted to get a better idea of where it was situated relative to the port and the rest of the island.

This was an esoteric interest. But, of course, I was aware of the rumours that had turned into a well-developed conspiracy theory that Cohen was right at the centre of a CIA-contrived mind control operation.

The circumstances leading to this somewhat far-fetched theory were just that, in my view: circumstantial. It has been suggested that the reason Cohen had gone to Greece in the first place was because he had met with Jacob Rothschild, whose mother had married a Greek artist who owned a big mansion on the hill. And Rothschild, of course, was a Zionist - as was Cohen.

South of Market

Then there's the 'fact' that Cohen was part of a MKUltra mind control experiment when he was just seventeen years of age and that he was a big user of psychiatry - and mind-altering substances - for most of his life. And that he seemed a bit flaky sometimes and his song lyrics were a tad cryptic. Oh, and that Prince Charles once admitted to liking his songs and gravelly voice.

But, for me, Leonard Cohen loved Greece, and especially Hydra. My wife also loved KD Lang's version of Hallelujah. She even asked that it be played at her funeral. And it was.

So, I suppose that my trip to Hydra was something of a homage. I wanted to say goodbye to Alice in the place where the man used to live who wrote one of her favourite songs. I don't think the fact that she liked a song sung by a slightly gender-bending artist was evidence that she had been subject to mind control. Or perhaps it was. But then, I also like the song and KD Lang's version of it. So, what should we make of this?

Anyway, I took the ferry from Spetses to Hydra. It's probably a lot more up-market now than when Cohen first visited in 1960. There are certainly more cafes and tavernas around the port. But the donkeys are still the main means of transporting luggage up the cobbled streets to the local hotels.

Mark Carlisle

I made my way to the Pirate Bar at the port. The sun was getting low in the sky, and I fancied a Negroni before making my donkey assisted way to my hotel.

When the Negroni arrived, I held it up and examined the huge cube of ice bobbing around in the scarlet liquid.

"That looks fabulous," a voice said. A man was standing in front of me peering through from the other side of my Negroni glass, with his hand outstretched. "I suspect you are Mark Carlisle. My name is Gordon. I think we have a mutual acquaintance. Would you mind terribly if I could interrupt your time with that fabulous looking Negroni?"

"Dear God, *you're* Gordon! I never dreamt that I'd meet you here. I thought you'd be long gone. Jenny thought you might be a spook."

"Nope. I'm still here, I'm afraid. And I'm just a retired doctor, as I told Jenny. I'm not packing a piece or anything like that. No license to kill or anything. Would you mind if I joined you? Please feel free to tell me to bugger off if you'd like to. But I really would love to have a chat."

"Gordon, of course. Have a seat and I'll order you one of these."

"That would be splendid."

Gordon spent the first and second Negronis getting me up to speed on his background. He had done his research on me. He seemed to have watched just about all content that had survived the social media culling. But I wanted to ask him why he hadn't asked Jenny for her number to arrange to meet.

"Well," he said, "I suppose I realised that you two were more than just employer and employee. I didn't want to cramp your style, Mark. Jenny is a very beautiful woman. And extraordinarily intelligent. I'm extremely jealous. But I admitted defeat by not asking."

"So, you were really just chatting her up?"

"I'm afraid so. You can hardly find that surprising."

"I don't but it doesn't help me. You could still be an agent working for the Foreign Office team at the embassy. Or you could be a field officer for the state security services. Think of it from my point of view. We have spent quite a few days trying to shake you off but here you are sitting beside me having cocktails."

"Indeed, but if I were a spook what would I have to gain from this meeting?"

"I suppose what you'd have to gain is my friendship and trust. You could be a state sanctioned confidence trickster. So, here's a test for you. Why did you target Jenny, in particular, in Piraeus?"

"Because she's beautiful and she looked to be English-speaking. I mean, she looked American. But, listen Mark, I'm sorry for elbowing in on your Negroni time. I can tell that meeting me here like this is making you uncomfortable and I can see things from your point of view. I'm a total stranger who has come into your lives. But it's just sheer coincidence that I admire what you've done and total coincidence that I chatted-up your wife to be."

"What did you say?"

I could see that the expression on Gordon's face had completely changed. He instantly reddened, realising that there was no possibility that he could have known about our plans to get married except if he had been listening to a wiretap or some other surveillance device. The smile and friendly demeanour fell from his face. He realised, instantly, that he had fucked up. I could see the realisation - and blind panic - on his face.

"Listen, Gordon, or whatever your name is, I'm going to leave you to pay for these drinks. But I want you to deliver a message back to whoever is handling you. This is a war you're not going to win. I can guarantee that. I'm way ahead of you. Oh, and thanks for the drinks."

With that I sneaked off into the dwindling light and made my way up the cobbled streets past the harbour and up to a headland above the port of Hydra. I stood on a layby to look out to the Aegean and a setting sun making the clouds the colour of a well poured Negroni. And then I dropped my mobile phone and knapsack into the sea - all the things that could possibly be used to track my existence on this beautiful island.

Mark Carlisle

And, for some reason, came into my head the words of Cohen's song, one of Alice's favourites:

I did my best, it wasn't much
I couldn't feel, so I tried to touch
I've told the truth, I didn't come to fool ya

And even though it all went wrong
I'll stand before the lord of song
With nothing on my tongue but hallelujah

Chapter 18: Rahul Vaidya

I'll admit, we were an odd quartet. Mark, Anna, Jenny and me. We had been thrown together but we stuck. So to speak. Don't get me wrong. There were times when I found Mark totally exasperating. I couldn't understand why he was spending so much time hopping around Greece and its islands. When he told me the story about being tracked by some weird guy on a Greek island, it kinda blew my mind. But it also confirmed that we were rattling them.

The four of us had come to similar conclusions from different directions. The Covid event, as far as I was concerned, was a hand being declared too soon. It took me a while, and things were very misty, very difficult to perceive, but it was clear that they'd made the matrix visible - to me anyway. And it was slowly coming into much clearer focus.

Mark had left me trying to deal with it. Negotiate with it. I had my feet in two different worlds. One world was awake. The other was still asleep.

When Mark told me about his theory that he suspected that geopolitics and empires were too complex to be orchestrated anymore by mere humanity, it struck a chord.

As a lowly developer just a few years ago I had noticed that it was becoming impossible to write code from scratch. So, machines were doing it for us. Our job was simply to arrange objects that interworked to create applications or solutions or control systems.

But the problem with running the world was that human beings couldn't really be told what to do. Or some of them anyway.

Those of us who were, increasingly, awake argued in the early days of the, er, awakening, as to who *'they'* were. I mean the controllers. But it was beginning to dawn on me that I knew. Mark's observation about a model - an immensely large data model - controlling things, really did plant a germ in my head. And I'm going to tell you why.

All computer programs are data models. All computers really do is perform computations. Digital computers have no real logic. They compute. They're glorified calculators. But they can do calculations very quickly. And these calculations create some type of output. But as computers have become faster, they have been tasked to perform lots of calculations - often simultaneously - and often in conjunction with other systems. This results in enormous complexity.

Only computers, themselves, can orchestrate this complexity. The complexity - when properly orchestrated - can result in increasingly impressive outputs. But it's up to the conductors to define how the orchestration should happen. The conductors can, in effect, define the nature of the output. And the conductors are human beings seeking outputs that may well suit some type of nefarious endgame.

The complex orchestration of computers running lots and lots of algorithms and being orchestrated to spit out 'answers' is typically, these days, called artificial intelligence or AI. But remember, AI is not intelligent. It's simply a system that can do a lot of very fast, orchestrated computing that has a level of complexity that no human brain could fully comprehend. But the output - the answers emerging from the complexity - need to be understandable to human beings.

Now it's clear that we could end up becoming very dependent on these types of systems - especially if they are made available to us almost free and can avoid us having to do too much thinking. Just think about it. Human beings often prefer simple answers. They don't necessarily want to be presented with lots of alternative answers. That's why AI systems tend not to give us different answers. They simply present us with exactly what we think we need.

They don't present us with any doubt.

But let's think for a moment. Try to imagine a world in which, if we ask any question, we're only presented with a certain response. A definitive answer. Do you think you might quite like that world? Might it start to feel more comfortable, less risky, less alarming, more paternalistic?

Rahul Vaidya

You see, I know how computers work. I know that the complex system is, more often than not, a Heath Robinson type construction. It doesn't really stand up to rigorous analysis. It's all band-aid and make-do. And it's typically designed in a way to provide the answers in a human-friendly way that the conductors have defined in advance. Or, to put it another way, the system, itself, has been badly programmed so that its human users become programmed in the ways the conductors have defined.

But the idea that Mark had presented me with was even more concerning. In effect, he was suggesting that the conductors might well have been using such systems well before the rest of us. It stands to reason that this would be the case.

We knew that every CEO of every major tech firm seemed to have an odd background. In popular culture every Tech Bro - it appeared - was some type of maverick genius. They were college dropouts, possibly mildly autistic, almost certainly had inhuman levels of intelligence, refused to suffer fools, and really liked to code in dark rooms. They were Machiavellian, highly innovative and were admired for their unique, and bizarre, communications skills. And their appeal to 'young people'.

But there seemed to be another common denominator that Mark and I had noticed - and one that was less well known to the general public, or the media.

South of Market

Just about every highly successful tech firm seemed to have a very close relationship with the intelligence agencies, the permanent state apparatus - especially of the nations of the 'Five Eyes' network - and many of the globally dominant corporations.

Therefore, it seemed to make sense that, given these relationships, that nation-states could well have been given a 'head start' in terms of its use, and conducting, of so-called artificial intelligence.

The Covid event showed the levels of orchestration that could be achieved. The 'lines' were clearly being articulated and amplified by every major media organisation. But to Mark, to me, to Jenny, to Anna, it seemed that these lines had been scripted by extra-human 'logic'. But for a very large percentage of the population the lines, the logic, the lies, represented a believable argument - and a far better alternative to doubt or uncertainty.

The conclusion I have reached is that artificial intelligence represents a level of dependence on stupid answers that I could never have comprehended. Much of humanity is now accepting its own incarceration in a prison of false narratives.

The Tech Bros, and the state for which they work, have clearly come to a conclusion that human beings are mere data points. And the system has answered - for whatever reason - that there are too many data-points to achieve any type of optimal output.

Rahul Vaidya

But the ghost in their particular machine is this. Human beings aren't data-points. True, they often cling on to certainty regardless of its dubious merits. But they're complex, nonetheless. And they're reluctant to be treated like livestock.

The conductors clearly have an ambition, however, for whatever reason, that they need to be adequately manageable via digital tracking and tracing and other herding techniques. AIs like to control via sensors and the internet of things. In human terms, no conductor-defined digital utopia can be achieved until biometric surveillance of every citizen on the planet can be achieved.

And that's why this has to be our battle: the battle for human autonomy off *their* grid.

I've said it before, and I'll say it again. I'm a Dev. But I think I'd prefer a future where the coding of our futures was in the hands of God - however we define God - rather than the Tech Bros and their Devs.

Chapter 19: Anna Sussex

It was a bit embarrassing when Harry and Meghan decided to call themselves 'Sussex'. I mean, who else just gets to choose their surnames like that? Apparently, there's a royal family tradition to just create or recreate dukedoms when they feel like it and for chosen families to adopt these titles as surnames. But it did seem odd that, on this occasion, they'd adopted *my* name. It's not exactly a common surname in England, but it's not uncommon either.

When I met with Jenny in DC - our first meeting in person - she asked me what I thought about sharing my name with a former small-part actor in *Suits*, now promoted to superstardom on Netflix. Admittedly, this question came after we'd downed a few Martinis before dinner in Cafe Milano in Georgetown.

"Is she though?" I asked. "Is she a superstar?"

"Well, we're expected to be interested in her. They expect us to gorge on this celeb stuff and royal tittle tattle as much as possible. Takes our minds off anything of any import. Bread and circuses. But I'm actually making another point. If you think about it, Anna, all media narratives are constructs. Conditioning. Diversion. Nothing to see here, so look over there. Meghan spilling the beans on 'the firm'. If there were no controversy, no intrigue, no upcoming new season of The Crown, we might just grow weary of it or, worse still, ignore it."

"I get your point, Jenny, but my issue is that I don't quite 'get' what the endgame is?"

"I suspect we're going to be given a lesson on the endgame."

Jenny was looking over to one of the tables on the other side of the restaurant where three men were beckoning over to us.

"It looks as though we're being asked over for a drink. I think I know the dude in the middle. He's the CEO of a company I did some work for a few years ago. I think you might find it interesting to join them for a drink."

We made our way over to their table, while Jenny muttered under her breath, "What's his fucking name?" The CEO dude then left his table to greet us both.

"Jenny McIvor! Great to see you. I think you worked for us for a bit a few years back. I'm Sam. And these are two great business associates of mine. Who's your friend?"

"This is Anna, Sam. She's a very special friend of mine. She's on the other side of the fence. Anna's a journalist. And a great one at that."

Sam and his two business associates shook my hand. I looked at the three spare places at the table. Sam quickly explained. "Hey, we're expecting three more guests but they're not due to arrive for a little while. Please, take a seat and have a quick drink with us." He pulled a bottle of Cristal out of the ice-bucket stationed at the side of the table. "Would this do," he asked, smiling moronically as he stroked the neck of the bottle like it was a sex toy.

My instinct was to flee from the three creeps who gawked at us like they'd never seen women before. However, as I sipped on the champagne, already quite giddy after my martinis, I decided to make the best of the situation - hoping that the new guests would arrive soon - and ask Sam about his business."

Sam pulled his shoulders back a little and smiled to reveal excessively white little teeth. I assumed dental implants.

"I'm in the small arms business, Anna. We provide light armaments to the military and civil protection sectors. We don't do the big stuff like General Dynamics or Northrup. We're more in the peashooter end of the business. He smiled and gulped back some Cristal."

"I presume they're pretty devastating peashooters," I replied. Sam and his two stooges laughed merrily at that.

"Well," Sam said, again pulling his shoulders back and grinning like a little boy who had just received a toy AK47 for Christmas, "I suppose they can do some damage when aimed at a Hamas or Hezbollah terrorist.

"So are all terrorists Islamic these days, Sam?" I retorted.

"They pretty much are, Anna. They pretty much are." He and his two friends laughed again in unison.

I could almost feel Jenny willing me on to goad these guys. But thankfully she stepped in, clearly enjoying the direction of travel of the conversation, to stir things up rather more quickly than I had expected.

"Anna, until very recently, worked for one of Jacob Stapelberg's media companies."

"Wow," Sam said, the smile disappearing from his face. "You've met Stapelberg?"

"I have, as a matter of fact. I had breakfast with him yesterday morning in New York."

"What the fuck? Can you believe this guys?" All three of them seemed to mutter, "respect" or some such word while nodding respectfully.

Jenny, interjected, "So what did you think of him, Anna?"

"Hmm, let me think now. Well, as you guys know, I think Stapelberg normally gets his way. He's probably a bit further up the pecking order than you guys and me. Israel pulls no punches and when you're a paid off lackey to Mossad it probably takes its toll on one's mental health. But, taking that into account, I still found him to be a loathsome creep. I certainly didn't find him to be a woman's type of man. More a man-baby and bully. But tell me, Sam? When do you expect your hookers to arrive?"

Jenny had kicked me under the table and tipped me off with her eyes that three very young women, who looked to be Ukrainian or some other Eastern European ethnicity, had arrived - wearing very short dresses and very high heels - and were asking directions to a table. I assumed them to be Sam's missing guests.

I turned my attention to Sam's two male guests. "So, tell me, you two, why are you both so important to be wined and dined by Sam here and his girls?"

I didn't receive an answer. Both Jenny and I were quickly ushered away from the table by Sam to be replaced by three ladies who were already laughing uproariously at nothing in particular. We returned to our recently forsaken bar-chairs and ordered two more Martinis.

"I'd just like to apologise for ever having worked for that guy's company," Jenny said.

"We've all done things we end up regretting, Jenny. I've just been fired by a boss I barely knew existed until a few days ago. But Sam and his peashooters at least prove a point. So many people are perfectly happy in their bubbles. Why should they question anything if they are happy? If the war machine pays for the Cristal and the hookers, why question a narrative that we are the good guys and Hamas are the bad guys? Or that Israel can do no wrong - or is the only proper, American approved democracy in the Middle East?"

"But the alternative to the SOMA induced state, Anna, is that we have to burn all our bridges. The world that you and I have inhabited is so vile, so debauched, so corrupt, and so filled with people in a stupor that we can no longer live in it. The democracy that we used to think existed is bullshit. The government, far from being the channel of the democratic will of the people, is actively hostile to anyone with the temerity to think."

"What am I to do though? Where do I go from here, Jenny? Seriously, what skills can I offer to the world? Do I become yet another PR, parroting the corporate lines? Or do I go work for another hedge fund creating the 'new media?"

"You don't need to do either of those things. Frankly you can pretty much do whatever you like. Mark and I were kinda hoping that you might join forces with us for a while. Help us flesh out our own thinking about how we might create a counter-narrative to the decades of propaganda about American global peace-making. What are your thoughts about bitcoin, for example? You've probably interviewed more bitcoiners than just about anyone else. What conclusions have you come to about the role that bitcoin is playing in the current narrative?"

"My goodness. That's quite the question for a girl who's on her third Martini."

"Okay, perhaps I'm taking advantage of you. But I'm genuinely curious to know what you think. It's clearly playing a role in whatever propaganda model they've created. US debt is now over $30 trillion. El Salvador is now basing its financial system on what they describe as digital gold. The dollar used to be gold-based, then petroleum based, now debt based. They've torn apart free speech. Are they going to tear apart the financial system so that only people holding bitcoin become the haves?"

"Before I answer that - if I can, I think I've forgotten the question already - you do realise that Mark gifted me 10 bitcoin a few years back?"

"Yea, he did the same with me, when he hired me. But I don't think he ever wanted you to think that there were any strings attached."

"That, I've taken for granted. But in interviewing all of those bitcoin maximalists over the years I couldn't help thinking that perhaps the discussion about what bitcoin is, or was, or will be, is all a bit brain-numbing. Most people own no bitcoin. I wouldn't have held any had Mark not given me some. But the more people I interviewed, the more I came to the conclusion that there was insider knowledge, that the price was being driven by hype, that the entire bitcoin concept was a neatly tied-up exemplar of what we've just been discussing. People are just discussing various perspectives on bullshit that the bullshit machine has defined.

"There's a passage in Gulliver's Travels where Swift, or Gulliver, I can't remember which, remarks that when there are gaps or silences in conversation that new thinking emerges, new innovations, new ideas. But I never find that with conversations about bloody bitcoin. It's all about Satoshi, the core network, hash rates and the halving events. It's intellectually stunting. And the reason is that the parameters are predefined. The conversations are conversations about certainty. There are rarely any silences, any doubt. Just certainty. Bitcoiners just repeat mantras, over and over again. There's a constant affirmation of the same point, over and over again.

"But, if you think about it, that's what we had during the lockdown period and the Covid scam. The mainstream media, and the so-called alternative media that we permitted to continue operating, had to delimit the conversation in ways that were defined from above. And that's still in play. Ask ChatGPT if Covid was a scam and it'll answer, definitively, 'No'. No ifs or buts. No nuance permitted. Only certainty."

"When I chatted with Mark in Greece," Jenny said, before sipping from her Martini glass, "and we discussed the point you've just made - about these canned narratives and pseudo-debates - he made the point that he was beginning to wonder if some or all might not have been spat out of some type of artificial intelligence.

Possibly one run by the CIA, DARPA or one or more of their contractors. What are your thoughts on us living in an algocracy?"

"A democracy defined and run by algorithm? I think it's becoming clearer that we are. When the dust had settled on the Covid medical emergency we were then assaulted by climate emergency bullshit, the Russian invasion of Ukraine - the most obvious example of a Military Industrial Complex construct that I could think of. No doubt we'll soon have more Israeli expansionism in the Middle East and more goading of Iran by the Americans and Netanyahu. It's the same old, same old, rehashed.

"But I want to return to bitcoin. Why did you raise it in particular?"

Jenny shifted in her barstool a little and stretched out her legs a little, stroking her own knees while she thought of the response. "Well, given all the things you've just mentioned are interconnected in some way, all outputs of the same algo, Mark believes that he has some specific insider information relating to bitcoin that proves the existence of the con-trick."

"How so?" I asked?

"Well let me answer with an observation that he has asked me to pass on to you. Do you know what the bitcoin price is as of today?"

"I think it's about $27,000 or so. But what's Mark's observation?"

"His observation is that bitcoin will pass the $100,000 valuation by the end of the year." At that point Jenny raised her glass. "And I think that means, my lovely Anna, that we're both going to be millionaires soon. But, let's face it, it's all nonsense. Bitcoin has no value. Mark likes to quote one bitcoiner who says that bitcoin is the crystallization of energy. Because of all the energy it takes to mine it or whatever. Who believes this? You and I are beneficiaries of a string of characters that will soon be worth a million dollars. But that's only because some people are too stupid to believe it's all an orchestrated market for nonsense. Although Mark's advice is that we sell as soon as it gets to $100,000."

I couldn't help smiling, of course. I'd been fired one day and then told I was about to be a millionaire the next. Our waiter then lifted our glasses from the bar and placed them on a tray and escorted us to our table. Thankfully, it was some distance from Sam and his table of hookers.

"How can Mark be so certain of these things?" I asked, when we were settled at our table.

"He wrote some model. He claims he can track the bitcoin price quite easily using a spreadsheet that he has built. Honestly, it goes way over my head. But the principle is this. If we know - and we *do* know - that the concept of bitcoin was created as a hedge against fiat by insiders, then it's possible to predict what's going on. But just as it's possible to predict price movements, it's also possible to predict its collapse. Mark claims that he invested in bitcoin right from the beginning because he knew it was ultimately a rigged and doomed market. They've got form, of course. They created fiat currency. And to be fair, it has worked. We have had decades of economic growth. But they knew that, inevitably, fiat was creaking. Where we are now is in an interregnum."

"My goodness, Jenny, that's a good word. You're going to have to explain."

"Well interregnum - another word much favoured by Mark - is a period of suspension of normal government between kings. Frankly, he stole this idea from me. But don't tell him I told you that. But this particular er, interregnum, has been in play for quite some time. In my view it started after the Kennedy assassination. Mark thinks it's a bit more recent. Perhaps after the 2008 crash or, possibly 9/11."

I decided to take a long drink of iced water to dilute the effects of the Martinis. I felt that I needed to paraphrase some of this to check my understanding of what Jenny was telling me. "Okay, wait, let me get my head round this. What you're saying is that at some point in the past a decision was taken to effectively suspend democratic government in favour of some type of intelligence agency control grid. And since that point democracy has just been play-acting to give the impression that the voting public can make change at the ballot-box. But, in effect, all the decisions are being taken by a secretive cabal."

"Yup, I'd say, Anna, that's a fair summary. But let me add some meat to those bones. You said that a decision was taken. I'm not sure that I'd agree with that. It's clear that there was a tipping point of some kind. But it didn't just occur in the US administration. I'm pretty sure that it was a thing that happened in the West. Certainly, the Five Eyes network. Have you come across it?"

"Yea, I've heard of it. The collaboration between the Brits, Americans, Aussies, Kiwis and Canadians. But surely that's more of an administrative thing?"

"I don't think so. I think what has happened is that the lines between all the various entities have blurred, the endgame has become confused, there's a huge amount of business interests and testosterone swilling around, yada. And a lot of Hollywood style psyops. And pet media. It would be impossible for me to try to draw some type of organisation chart or mind map for how the so-called 'global elite' works and chaos theory definitely applies but…"

Jenny was mid-sentence when Sam walked over to our table and kind've leaned over us a bit. He was quite obviously quite drunk. "Hey Sam," I said, "have you pulled yourself away from your little harem?"

"Listen," he said, a little slurred, "I just wanted to apologise. We invited you over to the table and then our guests arrived. I hope you understand that some of our customers and associates have high expectations in terms of how we should entertain them. I hope that, um, situation didn't embarrass you."

Jenny chipped in first, even though Sam was leaning very distinctly in my direction and was trying to give me a dreamy look. "Listen Sam," she said, "I know how this city works and how you guys work. Don't worry about it. I managed to swig at least half a glass of bubbles, so no hard feelings. Anyway, I'm sure I'll see you tomorrow at Capitol Hill."

"Oh, yeah, that thing. Yea, I'll hopefully get to that. I'll see you both there, hopefully." At that point he pushed himself into a perpendicular position again, wished us a good evening, and wandered back to his table while checking his hair was in order, for the lovely ladies.

Jenny watched him back to his table. Then turned her attention back to me. "Listen, Anna, I have no real understanding of how the system works but I know this to be very obviously true. There's a gameplay that works for the insiders. There is no discernible difference between the players. They all know that there's a lot of money, influence, prestige and free stuff to be had if they play the game and don't ask questions. In fact, no-one asks any questions. They all just assume their roles and say the lines that are expected of them. Why should they question America's role in Israel? What would the arms manufacturers do if the omni-wars ended? They'd have to create new wars. But they know that certain wars and warzones are preferred.

"Did you ever find it odd when you watched the James Bond movies that Bond had a very special relationship with his American counterparts in the CIA? Fleming essentially assembled the key players in the soap opera that was the Cold War. But could it be that on the world political stage they are all, essentially, actors too - dramatis personae? The play has been seeded into our psyches. 007 has a license to kill. The Americans are the good guys. The PM and the President want the best outcomes for their democratic nations. The Russians are bad. But they're just play-acting too."

"Yes, I get your drift, Jenny, but who was Fleming working for? And who is directing the real-world drama?"

"Well, I have my view. Mark has his. I'm sure you have yours too."

"What yours then," I asked.

"Mine is the mafia perspective. Just look around this room. You can see it in play here. You have government people, arms dealers, PRs, executives from drug firms, tech entrepreneurs, cyber-security experts, all schmoozing around, doing deals, making contacts, rubbernecking, getting hard-ons as the hookers' manicured talons graze their cocks under the tables. This is a veritable mart of sleaze and the various parties to it are all completely legit - as defined by the permanent government, or the establishment, the godfathers. It's not in anyone's interest to question the system or discuss its ethics. They know that there are other crime families in town, on the circuit, snapping at their heels. But that's all part of the geopolitical game. It's about turf protection and, where required, about respecting each other's empires. Geopolitics and empire - that's the most lucrative game in the world, and they all know it. But it's a game that comes with a license to kill, or even a license to commit genocide, if required. Just as long as the gameplay isn't interrupted."

"But from what I can see, there's just one mafia family, so to speak. It's pretty much them against us."

"That's true to some extent but I have a theory that the drama that emerged during the cold war was multi-polar. There was a turf war dimension to it. At the nation-state level. But now it's a corporate defined war. It's all about land-grabbing and competing psyops. But the prize is, whatever way you look at it, global government - as far as they're concerned. Because there are different corporate interests at play: the oligarchs in Russia, the Technocrats in America, and the Globalists in the EU. The fiefdoms overlap and the organisations they partner with vary. But essentially, it is a battle of them against us. And it's a battle that has ramped-up big-time since 2020."

I looked around the room. The general din in the restaurant was increasing as the booze worked on the diners. I could hear Sam's hookers laughing hysterically at every anecdote being told by Sam's special client guests. I could smell the truffle oil, could hear the tinkle of ice in shortballs and highballs, and I could feel the insider dealing being done all around me. But then I fixed my attention back on Jenny. She too was looking around the room. It was an opportunity for me to look at her. She was beautiful in a way that only women of her age and maturity can be beautiful. Her make-up was artfully applied. Her arms were toned and lightly tanned. Her fingernails were not too long but were adorned with a subtle gloss of clear polish.

"Why is it we're doing what we're doing Jenny?" I asked her when her eyes met mine again.

She hesitated for a few moments and looked away. But then she refocused on me again, smiling slightly, when she had decided on an answer.

"Honestly, Anna, I have no fucking idea. But there's no going back. When I look behind you and behind me all I see are burning bridges. Those are the bridges back to our old lives. We're not alone, of course. But we're imposters in this room. We're not with *these* people any longer. Our job - and I've no idea who gave us it - is to start building a new era that isn't really like the one we've left behind. The people in this room think they're in the ascendant. They think they have a ticket to nirvana. But they're actually building an Orwellian hell.

"But I have a question to ask you. Have you ever heard of an organisation called AIPAC?"

"You mean the Israeli lobby group that buys politicians?"

"Yes, that's the one. Well, they're having an event tomorrow in Capitol Hill, one of their regular briefing events. That's the gig I mentioned to Sam earlier. So, if you want to get a sense of how the Zionist mafia operates in this city it might be worthwhile for you to come along."

I looked at her quizzically and tried to raise one eyebrow.

"Oh, and one other little detail that I neglected to mention is who the guest speaker is at AIPAC's little event tomorrow. This might give you a particular reason for attending, I suspect. Because the guest speaker is none other than your old boss, Jacob Stapelberg.

Jenny had booked me into the Dupont Circle Hotel in DC and booked an Uber to take me back to the hotel when we finished eating at Cafe Milano. I was beginning to regret making the trip, especially when I heard that she had cornered me into the event on the Hill. But, at the same time, I was intrigued as to what Stapelberg might say in his presentation. I wasn't aware that he had any direct involvement in AIPAC. Perhaps he didn't. Time would tell.

Sleep was difficult. I regretted the martinis. They, and the jetlag, were playing havoc with my ability to sleep. There was so much going on in my head I just wanted an off switch. Instead, I decided to get up from bed, and have a long cool shower. I closed my eyes and let the water run down my face and body. When I towelled myself dry and lay in bed, I called Rahul. He told me to focus on nothing but us, and our impending trip to India (even though we had no idea when it would be) and how he was planning to cook me a Biryani. He was a terrible cook. But he made me laugh a little and I sent him mobile kisses, and he wished me sweet dreams.

Rahul's wish worked a treat. My mobile phone alarm woke me at around 9am DC time. The room was pitch black, but I pulled back the curtains to reveal Dupont Circle in eye-popping, sunshine-balmed Technicolor.

Jenny had left me a voicemail saying that she was meeting me for breakfast in the hotel and that we'd ride over to the meeting together.

I hadn't fully realised that I'd be attending a meeting in the Capitol, so the only dress I had was a white mini dress. I wondered if it might have been too short. But as I had just an hour to get ready for Jenny's arrival there was no time to debate the matter or acquire a new dress.

Jenny was already at the table when I arrived at the hotel's conservatory restaurant. She was wearing a much more demure business suit. "Holy shit, Anna, you may give some of our elderly elected representatives a heart attack when they see you," she exclaimed, as I sat at the table, tugging the hem of my skirt down as best I could.

"Is it too short, Jenny? I didn't exactly pack for a meeting with Mossad."

"Honestly, you look incredible. Jeez, those legs. Honestly, you look amazing. Although I do want them to hear what you're saying, rather than checking out how hot you are."

"More important than my dress, though, Jenny, is what Stapelberg is going to talk about. And what he's going to do when he spots me. It could be fucking embarrassing."

"Perhaps it would be best to stay out of view. Out of his sightline. The likelihood is that he'll just arrive, do his talk, then leave. I don't think he's the type to read-through the entire attendee list. But even if he has, he'll probably just ignore you."

Jenny then drove us to the Capitol building, dropping me as near the building as she could while she went off to park. She suggested meeting me at the top of the East Front steps.

I'll confess, I had only been to DC once before when I was in my mid-teens, with my parents, on a family trip. But walking up these steps, alone, gave me a distinctly strange feeling. I kept asking myself what I was doing here. What was I doing in DC? What was I doing in America? What was I going to do with the rest of my life? Was I really a bitcoin millionaire? And who the fuck is Jacob Stapelberg?

The security presence around the Capitol was a bit more obvious, I assumed, since the January 6 attack. When I got to the top of the steps, I spotted a USCP guard, rather obviously armed. I walked over to have a conversation with him.

"Hi there. I'm attending a meeting here. Am I in the right place?"

"You need to go to the visitor centre and go through security, Mam. What meeting are you attending?"

"Oh, I think it's a briefing in the Congressional Auditorium."

"Yes Mam. Just go to the Visitor Centre and go through security. It won't take long. You clearly don't have a lot of jackets or coats to go through the scanner. Just your handbag."

"Okay, thank you. Listen, I'm waiting for a friend to join me. She's just parking the car. So, I'll be loitering here. Just so you know."

"That's absolutely fine Mam. Your dress is the perfect colour. You match our beautiful Capitol. But I'll keep an eye on you as you loiter, just in case you're up to no good. We can't be too careful."

With that my armed guard wandered off and gave me a cheeky smile.

At the end of the National Mall, I could see the Washington Monument as I stood, almost alone, apart from a few tourists and my friendly guard.

The sun was getting quite high in the sky by now and the day was already getting hot. Although there was a gentle breeze. I could see Jenny arriving at the bottom of the steps. I closed my eyes for a moment to let the sun warm my face.

"Have you ever visited the Dr King memorial?" I opened my eyes, and the security guy was a few feet away from me. "It really is worth going to see."

"I haven't seen it, no," I replied. "It wasn't open when I was last in this city. I was just a young girl when I last came here."

"Well, Mam, I'd highly recommend it. It really is quite something. There are quite a few inscriptions from Dr King's writings and speeches. They're all worth reading. Do you want to know my favourite?"

"I'd love to know your favourite."

The USCP guy, who was probably over six feet tall, took a step closer to me, probably so I would be more certain to hear every word. And then he spoke.

"So, this is my favourite quote, Mam." For the first time he fixed his eyes on mine. "This is my favourite quote from Dr Martin Luther King, inscribed on the North Wall of his memorial." And then, after a short pause, he spoke the words to me. "The ultimate measure of a man is not where he stands in moments of comfort and convenience, but where he stands at times of challenge and controversy."

"Those are good words, officer. Those are good words. I think they're more important now than ever."

"I think they are mam. And I'd like to wish you a good stay here in our beautiful city. I think your friend has arrived."

Jenny and I bade farewell to my new friend and made our way to the auditorium where the meeting was being held. But just as we were about to enter the visitor centre and security scanning, I decided to bid my farewell.

"Jenny, I'm so sorry, but I just can't do this. I think I've better things to do with my time than to attend this meeting. I really don't want to hear what Jacob Stapelberg has to say about anything. There's no advantage for me being here. I'm going to go home to

California and try to figure out where I go from here. I have to move out of my home, for one thing."

"Well, thankfully, you won't have to pay movers. I gather Rahul lives next door. But I fully understand Anna. Get yourself home. I've a date with your old boss."

Chapter 20: Jenny McIvor

When I entered the conference room to attend the AIPAC briefing I felt very alone. I knew, of course, that Stapelberg had a very dim view of Mark Carlisle and his business empire - and, presumably, of his staffers, like me. But it wasn't immediately obvious to me why, in particular.

There were various other speakers before the star of the show took to the stage. I didn't hear much of what they said. I was thinking about Anna, Mark, Rahul and Alice. But more than anything else I realised that I'd asked Anna nothing about Rahul, and I'd told her nothing about Mark's proposal to me in Greece. We were all disorientated to such a degree that we obsessed about what we could do in the new world order that was being presented to us - but not show interest in each other's lives in the ways that we used to. I wanted Anna back so that I could have the girly conversation I should have had with her. But it was too late. Or perhaps the world had changed too much, I wasn't sure which.

But as far as AIPAC and Stapelberg were concerned, I didn't give a fuck anymore what they thought of me or how annoying I was. I positioned myself right on the front of the Auditorium, just a few feet away from the speaker podium. Stapelberg, I figured, would be certain to see me. I presumed that his aides would have made him aware of potentially hostile attendees. But I didn't care.

The room was pretty full when Stapelberg eventually took to the stage. He was greeted with muted applause. I suspected that many in the room wouldn't have been aware of who he was. Most of the delegates seemed to be congressional staff, a fair few Congressmen, and the odd Senate member.

Stapelberg's presentation style was strange. He started by welcoming everyone who had attended and stating his appreciation for people attending in person. He noted the number of delegates who were wearing face-masks - a reminder of the terrible pandemic we'd been through. He then went on to praise Israel's response to the pandemic - noting how it had become a test laboratory for the jabs, highlighting just how many jabs Israel's citizens had received - thanks to the Israeli government. This, he claimed, was a testament to the resolve of the Israeli people against aggressors - even virus aggressors. This was greeted by uproarious applause in the room.

But then, bizarrely, Stapelberg changed direction. He said he did not really want to discuss topics about which he presumed most people in the room would agree - such as the scourge of Hamas aggression against Israel and the importance of Israel being able to defend itself with the help of the United States. No, he wanted to discuss money. After all, he said, "I'm a money man. I'm going to leave politics to others."

What followed was remarkable. But also, rather dull.

Jenny McIvor

In meticulous detail he showed how the Israeli government had systematically appropriated cryptocurrency - but especially bitcoin - from people suspected of being involved in anti-Israeli activity. These, he claimed, were often Hamas operatives or sympathisers, and people operating within Gaza or the West Bank who were supposedly providing aid services to Palestinians. He spat the word "Palestinians" with utter contempt.

After rambling on about the brilliance of Satoshi - particularly the elegance of capping supply of bitcoin at twenty-one million coins, he then went on to praise the United States for busting the Silk Road network and ensuring that bitcoin remained a currency for freedom.

After quite some boring circumlocution about bitcoin becoming the ultimate store of value - *digital gold, but even better than gold* - he finally got to the main point. He essentially put out a call for American entrepreneurs to work with his portfolio of companies to develop new solutions for money that would allow Israel and America to embrace the opportunity for peer-to-peer money. He made clear that the best way forward was for both nations to start building secure, digital money wallets and custody frameworks to allow citizens to keep their money away from 'nefarious actors and terrorists'.

When his rambling discourse finished, he was joined on stage by the Chair of the event - a slim and earnest looking woman, probably in her late 60s with a slightly

Southern drawl. Remarkably, she asked if there were any questions from the floor.

I immediately had to drag myself out of the stupor induced by Stapelberg's rambling speech. I looked around the auditorium and there seemed to be no volunteers to ask a question. So, I stood up, noting that my skirt had ridden up somewhat causing me to reveal rather more leg than I had intended. Nevertheless, I ignored my clothing malfunction and waved at the Lady Chair. A nonchalant youth 'volunteer' was sent in my direction wielding a microphone. And then, suddenly, I was standing in the big auditorium about to ask a question of the guy who was now blinking into the audience trying to figure out who in the distant darkness of the auditorium was about to ask a question.

I tapped the microphone and got a bit of feedback. But then I held it up to my lips and asked my question that I had no idea I was going to ask until the very second I held the microphone.

"Mr Stapelberg, thank you for your presentation. I noted that you put quite a bit of emphasis in the early part of your presentation on the importance of your state intelligence services, and ours, sequestering the money of people suspected of wrongdoing. Handily, of course, because this money was held in digital form in digital wallets it was trackable by those intelligence agencies. That's one of the handy things about digital wallets over leather ones in that the funds inside tend to be rather easy to seize by snooping agencies and self-appointed moral guardians."

At this point the Chairlady intervened.

"Listen, we really would appreciate it if you could ask a question rather than making observations. Could I perhaps hurry you up to ask a question. We're lucky to have our guest speaker. But he doesn't have all day. Also, could you tell us what organisation you represent."

I took the opportunity to straighten-out my skirt and to stand a bit taller by slipping my feet back into my heels. And then I answered by asking a question.

"My apologies, Madam Chairwoman. Let me get to the point and ask a question. How does Mr Stapelberg think it would benefit society for people to hold money in digital wallets so that it could potentially be seized by agencies of the state? We saw - during the trucker protests in Canada - what so-called democratic institutions of state could do to people who disagreed with them. Will the Israeli government seize the wallets of Israelis who don't agree to be vaccinated, in future, or disagree with the Likud Party? Oh, and just to clarify, my name's Jenny and I'm a former hack who now works client-side for an energy company."

The Chairwoman looked to Stapelberg and asked him, "Well Jacob, I've no idea if you want to answer this lady's question. That really was quite the word salad. Do you want to answer?"

Stapelberg gripped the sides of his lectern and started speaking before the Chairwoman got her last words out.

"Indeed, I do want to answer. Frankly, Madam Chair, this is what we're up against. There's no sense of respect for our institutions of government. We are, today, having this meeting in a building that houses one of the world's greatest democratic institutions - the US Congress. America and Israel work tirelessly together to ensure that our people are protected from aggression and terrorism. Our great democracies are now seeking to protect the dollar and the shekel from the forces of evil. I'm offering my money and support to entrepreneurs hoping to help in that effort. So, how dare that young lady insinuate that we're working against democracy. Can I please have another question from the audience, and one that makes more sense, please."

Now I'm not proud of what happened next. It's what happens, I suppose, when I tend to lose my temper. I think it may have been the result of being referred to as a 'young lady'. I still had the microphone in my hand. I could see the green light indicating that it was still switched to the on position. I tapped it again and, again, got a little bit of feedback. And so, I raised it to my lips. I could see the panic on the face of the Lady Chair as I started speaking into it. Perhaps it was an act of God, but her own microphone feed seemed to be cut, somehow. And so, I said the following.

Jenny McIvor

"Thank you, Mr Stapelberg, for that mansplaining. I'm just a little lady that needed that clarification. Clearly, you're funded by Mossad. As a former intelligence officer, I can always spot the type. I managed to get out of my particular agency before they robbed me of my soul. You clearly didn't. And now you're left to tramp the boards lecturing people like the paid off sycophants in this room. I appreciate that you rarely hear dissent. Yes-men and women rarely dissent. There's no money in that. But thankfully, you've confirmed, for me at least, that you and your type are the enemies of the people. You thieve off them. You murder them if they don't comply. And you claim to do this in the defence of democracy. I'd suggest to you, Mr Stapelberg, that your experiments on your own people in the laboratory that you call Israel won't end well. We see what you are and what you're trying to do. And I, for one, won't stop trying to stop you until I cease drawing breath."

At that point I threw the microphone towards the stage where it landed, luckily, at Stapelberg's feet.

I was escorted off the premises by two burly security guards who were, thankfully, very gentle and ushered me to the exit door and wished me a good day.

And that was that. Or so I thought.

As I wandered back to the car park to retrieve my car I got a call from Anna.

"Dear God, Jenny, what happened? I've just had a call from Stapelberg's PA. Where are you?"

"I'm just walking back to the car. I think I lost my shit a bit in the meeting. It wasn't very becoming. But at least I didn't use any profanities. And I think you would have enjoyed my performance."

"I'm pretty sure I would have. I think, Jenny, I may need to stay another night in Dupont Circle. I want to have dinner with you. I want to hear every detail of what happened. I have no idea where you and I go from here. But we need to get to know each other just a bit better. I want to know more about Mark and you, and I want to tell you about Rahul and Tellicherry and what type of dogs we might get when we're married. Rahul has told me the news. About you and Mark."

"Frankly, Anna, I fucking hate dogs. But you're right. We've all been thrown together in this thing. I've no idea what *this* is but I know that I want to fuck them up and start living life again. I want to fuck them right up. I suspect you and I will be good for each other. We don't have to work anymore. We don't need to be serfs or yes people. We can annoy the man-tits off people like Stapelberg and his handlers. I think we need to finish what we started last night in Cafe Milano. Let's get, as you might say, royally pissed."

Unfortunately, however, that opportunity had passed us by. As I was about to get into my car I was intercepted by two suited men.

Jenny McIvor

"Ms. McIvor, we need to have a conversation with you about what just happened in the Capitol buildings. We need you to come with us."

Chapter 21: Mark Carlisle

It didn't help, of course, that Jenny had paid off the sound engineer to ensure she was given the microphone at the AIPAC event and that the sound feed for Stapelberg and the event Chair be cut off. I mean, it didn't help with her defence. Not that they pressed charges against her. And no newspapers or TV studios picked up the story. Until we forced their hands, that is. But it meant that she missed her dinner date with Anna.

There's a widely held misconception that news organisations will always pick up a juicy story. We thought we had the perfect one. But we knew it would be ignored, of course. So that's why we rigged it. And we rigged it in such a way that they couldn't ignore it.

Admittedly, it didn't really make it outside the beltway. But it had enough coverage for us to gather a huge amount of content. Our friendly sound engineer had also, helpfully, asked Stapelberg to wear a Lavalier microphone - one of those little wireless mics that they are so fond of using on the television. It meant that he was able to record Stapelberg's comments when he was on stage and thought that nothing he was saying was being put on record because his public address feed had been cut. So, it meant we had a sound recording, that we could sync up to the video recording of the event, where Stapelberg could - in crystal clarity - be heard muttering some pretty terrible and misogynist profanities.

Anna was good enough to make Stapelberg's personal assistant aware of all of this when she had called her to communicate Stapelberg's anger about what had unfolded at the event. I had made Anna aware of what had transpired, and our little sting operation, as soon as Jenny left the auditorium.

You see, this is what we refer to as a kompromat operation. It's the standard modus of the agencies. So we wanted to give them a taste, as they say, of their own medicine.

But they also make extensive use of false flag events where they blame, say, pariah states on certain high profile terrorist actions or aggressions. Case in point would be Nine/Eleven, of course. Within hours of the Twin Towers and Building Seven coming down the 'war against terror' had already started and the next phase of Anglo-British orchestrated regime change had commenced in the Middle East. Another case in point might be what happened just a few months after our minor success at Capitol Hill.

Mossad and the IDF will never permit the true story to emerge of what happened at the Gaza border on October 7, 2023. It's impossible for anyone to say definitively what happened. But the response - whether it was a genuine Hamas operation resulting in lots of bloodshed or a premeditated Hannibal Directive resulting in the killing of Israelis at the hands of the IDF - was genocide.

South of Market

By 2024, the US Presidential campaign was in full swing and, following October 7, the Trump campaign was beginning to ramp up its mudslinging against Iran. Because, in order to justify Israel's so-called Samson Option - its nuclear deterrence - America had to use every bit of propaganda it could muster, devoid of any evidence, that Iran was developing nuclear weapons.

My entire business model was to present nuclear energy as a solution. But now I was in virtual hiding in Greece and my Head of Comms was now on a CIA watch-list and was no longer permitted in or near the environs of Capitol Hill. The situation was far from ideal.

However, Rahul was a salvation. The strategy that he had come up with was simple. He started placing our people inside many of our clients as advocates and provocateurs. But jointly, we decided to fundamentally change direction in terms of the clients we worked with.

In the absence of any ability to get round the regulatory and geopolitical hurdles presented to us we turned our attention to hydrocarbons - helping, in particular, regional governments in India and China to develop clean and efficient energy and to open up supply chains. We provided seed capital to entrepreneurs building more efficient drivetrains for vehicles and we unpicked every bit of so-called evidence for man-made climate change. Instead, we elevated the voices of entrepreneurs in Africa and Gaza, Kerala and Bogota, who needed cheap dependable energy to achieve just some of the things that were taken for granted in London or LA.

We did all of these things outside of public view. Our mission was to do everything we could to undermine the impetus and noise of the Globalists and the Technocrats.

Like Jenny, like Anna, I often wondered why I had taken on this war. As far as the establishment was concerned, my reputation had been shredded. I was now hiding in the shadows, depending on Rahul to use his charm, intelligence and diplomacy to lead his troops. And, in the process, he was able to make profit, able to inspire his employees, able to make subtle change, against all the odds.

When I called him after the Jenny incident in Capitol Hill, he reintroduced me to a word I'd forgotten or fallen out of the habit of using. That word, *omerta*…the code of silence, adopted by the mafia to ensure that information would not be given to the police. But the word, he advised me, had been adopted, many decades ago, by the CIA to cover up the agency's involvement in the drug trade. I asked him to explain why it was relevant.

"It just dawned on me recently, Mark, that we needed to adopt the same strategy. Omerta. Our job is to keep to ourselves what we're up to. Because, ultimately, *they* only tell us what they want us to know. Therefore, everything they tell us, by definition, we know to be a lie, or a psyop or an act of manipulation. Omerta prevents them from ever telling us the truth. Omerta extends to their paid actors - particularly politicians and the legacy media."

"I get that, Rahul, but why does this apply to us? Why should we adopt the same approach?"

"Because think about it. We're who they're scared of. They're not scared of the results of the ballot box - because the results don't matter. Pretty much all the politicians are owned and signed up to the Omerta code. It's in their interests to do so. But the people they're scared of are those of us who know that they're full of shit.

"But if they know that we are the enemy we can't let them know what we're up to. There can be no endgame, as far as they are concerned. There can only be the results. The small wins. Rigging the system. Providing our foot-soldiers with the information they need. And organising non-compliance."

"Okay, I get it. But you need to turn that into a pity sentence for me, Rahul. I'm a child of the soundbite."

"Oh, it's very simple, Mark. Very simple indeed. Their chosen method of collecting everything they need to know about us, and sanctioning us, thieving our money, denying us energy - literally and metaphorically - is digital identity. By providing them with what they want - need - from us to achieve their totalitarianism they need to steal our identities. If we give them what they want, we have broken our collective code. Omerta. With digital identity comes digital surveillance, digital sanctions, digital prison. They'll have the ability to switch us off any time they wish. They can steal our money or switch it off. And there will be no nation states, no nationalities, no freedom, no independent humanity, no agency.

"I'll not permit our expertise to be used to further their objectives. I'm willing to pledge to you now not to help them get access to the energy they need to suppress us, or to make us slaves. But at no point will I admit to this. That's my pledge to you. Your job, now, Mark is to start building the team and the resources to stop them fucking us over. I'll take care of the business, as best I can."

"No pressure then, Rahul."

"No pressure Mark."

Chapter 22: Anna Sussex

Jenny made it her mission, after the Capitol Hill 'event,' to throw herself into an investigation of AIPAC influence in congress. She told me, in Cafe Milano, that my situation - being fired by the boss of a Zionist Hedge Fund - was something of a godsend. I couldn't quite see it that way.

But her investigations - that she made available to everyone - were meticulous. Using nothing but public domain information she carefully charted the relationships between money sources and beneficiaries.

While AIPAC funding of elected officials was relatively common knowledge, the extent of corruption wasn't fully appreciated. She revealed the extent. She published spreadsheets detailing payments, voting and speaking records for each recipient of such funding and other 'baubles' bestowed on politicians and NGO officials. These baubles included paid directorships on the boards of 'growth' companies - typically technology or 'cyber-security' companies funded, often, by venture capital funds themselves funded indirectly by the government of Israel or by Mossad.

But Jenny had a problem, no-one was taking any interest. Her work was ignored. After Capitol Hill they mounted a whispering campaign against her, claimed she was an anti-vaxxer, a conspiracy theorist, or a paid shill for the Palestinians, or Russia or even Iran.

But she found a new circle of very useful contacts in a community known as OSINT - or Open-Source Intelligence. She started reading every source of information she could find about Epstein, or 9/11, or funding sources for the tech firms that, as Trump got closer to the White House during 2024, seemed to be claiming more share of voice.

In November 2023 she rang me to tell me about how Mark's prediction that bitcoin would go through the $100,000 ceiling was correct. She advised me to 'liquidate my position' she said, obviously using a term that she had heard Mark use. She loved to use insider terminology.

And on her advice, I sold my 'position' and invested in gold, silver and Swiss francs - 'anything but shitty dollars' as advised by Mark, via Jenny. Rahul and I also decided to sell his little Cape Cod house in Santa Clara and to relocate to a rented house down the coast a little in Monterey.

I also upgraded my Miata to the latest model. This time it had a folding metal roof. But I opted, of course, for a petrol model, and thanked the guy in the dealership for not even trying to sell me a battery car.

Rahul made the point that it was completely impractical. He said we'd need to start thinking about casting off the trappings of our DINKY (dual income no kids) life - and that should include the Miata. But I was having none of it.

South of Market

California State Route 1, also known as the Pacific Coast Highway, afforded me the opportunity to play music very loud in my little open-top car and to push the engine very hard indeed.

I was doing just that in the late afternoon of July 13, 2024. I'd heard the news of the attempted assassination of Donald Trump before getting into the car in Monterey, intending to make the drive to Silicon Valley to meet my old Producer friend, Alex, who was now working for a production company making documentaries for CNN.

As I passed the junction for Half Moon Bay the phone rang, and the car-phone display told me it was Rahul. "Hey, have you heard the news," I asked him.

"Anna where are you?" he asked.

"I'm heading up to see Alex. Funny you should call me now, because I'm at Half Moon Bay. Do you remember that day…"

"Anna, I need to talk. But you'd need to be off the highway. Can you call me back when you aren't driving? Something terrible has happened."

Jenny and I never had the chance to have the conversation she so wanted to have with me, and I wanted to have with her, when I decided to spend that extra night in Washington DC.

Anna Sussex

I have no idea what they said to her or if they reminded her about the commitments she had made to 'the nation' when she served as an officer for the Central Intelligence Agency. Perhaps it wasn't mentioned. But whatever they said to her made little difference.

While Donald Trump was campaigning to Make America Great Again, Jenny was using every skill she had, and using every contact she had made, to shine a light into some very dark places. Her theory, of course, was that America and the UK were being governed, not by democratically elected governments but by the apparatus of the State - a glorified mafia bound by a code of silence.

But just as she knew that the same godfathers had created a currency hedge to serve the needs of the 'elite' - insiders bestowed wealth because of their compliance - so it was that they created the communications platforms used by people planning to expose their godfathers. And by Jenny. And by just about everyone. They funded the politicians. They funded the technology corporations. They funded the startups and growth companies.

When I parked my little car at the side of the road, near Half Moon Bay, Rahul told me that Jenny had arranged to go and see Mark in Greece. He had flown her, by private jet, to Kalamata airport and they had made their way to a little town on the Mani Peninsula called Limeni. They had gone for a swim in the harbour but - tragically - both had drowned. Their bodies were washed ashore some distance from the harbour and were discovered by a local fisherman. Their bodies lay, just a few hundred feet from each other, separated by the gentle lapping waves of the Aegean sea, coloured red as blood by the Sun, bobbing just above the horizon and the limestone massif of the Peloponnese.

Jenny stood tall in times of challenge and controversy. I wasn't sure where I had stood. I had lost a friend that I never had the chance to talk to about her love or her hopes. I had also lost a mentor and benefactor who saw something in me I had yet to discover.

Of course, the media barely made any mention of the deaths of Jenny and Mark. The news schedule was dominated by the assassination attempt on Trump.

Some of the local newspapers in DC carried the story - and those stories were remarkably consistent, almost as though the content was contained in a media release or briefing. They mentioned that the Greek authorities recorded deaths by misadventure. They claimed that both Jenny and Mark had been swimming despite forecasts for localised wind and rain. However, locals interviewed by Greek newspapers made no mention of any poor weather in the area at the time of their deaths.

I returned to Monterey and to Rahul as quickly as my little Miata would let me. And when I was in bed with him and we listened to the distant rumble of the Pacific ocean, I told Rahul about the Capitol Hill guard and that

Anna Sussex

quote from Martin Luther King and Rahul told me about his and Mark's pledge to work together behind the shadows.

Epilogue: Rahul Vaidya

I suppose I'd found Anna first when she pulled-up beside my little house in Santa Clara in her U-Haul truck. Then I introduced her to Mark, and then Mark introduced us to Jenny. Little, seemingly random, connections that changed our collective lives.

When Anna and I finally got round to getting married, in Kerala, in my hometown of Tellicherry, we knew that it would be both a wedding and a memorial service for my boss and his wife-to-be.

It was Anna's request that we have a secular wedding, but she wanted the vows to reflect some of the traditional practices of Buddhism.

She told me that Jenny had found an interest in Buddhism following a conversation she had with Mark when she first joined him in Greece back in 2023. Anna told me she wanted to incorporate a ritual from Thai Buddhism called Rod Nam Sang where water is poured over the hands of the couple and captured in a bowl. The water pouring represents the cleansing of the couple's past and the capture of the water in the bowl represents a new beginning together.

When we went to Greece to the village of Limeni to see where our friends had last lived together, Anna filled a bottle of water with seawater from the harbour. And this was the water that was poured over our hands and captured in the bowl.

Rahul Vaidya

We had planned, with Mark and Jenny, that we would have a joint wedding in Kerala. So, this was a way of achieving that and having Mark and Jenny with us.

Our wedding took place in July 2025 - almost exactly a year after we heard the news about Jenny and Mark. Just a few weeks before we were to be married, Israel launched an attack on Iran, supported by America. Trump's front bench team - almost entirely Zionist and supportive of Israel's war machine in the Middle East, talked of Iran's determination to build a nuclear arsenal. But no evidence was produced to that effect.

But it seemed that no-one really cared that much for evidence or truth anymore. Certainly not governments.

We had various readings at our wedding. And we asked Anna's father to read a short passage from a poem by Bertolt Brecht about war. Jenny had sent this passage to Anna in a text message, just a few days before she flew to Greece, and her death.

When it comes to marching many do not know
That their enemy is marching at their head.
The voice which gives them their orders
Is their enemy's voice and
The man who speaks of the enemy
Is the enemy himself.

But my duty, as I saw it, was to say something about the place that I called home. Not the nation. Not even the people, but the idea. The idea behind America, and Silicon Valley, and what I thought the Tech Bros were trying to achieve when I first arrived in California from India all those years ago.

America gave me a work visa and then the opportunity to live in the most thrilling, most wonderful, most dynamic city in the world. It gave me my opportunity to meet a wonderful English girl with a great tan and a fabulous attitude. It gave me the chance to drink hard liquor in the Redwood Room at the Clift Hotel and to meet Mark Carlisle, who took a chance on me and allowed me to thrive.

I wanted to say a few words about all the things America had given to me, and how we had to fight tooth and nail to fight for the soul of our collective humanity. But I knew, of course, that the wedding guests didn't want to hear all this. All they wanted was for us to kiss and to be happy in our lives together.

But later, as we left the wedding celebrations, and the blossom confetti was showered over us, and we walked into the night together, Anna kissed me and said, "I love this place. I love you and I love my life. But what about the Biryani you promised me?"

"Seriously, you want Biryani, just after getting married?"

"Well, you have made an issue, for years, about how great it is. I'm actually starving. Today has been a whirlwind. And I didn't get a chance to eat anything properly. I really could do with a big plate of savoury rice."

"You have just called one of the most majestic dishes, Thalassery Biryani, a plate of 'savoury rice'? Dear God, Anna, I have much to teach you."

"You do, Rahul. You do. And, frankly, I've much to learn. Perhaps I could wait until breakfast for my plate of rice. I presume it's possible to get some kedgeree around here. That makes for a really good breakfast, I think."

"On that we agree, my beautiful wife. You know, Anna, since what happened last year, I've found myself thinking about conversations I had with Mark. I can remember most of our conversations in incredible detail. And since we lost Mark and Jenny, I suppose I think that I have to remember those conversations as much as I can, otherwise I'll lose them forever. That would be too great a victory for their assassins. But for some reason I keep thinking of an anecdote Mark told me of a place he had been to in SOMA. A museum dedicated to books. A bookbinding museum."

"Yes, he told me about that place too. And it made him wonder about why it was that a big social media company was located South of Market. It was and is a valid question. But why have you been pondering that, in particular?"

"I honestly don't know, Anna. I honestly don't know. But something tells me that Mark knew that the instrument of war against the people was to deny them knowledge - or to make it very difficult to tell the difference between propaganda and truth. Or the difference between governments and democracy."

Anna wrapped her arms around me and looked into my eyes.

"Look, Rahul. What happened was appalling. For both of us this was the very worst possible thing that could have happened. But we can't undo what has been done. We can't give up our lives to make things better, or to right all the wrongs of governments we can't control. We both know we have parts to play. We know that there's about to be a battle for survival - for us and for our children that are yet to be born. But we can't make any promises right now to Mark, or Jenny or to anyone. Or perhaps we can. We have just made promises to love and cherish each other. But I'm prepared to add another promise to you."

"What's that?" I asked.

"It's this, my beautiful husband. It's this…

"I'm prepared to promise you that I'll always tell the truth even if no-one believes me, or even if no-one gets to hear it.

"But before speaking truth to power I need to find out what that truth is. But I'm not prepared to sacrifice my life any time soon. I love you, and I love myself too much for that. Because, my Dear Rahul, we found each other, and we now live near a great highway near the Pacific Ocean. Whatever the circumstances that brought us together, or the people we have loved that got us here, we have life to live. And some overdue joy to bring to each other. Now…where will you take me for kedgeree in the morning."

"Ah, my dear Anna, I know just the place. I know just the place."

About the Author

Jeffrey Peel spent most of his career working for information technology companies, in various communications roles, travelling extensively. He has worked for some of the biggest firms, headquartered in Silicon Valley or London. His job has taken him all over the world.

South of Market is his first novel, but he has written extensively about the merger of tech and geopolitics on Substack and X. He is also a regular political commentator and podcaster.

Jeff lives in Northern Ireland but travels widely.

Printed in Dunstable, United Kingdom

67236516R00194